CONSTANTINE CAPERS

Flashes of Memory

CONSTANTINE CAPERS

CAPERS

Flashes of Memory

NATALIE BRIANNE

Scarosi Press

MMXXII

To Clyde and Geneil and Joann and Dallas—my grandparents.

This is for the shelves of books I could peruse as I liked whenever I visited. For listening to me ramble about everything and nothing. For cucumber boats, quilts, and quiet moments watching the hummingbirds. For gooseberries, grass stains, and bottle rockets.

For allowing me to divert questions about my marital status onto my characters.

(Do they get married in this one? Well, I suppose you'll need to read it to find out.)

But most of all, it's for believing in me.

This one is for you.

October 9, 1888

MIRA'S LUNGS BURNED, SCREAMING AT HER TO stop. Six blocks of running, and Byron didn't slow down for a moment. She recognized the street signs as they raced down each cobblestoned alley. He kept a firm grasp on her wrist, pulling her along towards Palace Court. She risked a glance over her shoulder, still unsure of what or who they were running from, but no one seemed to be following them.

She returned her focus to her footfalls, each step stealing the breath from her lungs and replacing it with stinging fire. She stumbled as she continued to follow her detective. If she stopped, both of them would likely trip and fall.

They rounded a corner, and Byron finally slowed to a stop, pulling her up against the wall. He bent over, catching his breath as she did the same.

Throat aching, she managed, "Byron . . . why?"

He straightened himself, wincing at the effort, and adjusted his cravat.

"There was . . . well, a person I would rather not converse with. I can only hope he didn't see us," he said, measuring his breaths.

"An enemy, then?" Mira couldn't help her curiosity. In the month since she met Byron, he'd never mentioned having specific enemies. The threat of the Order of Circe loomed over them, but that was more of a general enemy rather than an arch nemesis. Of course, being a private detective, he was bound to have a few. And being Byron, he likely forgot some of them.

"Not an enemy, no. My brother, actually." He moved down the street again.

Mira gave him an incredulous look and followed. "Your brother?" She released a sharp laugh. "The way you ran, I thought we were in danger."

Byron ran a hand through his hair. "Well, no . . . I suppose we weren't. I just . . . well, I haven't spoken with him since the accident, you see. At least not that I remember." He lowered his voice, looking around. "Why don't we continue this conversation back at Palace Court?"

Mira turned, looking for any threats he may have seen following them, but came up short. She nodded, and he turned towards Kensington Gardens.

As they walked, Byron kept a keen eye on their surroundings, even staring at the pavement as if it were suspicious. Part of their daily routine included a walk through the gardens. From the outside, it would appear as if they were courting. In reality, both kept their eyes peeled for the mysterious gentleman that had stopped Mira in Kensington twice before. The haunting letter he had given Mira—*We Live On*—came up with nothing under Byron's tests. No silt, chemicals, or residue that could lead them back to Circe. No, the man was still their only lead to the criminal organization, but there was no trace of him.

The wind chilled her back as she followed Byron past the palace and towards Palace Court. When they arrived, he glanced back to see if anyone had followed them before opening the door and pulling Mira inside.

"Why haven't you spoken with him since the accident?" Mira asked as she placed her coat and hat on the hook in the entryway, grateful for the warmth of the interior.

"In a way," Byron took a breath and continued, "the accident was his fault." He turned away from her, moving over to the window. "Besides, we never were close."

"You mean you lost your memory because of your own brother?" She sat down on the sofa.

"Yes and no." He dropped the curtain in favor of pacing across the room. "While he didn't inherently cause it—well, it sounds ridiculous now that I'm saying it out loud."

"That's because it is." Mira pulled out her sketchbook. She glanced up at him, intending to make a quick sketch of his disheveled appearance, from the ruffled tufts of hair to the uneven crease of his trousers.

"Let me rephrase it, then. My brother works in parliament and happens to be in good graces with the Queen." He swallowed and ran a hand through his hair.

"You can't be serious." Mira's pencil slipped from her fingers.

"I'm afraid I am." He knelt to retrieve the pencil and placed it back in her hands as he sat next to her on the couch. "With his connection to me, that means I'm called upon occasionally to investigate matters of, well, greater importance." He stood to pace again, stopping at the window to scan the street before retreating to his armchair.

"But that's wonderful, Byron!" She closed her sketchbook and set it aside.

"I thought so at first, but that made things complicated when the only case I never solved was the one given me by

Her Majesty." He grabbed his journal from the side table and frowned at it.

"You don't mean to say that the accident happened . . . "

"Right as I was about to crack the case wide open, I'm afraid." He leaned forward and hit the back of the journal with slight frustration.

"That still doesn't explain why you haven't spoken to your brother after all these years."

"I suppose it doesn't." He sighed and placed the journal down again. "To be honest, I'd rather not see him again in general. After all, he was against my becoming a private investigator to begin with. The fact that I lost my memory just proves that point," he said, voice bitter and hard.

"But he's your brother! And it's been four years. Things are bound to have changed. I couldn't imagine not speaking with Walker for that long."

"I'm not as close to my family as you are to yours, Mira. And aside from that, I—"

A knock at the door interrupted him. "That will be him," he sighed, but didn't budge from his armchair.

"Aren't you going to answer it?" she asked.

"No. I think not." The knocking came again, but louder.

"Byron, you can't simply ignore him for the rest of your life."

He hesitated a moment before nodding. "Perhaps you are right. Why don't we . . . hmm . . . " He stood and moved as if to answer the door before ignoring the persistent knocks in favor of the stairs.

"Where are you going?" She stood and followed him as far as the entryway.

"I think it would be best if-if you were to be the one to speak to him." He skipped two steps and reached for the handle of his bedroom door.

"What? Me? Byron, I don't think that's a good idea."

"Yes. See what he wants."

"What do you want me to tell him if he asks for you?"

"That I'm not here and you don't know when I'll be returning."

"That would be a lie, Byron." She took a few steps up the stairs.

A new round of knocking sounded behind her, and she turned towards it.

"Good luck." Byron disappeared into his bedroom, and the door closed with a click.

"Byron! I . . ." She grimaced. She had seen him face death with less cowardice. Really, how bad could this brother be? With a roll of her eyes, she marched down the steps and onto the marble floor in the entry. Taking a deep breath, she slid the door open.

A tall, willowy gentleman stood before her on the front step. His posture matched the starched collar around his neck. Stiff and imposing. His blue eyes, so like Byron's and yet so cold, roved over her. His well-trimmed mustache twitched as he cleared his throat and spoke.

"Excuse me."

"Yes, can I help you?"

"This is 27 Palace Court, is it not?"

"Yes. It is." She opened the door another few inches.

"And a certain Detective Byron—em—Constantine lives here?" His expression soured at the word "Constantine" as if he had eaten something unpleasant.

"Yes, he does."

"Good." He pushed past her into the entrance hall, removing his hat and coat and giving them to her. His shiny black shoes clicked on the marble as he continued into the sitting room.

She stood startled for a moment, and then followed him, flustered. "Excuse me—"

"Yes, I would like some tea. Earl Grey, if you have it. Cream before tea, no sugar." He ran a finger over the mantlepiece and inspected it for dust before sitting in Byron's armchair.

Mira placed his belongings on the back of a chair. "That wasn't what I was going to ask. Who, exactly, are you?" Mira attempted to keep her voice level.

"Oh, pardon me. I thought you would know. Castel Sherard. I'm Byron's brother. He should be expecting me." His gaze wandered to the side table next to him and he picked up an unopened letter.

"That is, if he had actually read my letter." His lips pursed together as he straightened. "Is he here, by chance?"

Mira took a breath and moved to the window to feign a search for the forgetful detective.

"I'm afraid not. And I'm not sure when he will be returning." A moment of silence passed between them. She frowned, turning his name over in her head.

"Excuse me, but did you mean Castel Sherard *Constantine* by chance?"

"No. I meant Castel Sherard. Period." He paused to look up at her.

She shivered as his scrutinizing stare fell upon her. Byron was never this cold. A look of amusement crossed his visage.

"May I ask who you are? You are much too proper a lady to be his cleaning woman."

Was that supposed to be a compliment? Mira determined she well and truly disliked this man, be he Byron's brother or not.

"Samira Blayse. I'm his secretary." With one last glance out the window, she moved over to the couch and sat down.

A smirk flickered for a moment below Castel's well-trimmed mustache. "Now, how did Byron convince a lady such as yourself to work for him?" He leaned forward and cocked his head.

Mira averted her gaze fidgeting with her hands. "He helped

me solve a case of mine. I thought I would continue to help him for the time being."

"And how long have you been working for him?"

"Just over a month." She glanced at the stairs.

"And he hasn't told you?" He clicked his tongue. "How fascinating." His voice lowered as he tossed the unopened letter back onto the side table.

"Told me what?"

"I'm sure you wouldn't want to know," he said with disinterest. "Besides, if he hasn't told you, I won't betray his confidence."

"How very decent of you, Castel," Byron said as he strode down the stairs. Mira let out a slight sigh of relief.

Castel lifted his head. "Ah, Byron. How good of you to make an appearance."

"I could say the same to you." Byron sat next to Samira on the sofa.

"Your secretary said you were out. How curious that you weren't."

"I was out, in fact, until just a few minutes ago. I must have returned while she was in another room."

"How convenient." Castel tapped his fingers on the armrest.

Mira felt certain that they were having a silent conversation. She didn't like it.

"To what do I owe this visit, Castel?" Byron pinched the bridge of his nose.

"Can I not simply pay a visit to my younger brother?"

"Past experience would deem it unlikely."

"And who is to say that you haven't forgotten any prior visits?"

Byron flinched as if Castel had slapped him. His brow furrowed, then he leaned back and smiled. "I suppose you are right. Well, if you are staying, would you like a cup of tea?"

Castel narrowed his eyes, a hint of suspicion and surprise

evident behind them. But soon enough, his expression flattened, replaced by a smug upturn of his bottom lip. "That would be delightful."

"Would you like me to get it, Byron?" Mira could hardly wait to get out of this tense atmosphere. She needed to breathe.

"Oh no, Mira. I'll take care of it." Apparently, Byron felt the same. He moved into the kitchen and out of sight.

Her gaze flicked back to his brother. They sat in silence for a few moments, studying each other's features. The more she examined him, the more similarities she found between him and Byron. The way his mouth curved when he was thinking, and the way he drummed his fingers against the armrest. Slight mannerisms she recognized from Byron.

"You are pretty. I'll give him that." He leaned back in his chair.

Mira blinked at him. "I beg your pardon?"

"Excuse the observation. I'm trying to figure you out."

"And what seems to be stopping you?"

"Byron insisted he didn't need any assistance in his condition."

"You mean you have spoken since the accident?"

"Only twice before now. He wanted to keep his independence. I respected his wishes and kept my distance." Castel dusted off the arm of the chair, gaze distant and impartial. "Now it would seem that he needed help after all."

"He is perfectly capable of handling things on his own."

"Then why have a secretary?"

Mira's voice faltered. "This is only a trial arrangement, nothing more."

"And what are the terms of this arrangement?"

"I believe that is a matter betw—"

A crash came from the kitchen, as if a teacup had shattered. Mira started, poised to move into the other room if necessary. Some frustrated mumblings came from the door, and she stood to go help Byron.

"If you would excuse me."

She crossed the room, making out a mumble from Castel as she passed him.

"He certainly has you trained well, too."

Mira concealed a scowl and entered the kitchen and closed the door behind her.

"Byron, he is incorrigible. I see why you don't like to meet with him."

She surveyed the room and found Byron busy picking up stray bits of china from a broken teacup. She softened immediately.

"What happened?" She knelt next to him and helped stack the broken pieces on a tray.

"I was straining to hear what you two were discussing and managed to knock it over. Did he mention a particular way he liked his tea, by chance?"

"I think it was cream, but no sugar."

"Right. Right. Of course." He tossed the ruined teacup in the rubbish bin and turned back to the tea tray.

She moved over to his side. "Are you alright?"

"Perfectly." He looked up at her with a wavering smile.

"I don't believe you."

"Of course you don't. I'm a terrible liar. We ought to get this out to my brother before it goes cold, or he starts snooping through my files." He picked up the tray in one fluid motion and headed for the door.

She hesitated, then followed him back into the sitting room. Castel continued to sit in Byron's armchair. He leveled a glare of disapproval at them. She could only guess what he thought of the time she and Byron spent alone in the kitchen. Byron set the tea tray on the table and handed a cup to Castel, before readying two cups for himself and Mira. She perched on the couch, and Byron handed her a cup.

"You poured the tea before the cream, didn't you?" Castel

said as he took a sip of his tea. With a disapproving glance, he set it on the end table next to the discarded letter.

"I'm afraid I didn't know what you wanted. I made my best guess."

"I could have told you what I wanted, Byron. You only needed to ask."

"I'm asking then. What is it you want?" Byron asked.

The beginning of a smirk appeared on Castel's face. "A favor."

"And if I say no?" Byron crossed his arms.

"Her Majesty won't be pleased."

A stillness settled over the room, and the silent conversation continued. Mira sat there like an intruder, albeit an oblivious one, as the brothers played chess with their facial expressions.

"The answer is no, Castel." Byron stood and moved to the entrance hall, picking up his brother's hat and coat on the way.

He paused in the doorway as Castel stood.

"Byron, no amount of hiding, lies, and secrecy will change who you are. And being in that position, you have a certain responsibili—"

"No," Byron interrupted. "I don't."

"Whether you accept it or not, the responsibility is still there." His brother walked over to him, pulling out a letter. "At least read this. I had a feeling that you wouldn't want to see me."

Byron took the letter and placed it in his jacket pocket before handing the coat and hat to Castel. Mira sat there in silence and awe, uncertain of what to do.

"I hope that someday you can forgive me for what I didn't do," Castel said as he took his things and disappeared into the entrance hall.

Byron's jaw tightened, and he followed him out. Harsh whispers echoed from the hall before the door slammed. Byron returned to the sitting room, stopping for a moment to straighten his vest. After picking up his teacup, he reclaimed his armchair and settled in. Anxiety dripped off of him in waves as he took a sip and looked up at her.

"I'm terribly sorry about all that."

"As you should be, leaving me alone to confront him. And I thought you were a gentleman," Mira said, hiding a smile behind her teacup.

Byron's shoulders relaxed. "A gentleman and a coward, so it would seem." He sighed, leaning back in his chair. Mira softened.

"Not a coward, per se. I understand why you were so apprehensive."

"He's harmless, really. This, however," he said as he pulled the letter from his pocket, "is not."

"And what is that?" She leaned forward to catch a glimpse of the sender.

"An invitation from the Queen to meet with a representative about a case. At least, that is my hypothesis. Why else would he show up after all this time?"

"To check up on his brother?"

"He always has an ulterior motive."

"Always?" She raised an eyebrow at him.

"Yes."

"I see." She set her teacup on the tray and stood to retrieve Castel's nigh-untouched cup.

Byron stared at the envelope in his hands, and Mira glimpsed it over his shoulder; exquisite stationery with a wax seal closure.

"It's not going to bite you, Byron," she said, setting Castel's cup on the tray next to her own.

"No. Not if I don't open it." He continued to stare at it.

Mira faltered for a moment, coming up behind him again. "I will, then." In one smooth motion, she snatched it out of his hands and slipped away towards the window.

He jumped up, attempting to take it back.

"No, Mira, I'd rather forget the whole thing," he said, reaching for her hand.

She turned swiftly away and moved towards the entrance hall. "Is reading it going to hurt anything?" She slipped her finger beneath the wax and broke the seal.

He caught her wrist and held it tight. She looked up at him, waiting for his answer.

"It-I . . ." he stuttered, staring into her eyes.

She took that moment to use her other hand to free the letter from the envelope and flip it open. She looked back up at him as he loosened his grip on her wrist. Her resolve crumbled at his expression.

"I won't read it if you really are that adamant about ignoring it. I just can't see the harm in seeing what she wants you to do."

"I suppose you are right." His hand dropped from her wrist to her hand, fingers feather soft as he grasped it and led her back to the couch.

She sat down in silence, and he moved next to her. Careful not to rumple it, she folded the letter again and offered it to him. He shook his head and pushed her hand back.

"You read it. After all, you stole it fair and square." A half-hearted smile crossed his face.

She paused, then flicked the paper out. Her voice faltered as she spoke:

Request from Her Majesty Queen Victoria to Detective Byron Constantine. Your presence is required at Buckingham Palace on October Tenth of this year at ten-thirty sharp. You shall meet with a representative in order to discuss the nature of the agreement between yourself and Her Majesty and the content of the case. Do be prompt.

"And to think I thought this would offer some sort of explanation," Mira mumbled, closing the letter again.

"Didn't give us much notice to prepare, either. The tenth is tomorrow." Byron took the letter from her and looked it over.

"You're going, then?"

"You don't ignore an invitation from the Queen, Mira."

"Was that not exactly what you were going to do before I stole the letter from you?" She leaned back against the sofa.

"Ah, but I hadn't read it yet. I could have had an excuse if the letter had remained sealed in its envelope."

Mira glanced over at the sealed letter on his side table. He really had ignored his brother on purpose. She shook her head and picked up her sketchbook.

"So, you are going."

"Only if you come with me." He stood and straightened his jacket, walking over to the piano.

"The letter didn't say anything about you bringing your secretary."

"If Her Majesty wishes for me to solve a case of hers, then she will need to be alright with you knowing about it." His fingers danced across the keys.

"Very well," Mira laughed. "I'm afraid I don't know exactly what to wear to Buckingham Palace."

"Well, what would you wear to meet the Queen?"

"We aren't meeting the Queen, Byron. The letter says we're meeting with a representative. Besides, the court moved up to Balmoral estate weeks ago."

"How do you know that?" Byron stopped playing to look at her.

"My uncle's favorite pastime is following the lives of the nobility. It's easy enough to keep tabs on the movements of the court if you can get a copy of The Star."

"Does he keep a close watch on that, then?"

Mira laughed. "If you knew my uncle well, you'd realize

that he puts more credence into social standing and noble status than just about anything else. He has his own copy of the Peerage, which he reads for fun!"

Byron cleared his throat, the tension returning to his shoulders. "Well, then. Even if it is only a representative, we will be going to the palace in any case. You ought to look nice."

"I'm planning on it."

"Shall I let you off early today so you can get ready, then?"

"That might be for the best."

He left the piano and escorted her to the door, helping her into her coat. He left a gentle kiss on the back of her hand.

"I'd walk you home if I didn't have to get ready myself," he said.

"No. It's fine." She smiled. "I'll see you tomorrow."

SHE FOUND HERSELF ON HIS DOORSTEP, THE events of the previous hour puzzling her. Castel's comments about the secrets Byron kept from her gnawed at her insides. What hadn't he told her? And why was his last name different from Castel's? The name Sherard sounded familiar, but not in an extraordinary way. Had she encountered a different family member through acquaintances?

She walked through Kensington again. The sun set in her periphery, but the pond near the palace sparkled in the light that remained.

"Excuse me."

Mira jumped in surprise at the voice from behind her. Had she dropped one of her gloves? She turned, and the blood drained from her cheeks.

"You-you're . . ." she stammered at the mysterious gentleman.

His cold hazel eyes bored into her, and he smiled.

"Hello again."

"I—"

"May I walk you home?" He tipped his hat at a jaunty angle, showing the messy brown hair underneath.

"Certainly not." She found her voice again and turned away from him.

The man shrugged and continued his stroll at a slow pace, almost asking her to follow. Mira bit back a grimace and quickened her steps to catch up with him.

"What do you want?"

"To check up on you, Samira. Nothing more."

Mira's stomach turned in knots. If this man truly worked for the Order of Circe, she didn't want to have anything to do with him. But as he was the only lead . . .

"Check up on me? That's terribly kind of you." She played along with his game.

"Is it? I just thought that was something that friends do."

"How can we be friends if I don't even know your name?"

"How can you be in love with a man who doesn't remember yours?"

Mira clenched her jaw. How could he possibly know anything about her relationship with Byron? He stopped walking and turned towards her, eyes slipping from one feature to the next.

"Now that you've solved your own mystery, what's stopping you from leaving this detective business for good, hm?"

"I-how dare you presume that I—"

"You are an open book, Miss Blayse. But I would suggest if you want this book to end without heartbreak, that you stop this. And soon."

"Again, with the threats. Is that all that you do?"

"What?" He blinked at her.

"Is that the work you do for the Order? Threatening people into doing what Circe wants?"

"Is *that* what you think I'm doing?" he laughed.

"It won't work on me."

"I know. And if I know that, then why would I continue to do it? These aren't threats, Mira."

"Then why are you here?"

The man stopped and studied her for a moment. Mira's skin crawled with discomfort.

"If you aren't staying for him, then you're staying for the mystery of it. The thrill. Aren't you?" He cocked his head to the side.

"You haven't answered my question."

"Solve me, and that will be answer enough."

He tipped his hat once more and disappeared into the mist. Mira's steps faltered towards him, but she let it be. He could wait. The Queen, on the other hand, waited for no one.

October 10, 1888

WHAT COULD CASTEL HAVE MEANT? MIRA'S MIND swirled with possible explanations as she got ready the next day with Nero, her cat, mewling at her feet. His abrasive, if not rude, answer about Byron's supposed secret confused her. She found herself once again trying to puzzle out something about her detective that didn't make sense. If Byron's brother's last name was Sherard, then why was his Constantine? Were they only half-brothers? Was that why their relationship was so strained? She pulled her boots on in a huff. Why not simply tell her, then? Why would it be a breach of confidence? And if his brother did work in parliament—no, she didn't have time to think about it.

She braided her hair into careful plaits and pinned it into submission. The night before, she had picked out a nice blue skirt and bodice with floral patterns. She put that on first thing in the morning, but had opted to wait on her hair and accessories.

Once she pinned her hair in place, she added a blue feathered hat and grabbed her gloves. Today, she needed all the propriety she could muster. And not only that, she also needed to ensure that Byron had the same, if not more, himself.

"I'm off to Palace Court. Should be back before dark!" she called in the direction of her uncle's study.

He poked his head out. "I should hope so! I wanted to go over the plans for picking up your brother tomorrow."

"Tomorrow?"

"Tomorrow is the eleventh, yes?"

"Good heavens! Already?" Mira pulled on her coat in haste.

"Perhaps you would have noticed if you took some time to breathe," her uncle grumbled.

"Mustn't be late! Today we have an appointment at Buckingham Palace!"

Her uncle's face lit up. "You don't say? I expect a full report on the matter when you return home."

She called a hansom cab to take her around the edge of Kensington. For as nice of a day as it was, she didn't want to risk running into the man from Circe in the gardens again. He seemed to always pop up at the most inconvenient times. She didn't have the time for that today. She raced up the stairs of 27 Palace Court and took out her key.

The door opened before she could even touch the handle. Byron smiled at her and stepped out, placing his top hat on his head and brandishing a cane.

"Good morning, Mira! I was just coming to Swan Walk to get you."

"Well, I'm afraid I beat you to it, Byron. I see you read your journal this morning without trouble."

"Oh, I had loads of trouble. Trouble is my middle name, after all. Luckily, there were enough notes stashed around to get me settled. And, of course, some wonderful portraits to fill in some gaps."

Mira frowned, thinking about his name. For all she knew, his middle name could really be "Trouble." She shook the thought away. She could breach that topic later.

"Is something wrong, Mira?"

"Oh, nothing. A bit nervous to be going to the palace, that's all."

"Of course. And we ought to be going. Better early than late."

He paused, cocking his head at her. "You have freckles."

"Yes?" She laughed.

"But, your self-portrait . . ."

Mira took a breath. When she gave Byron her sketches to help him remember various people in his life, she knew something like this would come up. While useful in giving him a place to start, they weren't perfect by any means.

"Are you wanting me to add them in?"

He shook his head. "That's alright." His gaze fell to her dress, and he frowned.

"Give me a moment." He walked back inside, leaving the door wide open and removing his tie as he walked up the stairs to his bedroom.

"Byron, I thought you said we needed to leave!" she called after him, stepping inside and closing the door.

"I won't be a minute!" he called back. A few moments passed, and he reemerged sporting a cravat that matched her dress. She laughed.

"It is important to look our best. Matching our color scheme is certain to make a good impression." He opened the door for her again.

"You do look nice, Byron."

"And you look splendid. I'm sure you'll turn every head at court." He offered his arm to her, which she took with a roll of her eyes.

"You're such a tease."

"I'm only being honest. The blue compliments your eyes. Seems to make them greener."

She smiled. "Yes, but turning the heads of the entire court? Seems unlikely."

"I beg to differ." He called a hansom cab over and helped her into it.

They settled in next to each other as the cab moved towards the palace.

"Then, won't you get jealous?" she teased.

"If I've ever felt jealousy, I have since forgotten the emotion."

She laughed, and he smiled in return, turning his gaze to the road.

"To be perfectly frank," he said, softer, "I am more likely to be jealous of myself than anyone else."

"What do you mean?" She turned towards him.

"You are more than I ever imagined based on what I had written. And so, I am jealous of the selves I have left behind each day. Every me that has had the pleasure of knowing you."

His gaze deepened, and she fought the blush rising to her cheeks. She smiled and squeezed his hand.

"To me, there is only one you."

SOON ENOUGH, BUCKINGHAM PALACE CAME INTO VIEW, and the hansom cab came to a stop. Mira's breath caught in her chest as Byron led her up to the gates. A guard stood beside the main gate, upright and broad-shouldered. Mira shrunk back under his gaze, but Byron pulled her forward and handed the letter to the guard. The man read it, passed his gaze over them once more, and opened a smaller gate for them. He led them in silence to a side door, which he ushered them into.

"Wait here." He closed the door and left.

They stood in a long rectangular room with a door at either end. The door they had come from, and another that presumably led into the rest of the palace. They stood on a hardwood floor with a red and gold carpet running along the center. An incredible spray of flowers sat on a side table. Mira hesitated to sit in any of the opulent chairs, worrying that a stray bit of dirt from her skirt might sully the embroidered fabric. She opted to move towards the center of the room and study a painting depicting the English countryside.

"Are you nervous?" Byron asked, coming to join her in examining the painting.

"A little. Are you?"

He turned to lean against the wall. "If we were actually meeting with Her Majesty, I would be."

Mira fidgeted with her gloves. "This is out of my field of comfort, even if we aren't meeting her."

"You'd rather be chasing down a burglar?"

"No." She stifled her laugh.

"Jumping from a train then?" He smirked and leaned closer.

"Definitely not."

"What then would—"

The door opened, and Byron stepped back from her to face the person who entered.

"Ah. The young detective. We've been expecting you." A man, similar in stature to Byron's brother, entered and shook his hand. "And who is this with you?"

"This is Miss Blayse. She is my secretary and is invaluable to my investigations. You will allow her to attend this meeting?"

"Of course, of course. Right this way. The prime minister is waiting."

Mira's breath caught in the back of her throat, and she followed without thinking. She blinked, trying to bring her focus back to her surroundings. Byron fell into step beside her.

"Are you alright?" he whispered.

Mira remembered to breathe as she placed one foot in front of the other.

"Yes of course, but did he say prime minister?"

"I believe that's what he said, yes." He flashed a smirk in her direction.

"This is all rather extraordinary."

"It does take some getting used to."

Byron offered her his arm, and she took it to stabilize herself.

Their guide led them into a room styled as an office. An older man with balding hair and an impressive salt and pepper beard sat behind a desk. He stood as they entered.

"Detective Constantine and his secretary, Miss Blayse, to see you, sir," the guide said.

The prime minister smiled and moved over to them.

"A pleasure to meet you at last, Mr. Constantine." He shook Byron's hand, then glanced at Mira before gesturing to a cluster of sofas on the opposite end of the room. "Please, sit down."

Byron released Mira's hand from his arm and guided her to take a seat. Once Byron made himself comfortable, he turned to the prime minister.

"The letter that Mr. Sherard gave me indicated the Queen had some need of my expertise."

"It is less so the Queen, as it is the government, hence my involvement. It is a matter of procedure and tradition that Her Majesty extended the offer."

"Of course. What seems to be the trouble?"

"Before I continue, I must insist that what we discuss in this room stays confidential." The prime minister's gaze flickered over to Mira.

"I can assure you, sir, what we discuss will not leave this circle unless absolutely necessary." Byron followed his line of sight and frowned. "Miss Blayse helps me to retain my memory. If you wish for me to solve this case, she needs to be aware of the details."

The prime minister took a deep breath, then nodded.

"Very well. But allow me to correct you. Technically, there is nothing to be solved here. This is merely a precaution."

Byron removed his journal from his satchel and prepared to write, nodding for the prime minister to continue.

"In March of this last year, several European powers met to draft a treaty regarding the use of the Suez Canal in Egypt. As you may know, Britain fought to gain control over Egypt back in 1882. Since then, tensions have risen between our government and the governments of France, Egypt, and the Ottoman Empire. Most of the strain comes from the use of the Suez Canal, as it is one of the main trade routes into Africa." The prime minister paused to allow Byron to finish his notes.

"The treaty will allow all countries to use the canal in times of war and peace." The prime minister sighed.

"Isn't that a bit of a loss of control?" Byron asked, looking up.

"It's better to relinquish control to maintain peace between ourselves and the other European powers than to risk a war of this magnitude. And we will still have access to the canal."

"Which countries are signing the treaty?" Byron asked.

"Ourselves, France, Germany, Austria-Hungary, the Netherlands, Spain, the Russian Empire, and the Ottoman Empire."

"Quite the bunch. Seems everyone will be participating." Byron tapped his pen against his cheek.

"Indeed. Now, you are likely wondering why I would ask you here."

Byron nodded, and the prime minister continued. "There have been increasing anarchist threats as of late, as well as assassination attempts on government leaders. I'm concerned for the well-being of one of the ambassadors, Sir William Arthur White. He and his wife are visiting here in London before returning to Constantinople for the signing of the treaty at the end of this month."

Byron cleared his throat. "Are you wishing for us to keep an eye on things?"

"He needs to be protected. If this treaty falls through, the tensions at play could bring us to a global conflict. One that we are not exactly prepared to fight at the moment."

"What would you like us to do, sir?" Byron capped his fountain pen.

"I know Her Majesty requested you investigate the anarchist threats in the past. Even if there were no leads then, there may be some facts surrounding this one. I want you to keep close to Sir William and look for any threats that may arise."

"And why not use the police?"

"We want things to remain inconspicuous. And with your position . . ."

"You need a Sherard?" Byron said, softer.

"Yes. I'm not sure how to accommodate your secretary." The prime minister looked her over again.

"I'll take care of that," Byron said. "Do you have the address of where the ambassador is staying here in London?"

"Of course. I prepared a file for you. All the information you'll need is in here." The prime minister stood and retrieved a red briefcase from his desk. He opened it and pulled out a grey folder. "You'll help us then?"

"I'm not a bodyguard, but I'll do what I can. I can't promise you anything, especially since there isn't a crime for me to solve. But I can keep an eye out." Byron stood and took the folder.

"That's all we ask." The prime minister offered his hand, which Byron shook. "I'm glad to have you looking after this matter."

"Happy to help, Prime Minister." Byron looked back at Mira. "Shall we go, then?"

Their guide escorted them out of Buckingham Palace, but Byron made no move to stop a hansom cab. Mira found herself walking arm in arm with Byron back towards Palace Court.

"That was certainly unexpected," Mira said. "How curious that they didn't give us a case."

Byron remained silent. His gaze set on the ground in front of them.

"What's wrong?" She tipped her head forward to see his face better.

It took him a moment to speak. "Sorry, I'm caught up in my mind." He shook his head.

"Anything in particular causing you trouble?"

"I'm trying to determine the best way to bring you into high society." He gave her a half-hearted smirk.

"I've been to my fair share of balls and galas. I'm sure I can manage! Won't we have to find a disguise for you as well?"

"Something of that nature." His gaze drifted away again, searching the street.

Mira furrowed her brow. "Byron, are you certain that there isn't something else bothering you?"

"Not at all. In fact, I actual—"

Byron's voice cut off as they turned a corner, bumping headlong into a woman carrying a stack of packages. Said packages flew in every direction, and the woman lost her balance and fell with them. After steadying Mira, Byron immediately set to work retrieving the strewn cargo.

"I'm so sorry, Miss," he said, reaching for another lump of brown paper.

"Oh, please, it was an accident. No harm done." The blonde tucked a few additional packages under her arm and looked up at him. She blinked a few times, and the color drained from her cheeks.

"You seem quite pale. Are you sure you're quite alright?" Mira asked, extending a hand.

"Yes. But I need to be going."

Byron stood and offered the remaining packages to her, looking up at her fully. His eyes widened.

"Grace?"

"I need to go!" She snatched up the rest of her load and dashed across the street.

Byron stared after her, body tense as if ready to run after her. As the woman disappeared, his shoulders slumped and his brow furrowed.

After a few moments, Mira broke the silence. "Did you know her?"

"I-I don't know." He shook his head and blinked. "I don't think I remember her."

"You called her Grace."

"I suppose I did. I thought I recognized her for a moment, but how could that be?"

"You do recognize people from before the accident, don't you?"

"Yes, but not like this."

Mira looked off in the direction that the woman fled.

"She was certainly in a hurry. How would you have known her?"

"That's the thing. I don't know." He blinked again to clear his head.

Mira moved in front of him and centered her eyes on his.

"Are you unwell?"

His brow furrowed, gaze unfocused. She waved a hand in front of his face with no response. Sighing, Mira turned to the street and signaled a hansom cab to stop. She helped him into the carriage and settled in beside him. They sat in silence as the cab cobbled over the street. Halfway to their destination, he shook his head again and gave her a blank stare.

"What happened?" he asked.

"You disappeared for a moment, Byron. Mind telling me where you were?" Her eyebrow quirked up.

"I don't remember." He looked out the window.

Mira leaned forward to keep her eyes on his face. "What is the last thing you remember?"

"I'm not sure. My memory is a bit foggy at the moment, Grace."

"Grace?"

Byron's head whipped up, his eyes roving over her.

"Samira. Mira. Sorry. I . . ." He shut his mouth, eyes full of confusion.

"What's going on, Byron? Talk to me."

"I don't know. I really don't."

The carriage came to a stop, and he looked up. "This isn't Palace Court."

"No. It's Swan Walk." She alighted from the carriage and moved up the stairs.

He followed. "Why are we here?"

"I believe that some food would do you good, and I don't think either of us wants to be in public right now. I'm sure that Uncle Cyrus won't mind."

She opened the door, and Byron trudged after her.

"Miss Mira! I didn't expect you back so soon!" Landon Tisdale, the butler, greeted her from where he dusted the railings. He set his feather duster on the side table and moved to help her and Byron from their coats.

"Hello, Landon! Would you inform my uncle that we're here?"

"Of course. Shall I inform the cook that Mr. Constantine will be joining us for lunch?"

"By all means. Thank you!" She guided Byron into the sitting room.

She closed the door behind them and gestured to a chair. Byron eased himself down and stared into the fire. Mira sat across from him.

"Tell me what's happening in your head."

"I can't sort it out. It doesn't make sense."

"It doesn't have to make sense. Just tell me."

Byron stood to pace.

"It's Grace. She's come to me for help. I can't remember what it was for."

"When was this?"

"I don't know. This wasn't before the accident." Byron stopped at the window.

Mira stood. "You mean you remember something from after?"

"Her name is Grace Trimbell."

"Anything else?"

Byron squeezed his eyes shut. "I'm muddling my past and my present." He opened his eyes and looked at her. "Dash it all, Mira! I know it's nothing new to you, but I can't remember."

She laid a hand on his arm. "It's alright, Byron. You don't have to. It's extraordinary that you remember anything at all from after the accident."

"It isn't to me. It doesn't feel like any time has passed since then."

Mira looked down. A knock sounded at the door, and she turned towards it. Landon popped his head in.

"Lunch is served in the dining room, Miss."

"Thank you, Landon. We'll be there in a moment." She turned back towards Byron. "Let me know if you remember anything else. Maybe it can help us determine what happened to you."

"That was rather long ago. I doubt we'll find anything."

"I do believe you once told me you solved a case that was thirty-five years old. And we solved a case that was eighteen years old. Four years is practically nothing by comparison."

"That does sound like me," he hummed. "Very well. I'll keep you informed of any strange visions, memories, or the like that may come into my frazzled mind."

He extended his arm towards the door. "Shall we?"

Uncle Cyrus rose from his seat at the dining room table as the pair came in.

"Ah, Mr. Constantine, what an unexpected surprise!"

"I'm pleased to be here, sir," Byron said, looking Cyrus over. Mira moved to her place at the table.

"I heard you had a meeting at Buckingham Palace today."

Cyrus resumed his place at the head of the table and Byron took that as his cue to sit down.

"Yes, we did. Mira, would you like to tell him about it?" Byron took a sip of water.

"I'm afraid we can't tell you much, Uncle, as it is highly confidential. But the interior of the palace is gorgeous. I'm sure I would have gotten lost if we didn't have someone leading us through it."

"Did you see anyone of import?" Cyrus leaned forward in his seat as they all filled their plates.

Mira glanced at Byron, who gave her a slight shake of the head.

"No one to speak of."

"I see. Well, I'm sure I'll hear all about the case once it is finished and done with. And Mr. Constantine, I'm sure that this case won't be placing Mira in any danger?" Cyrus gave Byron a pointed look.

"Of course not, sir."

"Good."

"Weren't you wanting to discuss Walker?" Mira asked.

"Oh, yes!" Cyrus lit up. "I received his itinerary this morning. He'll be leaving from Dover at eight o'clock. Should arrive at Victoria station around ten."

Byron frowned. "Walker is . . . ?"

"My brother."

"Oh! Yes. Did I write that down somewhere?"

"It's quite possible that you didn't," she said, giving him a fond look. "He's been studying in France for the last year. He'll be home until next year when he will look for an apprenticeship."

"I see."

"You'll be coming with me to pick him up from the station, won't you, Mira?" Cyrus asked.

"Of course! I wouldn't miss it for anything." She glanced at Byron. "That won't be an issue, will it?"

"Not at all. It will give me time to go over the case file we received."

"Would you like me to come in the morning to make sure you read your journal?"

"I don't want to interfere with your family time, Mira."

Cyrus cleared his throat, "Speaking of that, there was something else I wanted to discuss."

"Yes?" Mira looked up at him.

"A former colleague of mine, a Mr. Sutherland, is holding a social gathering of sorts at his country house. We've been invited."

"Oh? When is it?"

"This Friday and Saturday. I expect you and Walker to attend."

Mira froze, dabbing a napkin to her mouth. "I'm not sure I'll be able to make it. After all, we do have a new case that we're looking into."

"You haven't been to a ball in over a year!"

"Uncle, I went to Maureen Harris' gala in February. That was less than a year ago."

"That wasn't when you spilled the punch bowl all over yourself, was it?" Cyrus laughed.

Mira's face burned. Byron looked at her with curiosity.

"What kind of punch?" he stifled a laugh.

"I wouldn't know. The incident occurred before I could sample any." She huffed a breath. "Honestly, Uncle, every time you bring me to one of these events, disaster follows. It would be best for me to stay home."

"Nonsense, Mira. Young people need to be out and about, getting to know each other. Not out solving cases for the police." He gave a disapproving glance to Byron.

"I agree, actually. Why don't you go, Mira?" Byron turned to her.

"Have you forgotten about our case?"

"It doesn't require immediate attention. Besides, it would be a good opportunity for you to spend quality time with your brother."

"Or with eligible gentlemen," Cyrus added with a knowing look.

Byron whipped his gaze to him, his humored mood dropping from his face. A pensive, worried look overtook his features.

Mira's mouth gaped open. "Uncle!"

"We can discuss it further when Walker arrives." Cyrus set his napkin aside and stood. "If you'll excuse me." He retired from the room.

Byron stared after him and turned to Mira. "Does he not think me eligible?"

Mira's face blazoned red once more. "I-I don't know. We haven't had many opportunities to discuss you. Although he has been molding me to marry up in rank since I was four." She averted her gaze.

"I see." Byron narrowed his gaze and stood. "Well, I ought to get back to Palace Court. I'm sure you have plenty to do here. Shall I see you tomorrow after you meet Walker or the day after?"

"Er." Mira's mind blanked. "Tomorrow?"

"Good."

He walked from the room, and Mira hurried after. He busied himself with his hat and coat. She went to do the same, and he took her coat from her hands and returned it to its hook.

"Shouldn't we look over the case file today?" She frowned.

"I'll take care of it tomorrow, Mira. Enjoy your time with your brother!" He fled out the door.

Mira moved to the parlor window, worrying her lip as he called for a hansom cab. The way he acted was so unusual. Could it be that girl, Grace? Or was he offended by Uncle Cyrus?

"Is something the matter, Miss?" Landon asked, walking in with a vase of fresh begonias.

"Everything," she breathed. "Just when I think I understand him . . ."

October 11, 1888

"Do you think he's here yet?" Mira buzzed with excitement as she walked into the train station arm in arm with her uncle. She swiveled her head about hoping to catch sight of her brother through the crowd and steam.

"If the train was on time." Her uncle checked his pocket watch and tutted at the time. "Wait here and I'll check with the stationmaster," Cyrus said. He patted her arm before walking off in the direction of the ticket booths.

Mira sat on a bench next to a mother and her child. She waited as passengers walked to and fro on the platform, keeping a careful eye out for her brother. It took all her self-control not to bounce in her seat.

A whistle blew, and the mother bundled up her baby, picked up a carpet bag, and left for a train. Mira turned her gaze back to the ticket booth. Her uncle had to have found something out. The bench creaked as someone else sat beside her.

"Been waiting long?" A deep voice asked.

The hair on the back of her neck bristled.

"Not long." Mira frowned, but didn't turn. Why did he sound so familiar?

"Maybe the wait is over then," the voice shifted, sounding almost like—

"Walker!" Mira whirled towards the man and launched into a hug. "It's you!"

The brother in question chuckled. "Hey, Mouse!"

She pulled back from the hug and smacked his shoulder. "I thought I told you to stop calling me that!"

"Not home for five minutes and she's already abusing me! Uncle!" he teased, beckoning Cyrus over to them.

Cyrus grinned and offered a hand to shake. Walker stood, shaking it, and pulled his uncle into a hug.

"It's been over a year, and I don't care if we're in public." He reached a hand out to Mira and pulled her into the hug as well. "I've missed you both too much!"

Mira laughed into his shoulder. "Shall we take you home, then, or leave you here?"

"Lead the way!"

Cyrus pulled back from the hug and picked up one of Walker's bags. Walker took the other and Mira took both of their arms and led them towards the waiting hansom cab.

"Now, I've been able to read about some of your adventures, little Mouse," Walker smirked as she rolled her eyes, "but it would be nice to hear them from your own mouth. Tell me all that has happened."

"That would take rather a long time to tell." She let go of both of their arms and climbed into the hansom cab. "Swan Walk, please."

Cyrus and Walker piled the luggage on the back of the carriage and pulled themselves inside.

"Then you had better get started."

Mira surprised herself by how efficiently she could tell the events of the past year. She glossed over some details of her first case with Byron, if only because her uncle was listening in. But the glint in Walker's eye assured her they would discuss it in its entirety late that night. The carriage rolled to a stop in front of Swan Walk as she came to the end.

"Based on all that you've said, I'd rather like to meet Mr. Constantine. He sounds fascinating."

"He is." Mira's heart soared for a moment before remembering the previous day's events.

Walker frowned at her expression. "Is there something wrong?"

"Not at all. I just thought of something." She schooled her emotions. "I'll be going to meet with him later today. Perhaps you'd like to come with me?"

"I'm sure your brother wants to rest after his journey. He's been on a train for most of the morning," Cyrus said, helping Mira from the carriage.

"Oh, throw that, Uncle. Get some food in me and I'll be right as rain!" Walker laughed, grabbing his bags.

The door opened, and Landon moved to retrieve the luggage. Walker intercepted him and pulled him into a hug. The butler, though surprised, embraced him readily.

"Landon! My good fellow, it's been too long!" Walker pulled back, shaking the butler's hand.

"It is good to see you, Master Walker. I trust your studies have gone well?"

"Splendidly. I wrestled them into submission like Hercules wrestled the Nemean Lion!" Walker pantomimed fighting such a creature.

Mira grinned, following her twin into the house. "Then why don't I see you wearing the pelts of books across your shoulders?"

"Good heavens, Mira! What kind of fashion would that be?"

MIRA HUNG OFF OF WALKER'S EVERY WORD as he described his travels in Switzerland, Belgium, and France over lunch. As the meal concluded, Uncle Cyrus cleared his throat.

"There was something that I wanted to discuss with both of you before you go off to who knows where."

"If this is about the party," Mira muttered.

"What party?" Walker said, eyes lighting up.

Mira chastised herself for being so careless. There was no way to get out of it now.

"The party is a piece of it, yes." Cyrus pulled out his pipe to examine it. "You see, both of you are, for better or worse," he glanced at Mira, "independent now. You don't need me around as much. So, I've been considering making some changes to my business plans."

"What kinds of changes, Uncle?" Mira leaned forward.

"Based on the current market, it is in the company's best interest for me to travel again."

"Aren't you getting on a bit to be traipsing about the world?" Walker asked.

Cyrus bristled up. "I may be older, but that won't keep me down. I still have plenty of good years left in me. The only reason I haven't before is because I wanted to make sure both of you were stable. And while the situation isn't exactly where I would like it yet," he glanced over at Mira again, "I believe that you both are independent enough that you don't need me overseeing all your affairs. For the most part."

Mira swallowed. She knew exactly what he meant, but asked anyway. "And what would be the ideal situation?"

"Well, Mira," Cyrus cleared his throat, blustering. "I'd like for you to be married."

Walker burst out laughing. "That's it? She's been living on her own for months just fine, Uncle."

"Until someone broke into her apartment, and she received threats on her life," Cyrus grumbled.

"That could have just as easily happened here. But if you feel like she needs to be married off, I'm sure I can arrange for her to meet someone."

His eyes twinkled with mirth as he looked at his blushing sister. Before she could protest, Cyrus continued.

"To answer your earlier question, Walker, the party is being held by a former colleague of mine. Mr. Vincent C. Sutherland. We're in discussions to merge our two companies for the greater good and profit of both. But while I would be going for business, I was hoping it would be a good chance for the two of you to mingle."

"What do you say, little Mouse? Up to some mingling with your brother?"

"I don't see what the appeal is," Mira huffed. "And besides, I have other responsibilities."

"Mr. Constantine made it clear yesterday that he approved of your coming." Cyrus raised an eyebrow at her. "He can do without you for a few days."

"It's an overnight affair? Even better!" Walker grinned.

"We'll be leaving tomorrow morning, and I expect both of you to be ready."

Mira stood with a groan and moved to leave the room.

"I'm going to Palace Court. I'll be back tonight," she called from the entryway while putting on her coat.

"Now wait just a moment!" Walker hurried after her. "If you think you are going without me, you are gravely mistaken."

"After taking his side? No. You can meet Byron when you and Uncle return from that ridiculous party," she fumed.

"Who says that I took his side entirely?" Walker raised his hands in mock surrender. "I just think that he's right about you getting out more."

"And what exactly am I doing now? Going out. Without you. So there!"

She opened the door to storm out, and Walker grabbed her wrist.

"Oh, come on, Mira. I just got home. Things have changed! At least let me come scope out the man that you are so obviously smitten with. I need to make sure that he's fit to know you."

Mira squeaked and looked behind him to make sure that Cyrus hadn't heard. She pulled him outside and closed the door.

"I never said I was in love with him!" she whisper-shouted.

"You didn't have to."

"What?"

"You called him by his first name."

"And that's enough to show that I'm in love with him?" Mira folded her arms.

"No." He chuckled. "Landon might have mentioned something when I went down to the kitchen to check on how lunch was coming along. And you just proved it yourself. Now, let's go! Can't keep Byron waiting, can we?"

He strode down the pavement towards Palace Court. Mira huffed a sigh and ran to catch up. "Remind me. Why was I excited for you to come home?"

"Because you missed me, that's why."

"Of course I did."

"Now, why are we keeping your feelings a secret from Uncle? Surely, you realize your problem could be solved if you explained to him that you're interested in Mr. Constantine. Or is it because your feelings aren't reciprocated?"

"It's complicated." Mira rubbed her arms. "My feelings are reciprocated. Most of the time."

He winced. "Ah. The memory loss?"

"Some mornings he doesn't even know who I am." Her shoulders slumped. "Every day is a gamble of whether or not he reads his journal."

Walker turned their path into Kensington gardens, the afternoon sun warming their backs.

"And then, of course, Uncle doesn't approve of me working with a detective, let alone courting him." She forced a laugh. "You know he's been preparing me to marry into a higher status! And Byron Constantine doesn't fit that in his eyes."

"There's only one person's approval who matters."

"Mine?" She looked up at him.

"No. Mine." After a moment, his serious expression broke into a grin, and he laughed. "Of course, yours! If he's a respectable gentleman who can take care of you, then you'll be better off than most of the married populace. Few can say they marry for love."

He caught her gaze again. "Although, you may want to work on his remembering you. I hate seeing you upset."

"There isn't anything to be done. And most days it's alright. Let's just hope today he's read his journal."

∽◦❦◦∽

WHEN THEY REACHED THE DOOR OF NUMBER 27, she gave pause. She pulled out her key and looked between it and the door before taking a breath and knocking. They waited. Footsteps came, and the door opened.

Byron Constantine stood before them in the flesh, dressed to perfection in his grey suit and dashing as ever. He smiled at them, and Mira felt the tension leave her.

"Mira! So, you came after all. Is this your brother?"

Mira nodded. "This is Walker. Walker, this is Byron Constantine."

The two men shook hands, and Byron stepped to the side to let them pass. "Do come in! There's work to be done."

Mira came into the sitting room with Walker following behind. She noticed that the filing system was open and that several papers lay scattered on the table. Had he already gone over the prime minister's case file?

"Give me a moment and I'll get us some tea." Byron hurried off to the kitchen.

"He seems chipper," Walker noted, taking Mira's usual seat.

She ignored that and moved over to the filing system.

"It seems like he didn't have any trouble reading his journal. He's usually more cheerful when he knows what's going on." She rifled through the folders.

"What are you doing?" Walker asked.

"If you must know, I'm doing my own little investigation. There's someone I want to look into, and I'd wager they're in here."

She moved slower in the "T" files until she found the folder labeled "Trimbell, Grace." She snatched it out with a glance to the kitchen and opened it, staring at it a moment.

"What's in it?" Walker stood to look over her shoulder.

"Nothing." Mira blinked at the empty folder before placing it back in its slot.

"Strange."

"Very," she said, noticing another file out of place. Cobden Club. What was a C file doing in the T's? She pulled it out and opened it.

The first item in the file was some sort of magazine. The top of the first page sported a round emblem with the words "Cobden Club" in the center and "Free Trade~Peace~Goodwill Among Nations" curving around it. An illustration resembling a belt encased the words. She frowned at it and thumbed through the publication. Other than a few circled words, nothing stood out.

Hearing the clinking of tea things, Mira thrust the file back into the system and moved to the window to act less conspicuous. Byron emerged from the kitchen, carrying a large tray. He moved several papers to the side and set it down, pouring out a cup for each of them and handing them around.

"How are you feeling today, Byron?" Mira asked.

"Fit as a fiddle and better!" he said, taking his usual position in the armchair closest to the fire.

Mira took her seat on the couch, and Walker sat beside her, sipping at his cup.

"You read about what happened yesterday?" she asked.

"Even better. I remember some of it."

Mira stared at him wide eyed and open mouthed. In her stupor, she had the wherewithal to steady her hand before she dribbled tea into her lap.

"What?"

"I remember." Byron grinned, and his blue eyes twinkled.

Mira's heart was fit to burst. "Truly?"

He rubbed the back of his neck and picked up his teacup. "Well, not everything. But bits. I remembered straight away this morning that I had to find the journal. And I remembered bumping into Grace Trimbell. The rest, the journal filled in for me."

"How is that possible?" Walker asked.

"I haven't the faintest idea! But if this keeps up, perhaps I'll remember everything at some point!"

"That's wonderful, Byron!" Mira said, focus still stuck on the empty folder in the filing system. Her smile didn't quite reach her eyes.

"Now for as excited as I am about my memory, I believe we ought to get down to business." He glanced at Walker. "We can trust you, of course?"

"It depends on the secret, but I am generally a man of my word." Walker leaned forward.

Byron looked him over. "Your demeanor suggests you are a trustworthy sort. And of course, being the brother of the lovely Mira Blayse does more for your credibility than just about anything."

"Didn't the prime minister request that this stayed secret?"

"You're working for the prime minister?" Walker asked.

"See, Mira, now it's necessary to tell him everything," Byron teased. "You give your word that you won't breathe a speck of this to anyone else?"

"I do." Walker placed a hand over his heart.

"Very good. Moving on. Based on the documents that we received yesterday, it would seem that Sir William and his wife are staying at rooms in Mayfair. They have two adult children living with them. Lila and Neville. They are leaving for Constantinople on October twenty-first, first taking an airship to France, and then the Orient Express. Our job is to keep watch for anything suspicious until they leave."

"What's our first move?" Mira asked.

"I've already taken it. I stopped by their rooms this morning and introduced myself. Asked the preliminary questions about if they've seen anything unusual. Nothing. So, I'd say our next step is heading over to the Yard to see if good ol' Fred can give some insight into any strange things happening in the realms of upper society."

"Things certainly happen fast around here, don't they?" Walker asked, placing his teacup down.

"There are only so many hours in the day! Best to make the most of them," Byron said, prepping his journal for the journey. "Shall we be off?"

"Let's!" Walker jumped up and hurried to the entry hall to retrieve his and Mira's coats.

Byron moved over to her and lowered his voice.

"He's eager," he chuckled.

"I think for as much as I envied his journeys in France, he envied our adventures here."

Walker poked his head back in, hat and coat already on. "What are we waiting for?"

"Absolutely nothing!" Byron moved past him to ready himself.

Soon enough, they all were on the street walking towards the main road. Walker signaled a cab and once they settled inside it, his questioning nature emerged. Mira looked between them from the center of the seat as they conversed.

"How long have you worked with Scotland Yard?"

"It's been about six years."

"And the memory troubles . . . ?"

"Well over four years."

"It's incredible that you're still able to solve crimes! Mira told me you've solved over forty since the accident!"

"I would say that I take it one day at a time, but, truthfully, it is rather incredible to me as well. I haven't the foggiest idea how I've managed. Although, I do know that recently it is due to the efforts of your sister that I've accomplished anything at all."

Mira blushed under the stares of the men on either side of her.

"You manage the detecting part quite well on your own, Byron. I only fill in the gaps when you need me to."

"And I'm most indebted to you as a result. But you are still selling yourself short." He glanced back over at Walker. "Your sister is one of the bravest women I know. I only wish I could remember all the instances I've read about in my journal."

Walker gave her a considering look. "I believe there are some stories I haven't heard yet, in that case."

The cab rolled to a stop and Mira let out a breath of relief. "Those stories will have to wait! Are you ready to see Scotland Yard?"

Walker brightened and hastened out of the carriage, helping his sister down after him. Byron paid the cab driver, and they all moved inside the building. Mira stifled a smile as her brother's mouth gaped open at the interior. She had a similar reaction the first time she entered the Yard, but she hoped she looked a bit more proper now. Byron led the way towards the front desk, eyes searching for his old friend. He grinned once he spotted him.

"Fred! There you are. Have you got a minute?"

The man in question looked up from the documents he held and smiled, moving over.

"I almost always have time for you. And Miss Blayse, of course. But who is the young gentleman with you?"

Mira caught a slight worry in his expression. She took her brother's arm and led him over. "This is my brother, Walker. He's just returned from abroad."

Walker offered his hand. "A pleasure to meet you, Mr. . . . Fred, was it?"

Fred laughed and took the handshake. "Frederick Wensley. But I prefer Fred."

"Now that we've taken care of introductions, I wondered if you could give us any information about the current goings on, so to speak. Particularly in the higher circles."

Fred frowned. "An odd request, that." He glanced around at the busy lobby. "Let's take this somewhere quiet. I think one of the interrogation rooms is open."

He led the group farther into the building, past offices, and other constables. Fred pulled open the door to an interrogation room and ushered them all inside. Byron pulled a chair out for Mira. The men remained standing.

"I can't talk for long," Fred said. "We're a bit busy at the moment."

"What seems to be the trouble?"

"Whitechapel, as always. It seems to be the only thing Commissioner Warren is interested in. He's taken great offense at another victim being found at the construction site for the new police building. We've been working like dogs trying to find the killer, to no avail. This Ripper fellow is running rings around us all!"

"I think I remember reading something about that," Byron

said, looking at Mira. "Wasn't our last case related to it?" Mira nodded.

Fred paced along the wall. "Thatcher mentioned you found evidence that there is more than one killer. But since it isn't conclusive, well, we're going to have our hands full until Circe decides to stop. And then we'll have the copycat killers to deal with." He leaned against the wall with a groan.

"I'm surprised you had time for us at all." Byron leaned on the wall next to him.

"Honestly? I needed a break. Was there anything specific you wanted to know?"

"Yes, actually. Has there been any strange activity near Mayfair?"

Fred frowned for a moment, then shook his head. "Not that I know of. Things have been uncommonly quiet outside of Whitechapel."

"Hmm. You'll let us know if anything comes up?"

"Of course. I ought to get back to work. Inspector Mayhew threatened to take a bunch of us out to the construction site again. Not that we'll find anything else." He blew a strand of hair out of his face.

"Best of luck to you." Byron clapped him on the back.

"You as well."

Byron turned left at the door and led the way to Chief Inspector Thatcher's office. Juliet Chickering, Thatcher's secretary, turned away for a moment as they approached. Mira suspected she was pinching her cheeks to put some color in them. She confirmed her suspicions as Juliet turned back around, face fresh and pink.

"Oh! Mr. Constantine! It's good to see you."

"You as well, Miss Chickering. Thatcher in?"

"Yes, of course! I'll let him know you are here." She stepped to the office door, knocked, and disappeared.

"This is all quite fascinating," Walker said, taking it all in.

"I'd read about the Whitechapel murders, of course, but Mira never mentioned that you were involved in the investigation."

"By the time we realized the connection, we'd already solved the case," Mira said

Juliet popped out of the office once more. "He has a few minutes. Go ahead."

The trio moved through the door, Byron leading the way.

"Good afternoon, Constantine. One moment, please," Thatcher remarked from his desk, not looking up from his paperwork.

He set his pen down with a flourish and glanced up, smiling. "And Miss Blayse! A pleasure, as always. Who's this with you?"

Walker stepped forward, and the two men shook hands. "Walker Blayse. I'm her brother."

"Ah. Come to see what she's been up to?" He chuckled before turning back to Byron and Mira. "I'm afraid I don't have any cases for the two of you just yet."

"That's quite alright, Inspector. I actually came to ask a favor." Byron leaned over the desk.

"Oh?"

"Can you keep an eye out for any shady dealings happening around Mayfair?"

"Certainly. I presume this is for one of your private cases?"

Byron nodded.

"I'll let you know if anything comes up."

"Excellent. Well, I'm sure you're just as busy as the rest of the yard. We'll take our leave."

"Be careful. All of you."

Byron and Walker exited the office, but Mira stayed behind.

"Erm. Chief Inspector, you wouldn't happen to recognize the name Grace Trimbell, would you?"

Thatcher looked up at her, brow furrowed. "Not exactly, no. Is she part of your case?"

"No. It's something I'm looking into about Byron. He's

had some memories resurface, and they are connected to her. I thought I'd look into it on my own."

The inspector's eyes widened. "He's remembering?"

Mira nodded.

"If there's anything I can do to help, let me know. I'll look into the name and see what I can find."

"Thank you."

Walker popped his head in. "Mira, are you coming?" He lowered his voice. "Miss Chickering is flirting up a storm out here and I think Byron could use some assistance."

The inspector chuckled behind her as she walked out.

"Sorry for the wait. Shall we go?"

"Yes, please," Byron said, offering her his arm.

Mira glanced over her shoulder, noting Juliet's burning glare as they left Scotland Yard.

"Thank you for letting me shadow you for the day. It was enlightening." Walker smiled down at her.

"I would say 'anytime' but I'm afraid some things are more confidential than others."

"I understand."

Byron called for a hansom cab but paused before giving the address.

"Don't you two need to get back to your uncle's? After all, you'll need to pack for your trip."

"Right! We're leaving tomorrow morning!"

"I never agreed to it." Mira folded her arms.

"You'd best go, Mira. We don't want your uncle to dislike me anymore than he already does." He turned to the driver. "Swan Walk, please."

"He does have a point, little Mouse."

Byron smiled. "Mouse?"

Mira hid her face in her hands.

"She's as small and shy as a mouse. I started calling her that after her first party. I think we were eight."

"If I go to this party and prove that I'm not a mouse, will you stop calling me that?"

Walker's lips twitched into a smile. "Deal."

"I can't promise that I won't," Byron said, laughing.

Walker joined in and soon Mira couldn't stop giggling herself.

THE CAB STOPPED IN FRONT OF SWAN Walk and Byron signaled the driver to stay while they all clambered out. He took Mira's hand and kissed the back of it.

"We'll see each other soon enough." He smiled at her.

"I'll be over, first thing on Sunday."

"I look forward to it." He tipped his hat and stepped into the carriage again.

Once the cab drove out of sight, she followed Walker up the stairs and into the house to pack. What a day! She pulled a small suitcase from the back of her closet and opened it. She should feel happy, ecstatic even. And yet, envy dwelled in the pit of her stomach. Who was Grace Trimbell, and why did Byron remember her? She perused her evening wear, hardly seeing the dresses at all. At least Walker was home. She smiled. Things always seemed more fun with her twin around.

A knock sounded at the door, and Walker stepped in. "You don't happen to have an explanation for why a good set of my clothes is shredded, do you?"

She laughed. "Help me pack and I'll tell you what Byron and I have really been up to."

October 12, 1888

MIRA PACED THE SITTING ROOM, WAITING FOR her uncle and Walker to finish with their preparations for the trip. With all their fussing about her being ready "bright and early in the morning," they didn't hold themselves to the same standard.

"Uncle! You didn't put my formal wear in the attic, did you?" Walker called down the staircase.

"It's at the back of your wardrobe!" she called up.

Walker appeared at the top of the stairs. "Why would you know that? How many of my clothes have you worn?" He glared at her, outraged.

"Ssssh!" Mira glanced at her uncle's study. "Keep your voice down."

Cyrus' door opened, and he peeked out. "What was that, Walker?"

"Oh, never mind. Mira helped me out."

"Well, hurry. I'm almost done here. Mira, are you ready?"

"I have been since seven," she huffed.

BEFORE LONG, THEY WERE EXITING A HANSOM cab at the train station, luggage in hand.

"I can't say that I'm particularly excited to be on a train again. I've had enough trains for a lifetime."

"Come now, Walker! What happened to your sense of adventure?" Mira teased.

"Must have left it back in France." He leaned closer as their uncle consulted the charts for their train. "Or on that airship." He winked at her, and she laughed.

Cyrus turned back towards them.

"Our train is on platform three and it's leaving in fifteen minutes. Come now, you two."

Mira could have sworn she heard him mumble something about "ridiculous children" under his breath.

After handing their luggage off to a helpful steward, they made their way into first class. Cyrus peered into each window, trying to find an empty compartment.

"Here we are." He slid the door open and gestured for the twins to enter.

They settled into their seats with Walker and Mira seated closest to the window, and Cyrus next to Walker.

Now that they were actually on the train, Mira relaxed, determined to enjoy the trip with her family. After all, she rarely saw Walker anymore, and his outgoing nature made him the most fun at parties.

"How long is this trip again?" Walker said, looking out the window.

"About two hours. Should go by fast enough."

Mira pulled a book out of her travel bag to occupy her time.

The train whistle sounded, and the soothing rumble of the engine shuddered through the car. She smiled to herself, thinking of the last time she rode on a train, and how she disembarked.

"What's caused that smile to grace your face, Mira?" Walker leaned over to her.

"I'm thinking, that's all."

"About anything or anyone in particular?" he prodded.

"Not at all."

She opened her book in an attempt to dissuade any further conversation on the subject.

The trip passed in a lazy blink, ending when Walker gave her shoulder a gentle nudge. She stirred awake.

"We've arrived. Shall we be off?"

SPENSTON PARK SPREAD OUT OVER SWATHES OF lush forest and lawns which glowed with the deep hues of autumn as their carriage trundled up the walk. The house itself loomed over them as they approached. Ivy trailed around the windows and onto the roof. The chimneys puffed, giving Mira hope for a warm interior. She held her ears for a moment to heat them up before they exited the carriage.

A tall man with greying hair and an amicable grin stood on the steps. He held a bit more girth than their uncle, but he seemed around the same age. His eyes lit up as they stepped out of the carriage and he moved to Cyrus in an instant, shaking his hand.

"Cyrus! I'm so glad you've come after all!" He turned to Mira and Walker. "And this must be your niece and nephew."

"Yes, indeed. Walker and Samira, meet Mr. Vincent Sutherland."

"A pleasure to make your acquaintance, sir." Walker shook the man's hand.

"Thank you so much for the invitation," Mira added.

"I'm just pleased I finally get to meet the both of you! Your uncle does talk a lot about you, you know. Now bring those bags inside before you catch cold!"

He escorted them into the entry hall and a butler helped them out of their coats and hats, taking them to a cloakroom. Mira marveled at the massive crystal chandelier, while Walker found interest in a strange box sitting on a side table.

"Is this what I think it is?" he said, excitement palpable in his voice.

"That depends on what you think it is." Mr. Sutherland smiled.

"It's a telephone box, isn't it?"

"It is indeed! One of the first in this part of the country. For as expensive as it was, I still haven't figured the blasted thing out."

"Can I take a look at it?" Walker vibrated with energy.

"As long as you'll teach me once you figure it out."

Walker set to work examining the object. Mr. Sutherland turned to Cyrus.

"Were you wanting to go over the particulars of the merger now?"

"That would be good, yes. Will you two be alright on your own?" Cyrus glanced between the twins.

"More than alright, Uncle!" Walker said.

"Quentin can show you to your rooms once that instrument bores you out. If you want a tour of the house or need anything, please let him know." Mr. Sutherland nodded to his butler before directing her uncle down one of the hallways.

"Mira, come look at this!" Walker beckoned her over.

She frowned at the brown box. She had heard of telephones, of course, but she'd never seen one before.

"What exactly am I looking at?"

"This is a marvel of technology! You see this?" He pointed to a black device attached to the side of the box. "This is a receiver. When you want to make a call, you pick up the receiver, wind up the box, and tap out the number you want to call."

"Number?"

"Well, you see, every telephone box has a number assigned to it. Used to be that you had a list of people who had telephones and you'd tell an operator who you wished to speak with. Some telephones are all connected to one another, so you can hear anyone's conversation whenever you like. Looks like Mr. Sutherland has a newer one that can connect to an operator to help you connect or dial a specific person outright."

Mira stared at the box. It was hard to imagine hearing someone's voice through it. Walker took her silence as a cue to continue.

"So, if you wanted to dial, you'd tap out the number in Morse code."

"You have to know Morse code to use this?"

No wonder Mr. Sutherland didn't like it. Walker felt around the table before opening up a drawer in the front. He smiled as he found a booklet and skimmed through it.

"Looks like a list of the numbers in the area, with the pulses drawn out. It couldn't be simpler!"

She looked over the booklet. The words "*Telephone Directory*" were typed at the top of the first page. Right below it was the word "*operator*" next to two zeros. She turned over the booklet and found the numbers zero to nine with the Morse code for each number typed in a column.

"Seems like a lot of trouble."

"Oh, but it would be worth it! Can you imagine what this technology could be like in just a few years? Why, I bet we could communicate clear across the country! Maybe even across the channel! Can you imagine instead of sending letters every day, we each had our own telephones and just spoke to one another?"

Mira tried to wrap her head around that. It would be wonderful. But how was everyone supposed to learn Morse code?

Walker expounded on the virtues of the telephone for

another fifteen minutes before he ran out of things to say. Quentin showed them around the house and finally to the guest quarters. Mira found herself alone in an enormous room. She moved past the rose-colored bed and set her luggage against the chest of drawers. She moved to one of the windows. Heavens, the grounds were lovely. She blew a strand of hair out of her face. If only she could go explore before the festivities.

A clock chimed three o'clock on the mantle. If she were younger, she and Walker would have already escaped to the back gardens. She sighed and turned back towards her luggage and the vanity. Another night of pretending.

THE GRANDFATHER CLOCK IN THE HALL CHIMED quarter past eight. Mira entered the ballroom adjusting her gloves, so they rested at her elbows again. Upper tier social gatherings were not the best way to spend an evening. Standing for hours, introductions to strangers, tiny little hors d'oeuvres, the heat of hundreds of people close together—her list of things she disliked grew longer as the evening did. Particularly since she hadn't seen her uncle or Walker since she came down.

Goodness, it took a while to style herself as a proper lady. Especially by herself. But her hair finally submitted to the curls and pins and pieces, and her dress came together rather well. The creamy pink complemented her skin tone without bringing out too much red in her hair, and the white, lace roses were a nice touch. With the conservative bustle, it was fashionable, functional, and most fortunate of all, comfortable. Even if there was the slight fear of tripping on the hem. She really should have taken it up before they left London.

She ventured over to the refreshment table hoping to find her brother (or something substantial to eat) but found gossip instead. Some young ladies conversed near the punch bowl.

"I've never seen him before. Are you certain they are brothers?" the first said.

"Positive! You can't deny the family resemblance, can you?"

"I suppose not. He is quite handsome, though I wish he'd turn towards us for the full picture."

"I heard from Lady Katherine that his name is Ambrose, and while he's not likely to take up the barony, he certainly has a fortune of his own," a third chimed in.

"Why, that makes him even more handsome!" All three burst into conservative laughter.

Mira rolled her eyes. Yet another reason to dislike upper society. Did everyone have an agenda? Not finding her brother, Mira moved back into the crowd. She glanced around the room until her eyes fell on her uncle. Straightening her posture, she moved over to him. When he caught sight of her, he broke into a wide smile.

"There you are Mira! For a moment, I thought you had decided to hide out in your rooms."

What a wonderful idea. Why hadn't she thought of that?

"Of course not, Uncle. We've come all this way."

"Well, let's find Mr. Sutherland and get him to introduce you to some of these lovely people. I already set Walker up with Miss Renaldi. Come now!"

Mira tucked a loose strand of hair back into her style. At least her brother was receiving the same treatment. She followed her uncle through the crowd.

"Ah, there you are, Vince. I'm afraid I need your services again!"

Cyrus pulled Mira into view and Mr. Sutherland grinned.

"I'm assuming you require some introductions?"

"If it isn't too much trouble." She fidgeted with her fan.

"I'm sure we could find you some eligible gentleman to dance with." Sutherland's eyes trailed across the ballroom. No doubt in search of someone he deemed eligible.

"Very good." Cyrus smiled. "I expect to see you on the dance floor soon enough, Mira."

Cyrus made his way back through the crowd, leaving Mira at the mercy of Mr. Sutherland.

"Well, let's see who is around, hmm?"

He turned in a circle before choosing a direction. He approached a man in a sleek black suit who seemed familiar.

"Mr. Sherard! May I introduce you to someone?"

"Of course."

The man turned towards them, and Mira glanced from his cold eyes to his well-trimmed mustache. Unmistakably, Castel. She resisted the urge to bristle in his presence.

"Mr. Sherard, this is Miss Samira Blayse, the niece of one of my colleagues. Miss Blayse, this is Castel Sherard, nephew and heir of the current Baron Sherard."

Baron? Mira's eyes widened, and a gasp stuck in her throat before she composed herself.

"A pleasure to meet you again, Mr. Sherard." She inclined her head.

"Oh! You've already met? Splendid!" Mr. Sutherland clapped his hands.

"Yes, we have," Castel smirked and continued. "But I don't believe that you've met my brother, Ambrose Sherard."

Castel stepped to the side, and a strikingly familiar gentleman turned from his conversation to join theirs. Mira's heart leapt. No wonder the girls had been gossiping.

"Ambrose, this is Samira Blayse."

Ambrose's blue eyes lit up, and he took her hand in his, kissing the back of it.

"Do you mind if I call you Mira?" His eyes twinkled.

She bit back a smile. "As long as I may call you Byron."

He grinned and leaned closer to whisper, "Perhaps not in this setting."

Mr. Sutherland gave a booming laugh of triumph. "Well, I'll leave you young people alone. Let me know if you require any additional introductions, Miss Blayse!"

Castel looked between the two of them and scoffed. Mira thought she made out a "hopeless, simply hopeless," before he left their company as well.

"What brings you here, Mr. Sherard?" She raised an eyebrow at him.

"I heard that one of the most beautiful young ladies in the country would be in attendance, and I knew I had to see it for myself."

"Flatterer. Why are you really here?"

"You'll never believe it, but Sir William happens to have been invited."

"Is that so?"

He nodded and turned back to the gentleman he had been conversing with before.

"Sir William, allow me to introduce Miss Blayse. I believe I told you about her at our last meeting."

Sir William smiled. "A pleasure to meet you, Miss Blayse. You are just as lovely as Mr. Cons—I beg your pardon—as Mr. Sherard said you were."

"Thank you." She smiled. "Are you enjoying the party thus far, Sir William?"

"Most definitely. I believe this is the last gathering we'll be able to attend before we leave for Constantinople. For as much as I enjoy travelling abroad, there is something to be said of home."

"That's true. Although, I'm afraid I haven't travelled much myself," Mira said.

"We should remedy that." Byron smiled at her.

Sir William chuckled. "I'm afraid I need to speak with Mr. Sutherland, but it was so nice to meet you, Miss Blayse. I'm sure I'll be seeing more of you before the month is out."

He bowed his head and disappeared into the crowd. Byron turned to Mira.

"You really do look splendid this evening. We ought to go to more parties."

"I'd be more inclined to do so if I knew you would be there. Did you know about this yesterday?"

Byron grinned. "I thought I could surprise you. That is, according to what I+ve written in my journal."

"Incorrigible." She hid her smile behind her fan.

"At least I remembered what I was doing today! And I remembered bumping into Grace two days ago. My memory seems to be improving."

A strange blend of jealousy and relief rushed through Mira.

"That's brilliant! I hope it keeps up."

"Me too." He leaned closer. "I can't wait to remember you. Although, it was a pleasant experience to be introduced to you again."

A warmth spread over Mira's cheeks, and she lost her words. Byron looked out into the crowd.

"I shouldn't let Sir William get too far out of sight, but may I reserve a dance on your card?"

"Of course, Mr. Sherard."

She slipped the card off her wrist and passed it to him. He removed a pen from his inner pocket and wrote his name under two slots.

"Until we meet again, Miss Blayse."

Byron kissed the back of her hand and drifted into the crowd. Mira's gaze stayed with him until he disappeared, then she turned back towards the center of the room. She caught a few frosty glares from the refreshment table, but shrugged them off to find her brother. He could probably use some rescuing.

There were fewer people invited to this ball than the last one she had attended. At Maureen Harris' gala, it had seemed that the people filled the ballroom like wall-to-wall carpet. Stifling, to say the least.

Here, there were plenty of people to be sure, but it was simple enough to navigate from one side of the room to the other. Or so she had thought as she walked along the wall searching for Walker. In a heartbeat, her hem caught on a table leg, and she fell, sprawled on the floor in a heap of fabric and embarrassment. Her skirts twisted around her legs. She sighed and tried to free herself from her predicament.

"Might I lend a hand?" a gentleman offered from above.

Without looking, she took his hand, and he helped her to her feet as she rearranged her skirts.

"Thank you very much! I'm afraid I had quite the" —Mira's blood ran chill as she met dangerous hazel eyes— "fall."

"Yes, you did, Miss Blayse."

He smirked and kissed her hand. She discreetly removed it from his grasp.

"I'm afraid I need to go."

Her gaze darted across the ballroom. The lead they had been chasing for weeks was right in front of her, and Byron was nowhere to be found! No. He had to be somewhere.

"Your dance card says otherwise."

She turned to see him examining her dance card. A glance at her wrist told her it had fallen when she tripped.

"Would you be so kind as to return it to me?"

"Of course." He took a pencil and wrote his name in next to one of the dances, before handing it back to her.

"You do realize that it is a breach of etiquette to ask a lady to dance when you haven't been properly introduced?"

"Would that be a problem if Mr. Constantine was the one doing the asking?"

Mira bit back the comment that Byron had, in fact, asked her to dance. And that they had now been properly introduced. Instead, she turned away from the mysterious gentleman in a huff and continued scanning the area. Hadn't Sir William mentioned that he was looking for Mr. Sutherland? And wherever Sir William was, Byron wouldn't be far.

As she put some distance between herself and the Circe spy, her uncle caught her arm.

"Mira, I knew you had it in you!" His eyes filled with joy and pride.

"Whatever do you mean, Uncle?" Mira's gaze continued to flit over the crowd.

"Mr. Sutherland informed me of how well you got on with the youngest Sherard! Why hadn't you told me you had met Castel before?"

"It didn't occur to me."

"No matter. Did his younger brother ask you to dance?"

"Yes, he did."

"Very good. Have you met any other gentlemen?"

"Only one," she muttered, glancing at her dance card.

A. D.

Ambrose Sherard

Ambrose Sherard

"Keep it up, and do remember to smile!"

"Of course, Uncle."

Cyrus patted her on the back and nudged her in the direction of another gentleman. She gave him a polite smile then continued her search for Byron.

She wandered into the drawing room, hoping to find him there. Instead, she found it empty, save for Byron's brother. Castel smoked his pipe by the window. Mira took a breath and moved over to him.

"I'm sorry to bother you, Mr. Sherard, but do you know where your brother is?"

"I'm afraid I don't. I'm surprised that you lost him."

"Whatever do you mean?"

"Allow me to rephrase." He turned towards her. "I'm surprised that he let you out of his sight. He hardly spoke of anything else since I picked him up this morning."

"Really?"

"I don't speak falsities to make others feel better, Miss Blayse. Even for the happiness of my brother."

Mira took pause. "Please forgive my curiosity, but why are things so strained between you two?"

"He hasn't told you?"

"I'd like to hear your version of it. Byron's memory isn't the most reliable."

Castel gave a disheartened chuckle and puffed on his pipe for a moment. "That's a major part of the problem, you know."

He turned towards her. "Shortly after I received my seat in parliament, Byron came up with this crazy idea to become a detective. We all knew he was brilliant. And he did well with the tips to the police. But then he suggested he move to London to investigate crimes. I suppose it comes from him having three older brothers. It's quite unlikely he'll inherit the title. With our brother Philip off traveling the world and our brother Ralph in the military, there isn't much for Byron to do. For as much as our father would have wanted Byron to take up the cloth and follow in his footsteps, well, you can imagine how well that would have gone over."

Mira tried to imagine Byron as a reverend and couldn't.

"When he was fifteen, I suggested he find some way to make a difference in the world and to make a name for himself. And then he literally made a new name for himself. At least that way he never brought disgrace upon the family name."

"I highly doubt that Byron would disgrace your family in any way."

"You don't think a detective with memory loss is laughable?"

"That isn't his fault. And he does a splendid job in spite of it."

"I can be grateful for that." He sighed and tapped the side of his pipe as the flame died down. "I wanted to support him in the only way I knew how. When I heard the Queen wished to look into the attempts on her life, I immediately thought of Byron." A pained expression crossed his face, and he turned away from her. "Of course, that would be the case that took his memory."

She softened. Perhaps he wasn't as severe as she had previously judged.

"You're not to blame either, Mr. Sherard. And while Byron may blame you, he's wrong to do so. I think you're both hurt, and that's making it impossible to reconcile."

Castel looked up at her, brow furrowed.

"Bold of you to speak such things to a member of the House of Lords."

"I care about Byron. And I think deep down he still cares about you."

His mouth fell open as she smoothed out her dress.

"Thank you for telling me your side of things. He's been remembering bits of what happened to him. I want to help him as much as I can."

A ghost of a smile appeared on his lips.

"I had wondered what he'd seen in you." He relit his pipe, shaking the match. "I'm glad he's in good hands, at least."

"I ought to go find him. Good evening, Mr. Sherard."

She moved to the door and took a deep breath to calm her nerves. Peering out the door, she glanced both ways to ensure that the mysterious gentleman wasn't in sight. To her relief, he wasn't. She moved up the stairs to explore the upper sitting room.

As she entered, she noticed Walker in the corner, engaged in conversation with a man in a sharp, blue suit. So, he had escaped the attentions of Miss Renaldi after all! He lit up as she approached.

"Mira! I have someone I'd like you to meet!"

The other gentleman turned, and a sour taste entered her

palate. She swallowed a grimace and smiled, floating over, graceful as a dove.

"This is my sister, Samira Blayse. Mira, this is Alexander Durant."

She filed away the name for when she encountered Byron again, even if it was likely to be an alias.

"It's a pleasure to meet you, Miss Blayse. I've heard so much about you." His eyes seemed warmer in this light.

"And I so little about you. Other than a name, so it would seem."

She glanced at Walker, who rocked back on his heels, far too pleased with himself.

"I'm sure with adequate time we can get to know one another." Alexander reached out and left a burning kiss on the back of her hand.

"Perhaps. But finding that time is a bit of a difficulty."

"Not necessarily, Mira," Walker chimed in. "Alexander has offered me an engineering opportunity that I just might take him up on."

"Oh? What kind?" Mira asked.

"I have connections with the remnants of the East India Trading Company, and they are always looking for new inventors for steamships and the like."

"Can you imagine it? I'd be following in father's footsteps."

As long as he didn't follow them too closely. Mira kept her gaze level with Alexander's.

"Sounds like a wonderful opportunity, Walker." She tried to keep her voice from sounding too hollow. She failed.

"Yes, I believe it will b—oh, I must dash. I think Miss Renaldi has caught sight of me again. Good to speak with you, Mr. Durant! Keep out of trouble, Mira." He pressed a kiss to her cheek and fled from the room.

Mira turned back to Alexander, crossing her arms over her chest.

"What are you playing at?" She drummed her fingers on her arm.

"Can I not take an interest in a fellow engineering student?"

"You study engineering?"

"Among other things." His gaze traveled down the row of lace flowers on her dress.

Mira glared, and he smirked at her as his eyes found hers again.

The music for a two-step drifted up from the lower floor, and Alexander offered her his hand.

"I do believe that I'm the first on your list. Shall we return to the ballroom?"

"For the sake of propriety, let's."

She offered a thin smile and took his arm. The grandfather clock chimed for half past nine as he led her down the stairs to the ballroom and pulled her into dance position.

"Since when do you care about propriety, Miss Blayse?"

"My uncle is watching."

"Thank goodness for your uncle, then."

They swayed to the music, and Mira found him to lead rather well. She bit back her annoyance and struck at why she actually allowed him to dance with her.

"Why are you here?"

"I was invited, same as you."

Mira scowled. "Well, stay away from my brother."

Alexander sucked in a hiss of air, "Mm. Sorry. Can't do that, I'm afraid."

"And why is that?"

"You aren't exactly threatening. And I made a promise. Despite what you might think of me, I'm a man of my word."

"A promise to who?"

"Your brother, of course. I promised I'd look into a position for him."

"And what are your other motives?"

He chuckled. "Why on earth are you so suspicious of me?"

"Oh, I don't know. Perhaps because you work with Circe?"

Alexander smiled, eyes full of mirth. "You are quite unlike any other woman I've ever met, Miss Blayse."

Mira's cheeks burned without her permission. "What, do other ladies swoon at your feet?"

"Actually, yes."

"So, you are conceited as well as a traitor to the crown."

His brow furrowed. "Where did you get a notion like that?"

"The warnings, the letters, the cryptic messages!"

He led her into a spin, confusion evident when she came back to face him.

"Then this game has gone on long enough. I ought to explain myself," he said, softer. As the dance ended, he pulled back from her but kept a firm grip on her hand. "But not here."

He slipped a piece of paper into her palm. She pulled back and concealed the paper in her fan.

"Until later, Miss Blayse."

He nodded to her and walked away, leaving her dumb-founded. Retreating to the hall, she removed the paper and unfolded it.

Meet me in the conservatory at one.

She glanced at the grandfather clock. The hour-hand rested between nine and ten. She bit her lip. Only a few hours to decide. Was it wise to go? On one hand, she could gather valuable information about Circe. On the other, well, what were his intentions exactly?

"I heard you were looking for me?"

She relaxed hearing Byron's voice and turned towards him. "Oh, yes. Well . . ." Should she tell him? She chewed on her lip.

"I wanted to see a familiar face." The orchestra struck up a waltz, and she smiled. "And I believe our dances are next."

"Quite right you are." He took her arm in his and led her

out into the center of the ballroom again. Her skirts swished around her ankles as he led her through the steps.

"You dance beautifully, Miss Blayse."

"As do you."

"That comes with the territory of being a Sherard."

"Oh, of course!" She glanced up at him through her eyelashes. "Were you ever going to tell me?"

"I prefer the anonymity of Constantine. It's safer that way."

"That doesn't answer the question. I had my suspicions about your real last name after Castel came to visit. But didn't even consider the thought that you could be related to Baron Sherard. Would you have told me if it weren't for Castel?"

Byron sighed. "I'm not sure. Even if I chose to tell you about it, I'd forget before I saw you again. And when I first meet you each morning, I can't imagine that I want to give up a secret I've been so keen on protecting. Only my family knows."

"I didn't realize it was that serious."

Byron nodded and continued. "Aside from that, I'd rather make my own way, so to speak. There are fewer expectations."

Mira nodded. "I understand."

He smiled at her, expression softening. "Were you surprised?"

Mira thought on that a moment and shook her head. "No. Not really. You've always had a noble air about you. But this doesn't change a thing. I prefer the sound of Constantine, anyway."

He grinned and twirled her out onto the dance floor before pulling her back towards him. She laughed as she followed his lead.

"Wait! This does change something."

His smile disappeared. "What?"

"My uncle might find you eligible now!"

Byron's grin was never brighter.

October 13, 1888: Early Morning

THE GRANDFATHER CLOCK IN THE HALL STRUCK one. Mira stood outside the conservatory. The silence of the night swelled in her eardrums in contrast to the din the party had made only a few hours before. Swallowing, she slipped through the door. Moonlight drifted through the glass, highlighting the plants in a ghostly aura. A small pond lay at the center of the room. She shivered. Why had she come? And why hadn't she told Byron? Or anyone, for that matter?

She yawned. Should she just go to bed? Everyone else had, save a few servants and caterers left cleaning up the mess in the wake of the guests. Somewhere in the house, Byron's memories were slipping away like dreams, and here she was, potentially walking into a trap. She really should just leave. Mr. Durant could wait until morning for all she cared. And yet her insatiable curiosity couldn't be dismissed so easily.

As she stepped into a spot of moonlight, glancing around for any trace of him, a shadow moved.

"I was afraid you wouldn't come,"

She froze. What could she say to that?

His figure moved into the light. "I believe I owe you an explanation."

"That is what I came for." She folded her arms and sat on the edge of the pond.

He sat next to her, allowing about three feet of space between them. Mira kept her gaze on the pond as the koi fish swam in circles.

"It started a few months ago. I received an anonymous letter saying that if I delivered a message to you, I would receive fifty pounds."

"That is quite a sum," she hummed.

"Yes. It is. I'm apprenticed at the moment and extra money is always welcome. The letter also informed me of where and when to find you and contained a photograph." He caught her gaze and smiled. "I must say, that even without the money, I was entranced. Curiosity fueled our first meeting, nothing more."

Mira swallowed and fiddled with one of her wayward curls, looking away. How had Circe come into possession of a photograph of her?

"Did they say why they needed the message delivered?"

"From what I could tell, it was part of an elaborate prank." He fiddled with the brim of his top hat. "The sender said that it wasn't meant to do any harm. They wished to remain anonymous so no one could trace it back to them if I decided to reveal myself as I'm doing now." He moved closer to her. "I received another letter later instructing me to deliver the last message to you."

"And I suppose you received another one instructing you to 'check up on me?'"

"No. I did that on my own."

Mira stood and walked over to the main window of the conservatory. He stayed by the pond. She mulled it over. Everything she knew about this "mysterious" man flitted to the forefront of her mind. His story made sense, but only if she could trust him. Could she? She glanced back at him as he looked up at her in earnest. He even kept his distance. Her gaze drifted back to the conservatory window.

"If this is true, how do you know about Byron?"

"They included a bit of personal information in the first letter—including your relationship with Byron."

She furrowed her brow and turned back towards him. "Then, you don't know anything of Circe?"

"I heard of it first from you."

"Why are you telling me this now?" She paced along the window, skirts trailing on the brick beneath them.

He sucked in a breath. "That is where things get awkward."

"Try me."

"Well, I found myself becoming jealous of Mr. Constantine."

"What?" Her breath caught in her throat.

"Because of how we met, you hated me. If we had met in any other fashion, I might have had a chance to get to know you. We could have been friends." He stood and moved over to her, then added, almost to himself, "Or more."

Mira huffed and turned away to hide a blush. He continued.

"I thought I could gain your interest by sparking up a different mystery for you to solve: to figure out who I was. It could have been fun."

"This isn't a game, Mr. Durant," she said, voice wavering.

"No, it isn't." He leaned closer.

The moonlight brought out the gold in his eyes, and that warmth spread to the rest of his face. "I realized that when I found out that Walker was your brother. I had no idea of your connection. I only wanted to give him an opportunity, as he seems bright and able. And since we would likely see each other more, it would be prudent to end all this before it started." He sighed and dropped his gaze to the floor. "And I am sorry."

He glanced up at her, hope in his eyes, but Mira couldn't take him at his word. Too much was at stake.

"How can I trust that you're telling the truth?"

"I suppose you can't, but—"

BANG.

Mira let out a stifled shriek. "What was that?"

"It came from the room above us. Do you know what's there?"

Alexander rushed towards the door, Mira at his heels.

"I think it's the study. Was that a gunshot?"

"I certainly hope not."

They ran up the stairs to the study. Alexander jiggled the handle.

"It's locked. Stand back. I'll see if I can't break it down."

Mira stepped aside as Alexander examined the door. His hands feathered over the lock, hinges, and handle, then he stood back and straightened. With a wide stance, he lifted his foot and kicked his heel into the door with all his force. The door splintered, and a metallic tinkle rang out. Two more well-placed kicks and the hinges burst. They entered the room together. Mira's stomach roiled as she stopped on the threshold. The curtains swayed as a cold October breeze swept through the room. A man slumped over a mess of papers, blood clotting onto them. She looked away and swallowed a mouthful of acrid spit.

Alexander tested for a pulse.

"There's something, but it's fading. He must have fainted from shock and blood loss. Miss Blayse, I believe I saw a telephone in the main entry hall. I need you to call the police. I'll go see if there is a doctor among the guests."

She ran out of the room, stumbling down the stairs. She cut across the ballroom, hoping to take the shortest route to the entry hall. The grandfather clock chimed quarter after one. Brushing past a caterer as she moved through, she caused a tray of pans and dishes to crash to the floor.

"Oh, I'm so sorry!" She continued to run.

The sooner she called the police, the better. She almost slipped as she reached the entrance hall, but she righted herself and moved to the telephone. She shook out her hands and flicked on the light switch with a buzz.

"Come on Mira. You can figure this out."

She picked up what she thought was the receiver and rummaged for the booklet in the drawer. After retrieving it she ran a finger down the listings for any sign of the police. Nothing. She turned it over to ensure she remembered the number of zeros for the operator, then flicked back to the Morse code. Five dashes. Twice. She wound up the box and took a breath. Placing her finger on the tapper, she counted out ten dashes. The phone hummed for a second.

"Hello?"

No response. She tapped out ten dashes again, faster this time.

The main door opened behind her as her uncle came in.

"Mira? What are you doing up?"

She opened her mouth to respond, but the phone buzzed again.

"This is the operator for the East Sussex telephone line. How may I help you?" a tired female voice crackled through.

Mira could have cried in relief.

"I need you to call the nearest police station to Spenston Park."

"Has there been an incident?"

"Someone has been shot. Please hurry!"

Her uncle gasped beside her.

"It looks like there is a police house just down the road from you, but they don't have a telephone. Do you have someone you can send?"

Mira held a hand over her stomach as a queasy feeling passed over her. Commotion spread through the house, with people running about.

"I'm sure I can find someone. Thank you."

She dropped the receiver on the table and looked up at her uncle.

"I have to find someone to get the police."

A myriad of emotions crossed her uncle's expression.

"I'll take care of it. You stay safe." He kissed her forehead and put his coat on. "I'll take one of Sutherland's horses. I should be back soon."

Mira nodded to him and ran back to the study. Several bleary-eyed houseguests crowded the hallway. They stood there in their nightclothes, bickering with one another.

"What do you suppose has happened?"

"That man was asking for a doctor. Is someone sick?"

Despite the damage done to the door, Alexander had managed to close it again. The frame stood splintered and cracked from where he kicked it in, but otherwise there was no sign of anything off. No one could know what had happened. Mira searched the crowd for any sign of Byron or her brother.

"Has a doctor been found yet?" she asked the person nearest to her.

"Not yet."

Mira fought the urge to panic. She thought she did rather well, considering.

"Do you know what happened, Miss?" the housekeeper asked.

Mira hesitated. "I need everyone to stay calm, but someone has been shot. We've sent for the police."

She moved to the study as the crowd burst into new exclamations. Mira ignored them, opened the door, and moved over to the injured man. She recognized him as Mr. Sutherland as she got closer. Poor man! Why would anyone want to shoot him? She held her breath as she checked him for signs of life. Despite the warmth of his wrist, there was no pulse beneath her fingertips. She pulled her hand away with a gasp.

"Let me through."

A tall, stern man with dark whiskers and spectacles stepped through the crowd at the door, Alexander right behind him. The doctor moved to the body to examine it.

"I'm afraid there's nothing I can do. He was shot clear through the heart, it would seem. I doubt he lived much longer after you first found him."

A hush fell over the people in the hallway. Byron pushed through the crowd and moved towards the desk. The tension in Mira's shoulders dissipated.

"Have the police been notified?" he asked Mr. Durant.

Mira stepped forward. "I tried to phone, but the nearest police house doesn't have a telephone. I sent my uncle."

"Good. For now, we ought to keep everyone out of the room. We don't want to disturb any evidence." Byron moved to the window, adjusting the tie on his housecoat.

"And who are you?" the doctor asked.

"Byron Constantine, private detective." Byron shook hands with the doctor.

Alexander glanced in Mira's direction. Byron continued enumerating items on his fingers.

"Now, before the police get here, we need to do three things. One: We need to bring everyone into the ballroom to make sure everyone's accounted for. Two: We need to seal this room to prevent any issue with evidence tampering. Three: We need to get this woman a chair. She's fit to fall over any second."

Mira hadn't noticed she was shaking until he steadied her arm with his hand.

"Were you the one who found the body?"

"Y-yes. Mr. Durant was with me." She nodded to Alexander.

"Good of you not to scream. What was your name?"

So, he didn't remember her again. She swallowed.

"Mira Blayse."

"Let's get you to a sitting room, Miss Blayse."

He took her by the arm and escorted her to the door. Looking back at the remaining two gentlemen in the study, he gestured for them to follow.

"Come on then, let's get everyone settled and see if we can't parse this out."

MIRA SIPPED AT HER HOT CHOCOLATE AS Byron paced with his journal. In his rush to see what the commotion was about, it seemed that he didn't have time to catch up. At least his memory seemed to serve him a little. He remembered about the journal. They were in a sitting room right off the ballroom. The other party guests milled about, talking. In a prudent course of action, the housekeeper brought out a variety of hot drinks to keep everyone awake until the police could come. Despite that, Mira felt herself drooping. Mr. Durant sat opposite her, and the doctor, who she now knew was Dr. Lorenzo Kelley, stood at the window.

Mira wanted to run to the ballroom to look for her brother and uncle, but at the moment, that wasn't possible. Particularly since her uncle hadn't returned with a constable yet. Byron snapped his journal shut, startling her.

"You could have told me."

He sat next to her on the couch as he glanced over the sketches she had made for him. Mr. Durant's gaze bored into the two of them.

"I was a bit preoccupied."

Byron softened. "I suppose that's true."

He paused a moment to compare one of the drawings to Mr. Durant, eyes narrowing before he turned back to her. "Can you tell me what happened?"

Mira glanced up at Alexander, then back to Byron.

"I had met Mr. Durant in the conservatory to discuss something. That was around one. We couldn't have been talking for more than five or six minutes before we heard the gunshot. We ran to the study. Mr. Durant broke down the door, and . . ."

Mira closed her eyes. For as much as she had been through with Byron, somehow, this rattled her more than anything. She took a breath.

"We saw the body. Mr. Durant directed me to the telephone while he ran for Dr. Kelley. While I was trying to telephone, my uncle came in. When I found out that the police house didn't have a telephone, he offered to go fetch a constable. Then I returned to the study."

Byron wrote notes in his journal, tapped the fountain pen against his cheek, and looked up at Mr. Durant.

"What do you remember?"

"It's exactly as she tells it. We heard the gunshot and discovered the body together. Then she ran for the telephone while I ran for a doctor. Of course, I didn't know if one was in attendance, so I ended up waking up a handful of guests before I found Dr. Kelley."

Byron nodded. "Well, I ought to have a look at the crime scene. Mira, are you feeling up to coming with me?"

"Of course."

Now that the hallway was clear and quiet, and it was only her and Byron, she took her time to take in the details of the room. The curtains still swayed in the window, and she rubbed her arms against the autumnal chill. This early in the morning, it felt more like winter. A fire crackled in the hearth, flames licking at the logs placed there. Books lined the bookshelves, though none seemed out of place, or even dusty. A display of pistols, minus one, hung on the east wall. Mr. Sutherland had removed his suit jacket and placed it on the back of the chair. It seemed he was looking over some paperwork before he died. The documents were covered in blood—more of it than before. Byron leaned over the corpse's shoulder.

"These documents have your uncle's name on them."

"They were working on a merger between their companies. They finalized the details yesterday."

"Hm. What do you think happened, Mira?"

She swallowed and stepped into the middle of the room, turning in a slow circle.

"It looks like Mr. Sutherland was working late. Maybe he wanted to make sure they hadn't missed anything before my uncle left the next day. The murderer came in, shot him, and fled out the window."

"That is the logical conclusion. You didn't see anyone in the hall?"

"No." She shook her head. "Not at all."

"How long would you say it took you to get from the conservatory to here?"

"Less than a minute."

Byron moved over to the front of the desk and grimaced. "Do you remember what the blood looked like when you first came in?"

"It was dark and clotting. I didn't see much before I ran to the telephone."

Byron gave the room another appraisal before heading out to the ballroom. His eyes flicked to each of the twenty or so guests, still dressed in their nightclothes. A few older men dozed on sofas against the walls. Castel approached.

"Well, Ambrose, are you making use of your talents, yet?"

"To the best of my ability. And it's Byron now. No reason to keep up the act."

"Depends on which version of you is the act." He raised a brow and turned to Mira. "Good evening, Miss Blayse. Seems that murder follows my brother around."

"For the record, Castel, this is the first time this has happened," Byron said, rubbing his temples.

"That you remember."

Byron looked heavenward. "Are you only here to get a rise out of me?"

"No. I'd like to know when we can go back to bed."

"Can't say for sure. I get the feeling most of us won't be heading back to bed."

"Wonderful." He stalked off.

"Where are you going?" Byron called after him.

"To see if there is any scotch lying around. Heaven knows the coffee needs it."

Byron groaned. "And here I thought he would be useful for once."

A startling, brother-shaped force gripped onto Mira just then. She would have fallen over if Walker wasn't trapping her in a bone-crushing hug.

"There you are! I was terrified when I couldn't find you." He pulled back and frowned at her party clothes. "Did you never go to bed?"

"No. I'll explain later."

She knew she shouldn't have met up with Mr. Durant! What would people think?

"Are you alright, Walker?" she said.

"Other than giving me palpitations? Perfectly fine. Have you seen uncle? He's missing, too."

"I sent him for the police."

"Brilliant. You two are knee deep in an investigation, while I'm asleep! At least this will be a story to tell Mr. Constantine when you get back to London, eh?"

"Well . . ." She turned towards Byron.

Walker grinned. "How'd you get here before the police?"

"I was already here." Byron stepped closer. "I can only be grateful that my client wasn't the victim. Although I'm certain the investigation will stall his travel plans."

Mira frowned. Where was the ambassador? Her eyes flicked from person to person until she spotted him and his wife across the room. Good. They were safe.

A commotion appeared at the door to the ballroom as two constables arrived at a quarter to two. Byron glanced at Mira.

"Stay here. I'll brief them on the situation."

Mira opened her mouth to argue, but lost her fire as she caught sight of her uncle.

"Thank goodness the two of you are safe!" Cyrus gripped the twins' shoulders and pulled them over to a couch. "Now, tell me what happened?"

As Mira delved into the story once again, her uncle's features grew even more worried and tired.

"Poor Vincent. He was a good man. There's no reason for him to have gone out in this way."

Mira yawned and nodded. Walker put an arm around her.

"Why don't you sleep for a while, Mouse? You've had a particularly long day."

She couldn't help yawning again, but she shook her head. "I've got to stay awake to help Byron."

"Mr. Constantine is here?" Cyrus asked.

"He was invited on behalf of one of our clients."

"Seems you can't have a day off after all," her uncle muttered. Mira gave a light laugh and nestled into the crook of Walker's arm.

October 13, 1888: Morning

A SORENESS SPREAD OVER MIRA FROM FALLING ASLEEP in all her finery from the party. She groaned and sat up. Strands of hair fell into her face, and awkward lumps dug into her side from where her dress bunched beneath her. That would teach her to close her eyes. She blinked a few times and took in the ballroom.

She couldn't have been asleep for long, feeling as exhausted as she did. Then again, Walker and her uncle had vanished, so she must have been out of it enough for them to have moved. She was alone in the ballroom, save for a few straggling potential suspects in the corner drinking from an amber-colored bottle. Where was everyone? Had the police allowed everyone to return to their rooms after all? She stood and went in search of a clock.

The grandfather clock in the hall showed half-past six. Hours since she had last walked the waking realm. Had the police or Byron found the culprit? She passed by the library door. It stood ajar. Low rumbling came from within, and she stopped outside.

"There has to be another explanation!" Her uncle's voice called out, clear as a church bell.

Why was he so upset? She stifled a yawn. Right, his business partner was killed. Murdered, actually. She leaned forward to listen.

"I'm afraid that going off of our current evidence, there isn't much we can do," the constable said.

So, they hadn't found the killer after all? The constable continued.

"Unless, of course, you can provide an explanation as to your whereabouts this morning?"

"As I said, I couldn't sleep, and so I thought I'd take a walk. I started to feel tired around the edge of the forest and turned back. That's when I heard the first shot, and I ran back towards the house. When I was halfway across the green, I saw a man climb down the ivy and retreat around the side of the house. I was on my way to investigate when I heard another gunshot and decided it was more important to get to the house and see what was going on."

"And what did this man look like?" The scritch of a pencil on paper reached her ears.

"Well, at first I thought it was Vincent. Evidently, it wasn't since he is dead. Tall. Darker hair. Barrel-chested."

The voices went quiet, and she leaned in closer.

"Cyrus Griffon, I'm afraid that you are under arrest until further investigation can take place."

Mira froze in the hallway. That couldn't be right. Her uncle? A murderer? She pressed against the door and made herself known to the occupants. Her gaze drifted over the constables, her uncle, her brother, and Byron. At some point, her brother and Byron must have changed into day clothes, as they looked impeccable. She must have looked a fright based on the way the group stared at her.

"You're mistaken. It can't be him," she said, her timorous voice betraying her emotions.

Her gaze settled on her uncle, pleading for him to assure her that she was right. He took a breath and stood tall. She blinked back tears.

"Can you provide an alibi for him?" The constable looked up at her from his notepad.

"Well, no. But—"

"My sister's right." Walker stood and moved next to Mira. "Our uncle had no reason to kill Mr. Sutherland."

"You're certain of that?"

"Yes," the twins said together.

"Then you have nothing to worry about. We'll continue our investigation, and once new evidence comes to light to clear him, your uncle is free." A constable stood and moved to Cyrus' side. "I trust you'll come willingly?"

Her uncle's jaw tightened, but he nodded. The constables made their way towards the door, Cyrus between them. Mira stepped in front of them and gripped her uncle in a hug.

Cyrus ran his hand through her loose hair. "It'll be alright, Mira. The truth will show soon enough," he whispered in her ear.

He kissed her forehead and looked between her and Walker. "Take care of each other?"

MIRA SAT ON THE COUCH IN THE ballroom, not seeing a foot in front of her because of her tears.

No. It couldn't be. There had to be something else. A pressure landed on her shoulder and a buzzing rang in her ears. She whipped her head up to look at Byron and wiped at her tears. His hand stayed on her shoulder. She squeezed her eyes shut, but the image of her uncle in the back of the police wagon burned in her mind.

"Mira."

"Why didn't you stop them?" She turned away from him.

"I'm sorry."

"He didn't do it." Her words caught in her throat, and she blinked more tears away.

"I know."

"Then why didn't you do something?"

Byron's gaze softened at her bitter tone, and he sat next to her, taking her hand in his.

"We'll need evidence, Mira. And that requires time. I'll ensure that he doesn't hang. I can promise you that."

"We'll hold you to that promise," Walker said from her other side.

Mira jumped up, pacing out her nervous energy.

"It doesn't make any sense. Why would they suspect him?"

"Perhaps it's because his name is on the documents and he is the only one who was outside for certain," Walker said.

"What about the man he saw?"

"Unfortunately, everything is circumstantial at the moment. Of course, we'll look into it. But based on the evidence the constables had, it was a likely conclusion that your uncle was the killer." Byron drummed his fingers on his journal. "Setting the evidence aside, the only people who are not suspect are the caterers, yourself, and Mr. Durant. You all have someone to corroborate your locations at the time of the shot."

"But my uncle admitted he was out for a stroll." Mira threw her hands up. The gesture wasn't ladylike, but she didn't care. "If he killed Mr. Sutherland, he wouldn't likely admit to being outside!"

Byron sighed. "He had to because you saw him come in."

The blood rushed from Mira's cheeks, and she sat down again. "Oh, no."

"So. We need to make a plan of action. First, we need to search the grounds and the rooms for any trace of the gun. I'd imagine the killer would have disposed of it as soon as possible, but you never know. We need to finish up searching for any clues that we can find, and see if the police here have access to a camera. Then we need to get your uncle transferred to Scotland Yard. He'll be closer to home, and we'll be better able to work from there."

MIRA RUSHED OUTSIDE AFTER CHANGING INTO SOMETHING more suitable for romping around on the grounds. She found Byron beneath the window to the study, eyeing the ivy. The rising sun had begun to melt the frost that hung there. Byron took off his jacket, despite the fact that they could both see their breath.

"Hold this, will you? I'd like to test the strength of this trellis."

Mira took the coat from him and held it close to her for warmth. "Be careful, Byron."

"I'm always careful." He placed one foot on the trellis, then the other, testing it before climbing up halfway.

"See anything?" she called up.

"A handful of sturdy footholds."

He searched through the ivy with one hand, and Mira stifled a chuckle. It reminded her of when she first met him. Byron and shrubbery just seemed to get along.

"Not even a scrap of clothing!" He climbed down and Mira noted how the ivy clung to him.

"You seem to have some stowaways." She smiled and brushed some sprigs of ivy off his shoulders and back.

"Just as well that I left my jacket down here, then."

He took the jacket from her and shrugged it back on as he looked up at the house again.

"Hey!" Walker called from further down the green. "I've found the gun!"

"Don't touch it!" Byron called back.

Walker strode towards them, holding a white bundle.

"Why would I touch it? I know you've got some detective-type things to do with it. I've wrapped it up in my handkerchief."

He opened it up for them to see. It matched the pistol display in the study.

"Where did you find it?" Byron leaned over the bundle.

"Just off the gravel path. Left a sizable dent there."

Byron hummed. "Well, put it back. The constables have to find it there, otherwise they'll think you did it."

Walker opened his mouth to object, thought better of it, and left to put the gun back.

"You'd think this was his first murder investigation," Byron teased.

"It *is* his first murder investigation." Mira bumped her shoulder into him. "Come on. Let's follow the path of the man my uncle saw."

She ambled up the side of the house, Byron and Walker close behind.

"I don't understand why anyone would kill Mr. Sutherland," Mira said. "I mean, I don't understand why anyone would kill at all, but there doesn't seem to be any motive here."

"But suicide doesn't seem likely either. The angle would be awkward. And why go for the chest when you can get it over faster by aiming for the head?" Walker stopped to inspect the brick of the building.

The ivy wasn't as thick on the side of the house, and it stopped halfway around.

"And, of course, the gun was out here, rather than in his hand." Byron mentioned as he stooped in the grass, picking up some bits of ivy.

"Er, right." Walker shuffled his feet from side to side.

"You didn't hear any loud voices, did you, Mira?" Byron asked.

"No. Just the gunshot."

She rubbed at her arms. Why did it have to get so cold in October? Byron noticed and removed his jacket again, this time to offer it to her. She hesitated before taking it, catching a whiff of sandalwood as she settled it around her shoulders.

"In that case, it couldn't have been a murder committed in rage or in a fight. You would have heard it."

"Well, the caterers were loud in the ballroom. It would have been hard to hear."

Byron nodded, noted their surroundings, then moved back towards the front of the house.

"I don't think we'll be finding anything else for the time being. Let's go back to the study."

MIRA STOOD BY THE SPLINTERED DOOR. THE constables had returned with a medical examiner. Walker was in the entry hall, waiting for the region's inspector. The constables said he should be there by one. A glance at the clock in the study told her he was fifteen minutes late. After taking photographs of the scene, the medical examiner removed Mr. Sutherland's body with the help of one of the constables. Byron stood by the fireplace, observing their movements. The last constable gathered up the rest of the bloodied papers and took a final appraisal of the room.

"While you were gone, we had a look about the grounds," Byron said. "We found a gun near the gravel path out there." He pointed out the direction through the window.

"Very good, sir." The constable beamed. "A pleasure to be working with such a distinguished detective."

"Of course. Would you mind if I scoped the room out a bit?"

"You think I missed something?"

"I like to be extra thorough. May I?"

After a nod from the constable, Byron moved about the room. He stooped to the floor and ran his fingertip along the boards. He glanced at the fireplace, which had been poked to a roaring state, then moved to the window and examined the sill. Picking up Sutherland's orphaned jacket, he looked through the pockets.

"Ah. A pocketbook. These are always useful." He thumbed through it. "Looks like most of these are business meetings, but we ought to check up on them."

He handed the book off to the constable and pulled out a pocket watch.

"Pity it isn't engraved. But he kept it in top condition." He placed it on the desk along with a fountain pen.

"What else do you see?" Mira stepped forward.

"I found traces of gunpowder near the fireplace. I would think that the murderer shot him from about" —Byron placed himself right in front of the fireplace— "here, I'd say."

He moved to the window. "I would also think that the window was open before the shot. There are no traces of gunpowder from the killer's hands or clothing on the window frame or sill."

"Does it matter?" the constable asked.

"Makes me wonder why Mr. Sutherland had the window open on such a chilly night. It certainly wasn't for his health."

"Hm." The constable furrowed his brow.

Byron moved to a closet in the room and opened it, peering inside. He closed it, inspected the hinges, then walked over by the main door and poked around in the splinters.

"You haven't seen a key lying anywhere, have you?"

"No?" Mira frowned and picked up her skirts, glancing around the floor.

Byron turned to the constable.

"Make sure you check the corpse for a key. If you don't find one, let me know."

The man nodded, picked up the gathered evidence, and left the room. Mira moved to the window.

"Do you think my uncle could have climbed this trellis?"

"I think if he put his mind to it, he could have. But that doesn't mean he did."

Byron continued to mull about in the bits of wood. Mr. Durant appeared in the open door.

"Any luck finding anything?"

"A bit here and there." Byron gave a terse smile to Alexander and continued to look.

Mira turned towards them. "At the moment, he's looking for a key."

"Is a cabinet locked or something?"

"Or something," Byron mumbled.

"Why does the key matter?" Mira asked.

"You said that you had to break down the door?" He looked up at Alexander who nodded. Byron continued. "If it were locked from the inside, the key would likely be in this room still or on the body. If it were locked from the outside, then the murderer likely locked the door and took the key."

Alexander frowned. "So, if we find the key, we could find the murderer?"

"Exactly."

Alexander stooped to help sift through the pieces and look under furniture while Mira moved to examine the set of pistols again.

"These pistols are rather old. Do you think the murderer had to bring their own bullets for them?"

"That would be easier than bringing their own gun," Byron said, standing to come study them again.

"So, then the murder had to have been planned!"

Byron nodded as Alexander gave a huff of victory.

"I found it!" He brandished a small brass door key.

Byron took it from him and compared it with the lock on the door.

"It must have jostled loose when you kicked the door in." Byron set the key on the desk.

"Then we're back to square one." Mira swept some hair behind her ear.

"Maybe not. I have some ideas." His eyes sparkled.

He turned towards the door as a new set of footsteps approached from the stairs. Walker's face appeared in the doorway.

"The inspector has arrived. He's asked to speak with you, Constantine."

"I'd best get down there then. And it might be best if we vacated this room for the time being."

He glanced between Alexander and Mira before following Walker out. Alexander moved to Mira's side.

"I wanted to see if you were alright."

"I appreciate your concern."

If she said that everything was fine, the bubble of emotion was certain to erupt. She gestured for him to lead the way out of the room, which he did.

"I was shocked, coming in and seeing the body like that," he said.

Mira looked up at him as she closed the door behind them and continued down the hall.

"It was traumatic, to be sure."

Alexander nodded and looked over the bannister.

"I've heard of these kinds of things happening, of course. I just never thought I'd be involved. I mean, a murder investigation? Is this what it's always like?"

"Well, I've only helped Byron with one, and this one is rather different."

"Because you weren't there at the time of the murder or . . . ?"

Her eyes flicked over to him. "Because my uncle wasn't a suspect before."

"Oh." Alexander stopped walking. "I didn't realize! My sincerest apologies."

She straightened and walked faster.

After a questioning glance, he fell into step beside her. "You still don't trust me, do you?"

"You haven't given me reason to."

"Then I shall work harder to earn your favor. Is there anything I can do to help with the investigation?"

"That's more of a question for Byron than for me, but I think we have it handled. Thank you, though." She stopped in the ballroom, catching the gaze of her brother. "If you would excuse me, I need to speak with Walker about the situation."

"Of course."

Mira made her way across the ballroom. Walker smiled.

"You two seem to be getting along well."

"I suppose." She lowered her voice. "One does bond over discovering a corpse together."

"He was with you? Why?"

"It doesn't matter." She shook her head. "Is Byron still with the inspector?"

"They're going over all the particulars, yes. Last I heard, he was trying to get Uncle relocated to London, which would make things quite a bit easier, if you ask me."

Mira took his arm as they walked towards her room.

"I still don't understand how this happened at all! If only he hadn't gone for a walk last night. Who walks at one in the morning, anyway?"

"You were up." He quirked an eyebrow at her.

"Well, that's different. And besides, I wasn't outside," she huffed.

"There is something else odd about Uncle's story. Didn't he say that he heard two shots?"

"Oh." She furrowed her brow. "He did, but I only heard the one."

Mira opened the door to her room and stepped inside. The bed looked too comfortable, and she flopped onto it unceremoniously. A dip in the mattress next to her told her that Walker followed suit. She rolled onto her side.

"How many shots did you hear?"

Walker's voice was muffled through the blankets until she hit his shoulder and he turned.

"I was asleep, like any normal person should have been."

That earned him a hit from a pillow, and he laughed. "I didn't wake up until a bunch of people were making noise out in the hall."

"You always were a heavy sleeper." She bit her lip. "Do you think anyone else heard two shots?"

"Possibly. Depends on if they were up or not."

Mira sat up and smoothed out her dress. "There's one way to find out."

Seeing as the police weren't keen on letting anyone go, a majority of the guests occupied the dining room for a late lunch. Walker and Mira fanned out, questioning everyone they could about how many shots rang out the night before. Unfortunately, most people hadn't even heard one. Mira slowed her pace as she passed the ambassador and his wife.

"This is beastly business," Lady Katherine said with her slight German accent. "Being caught up in a murder scandal is a bad omen for the treaty signing."

"Now, now, my dear. As long as the investigation wraps up soon, we'll be on schedule."

"William, you don't understand. I saw a ghost last night!"

"Just another nightmare, I'm sure."

Mira stopped and moved over to them.

"Forgive me for eavesdropping, but did you say that you saw a ghost?"

"I'm sorry Miss Blayse. It was just a dream," Sir William insisted.

"I wasn't asleep!" Lady Katherine tapped her fan on the table. "I was as awake as I am now."

"What happened?" Mira sat down in an empty chair.

"I was startled awake; I think from William turning over. Or perhaps there was a noise, I'm not sure. But I was wide awake, and a bit cold. I thought I'd grab another blanket from the drawers. As I came around the side of the bed, I saw that the light from the moon was bright. How was I to fall asleep with the moonlight dripping everywhere? So, I moved to the window to close the curtains. That's when I saw it. A ghostly figure of a man with a white shirt mangled with blood just over the heart. It moved quick as anything around the side of the house."

"And then?"

"I heard the gunshot, and I woke William up to see what the matter was. I almost completely forgot about the ghost until I realized it must be a sign. We can't go to Constantinople." She gripped her husband's arm.

Sir William rubbed at his temples. "I think I'm getting a headache. Could you see about finding me something for it?"

After some prodding, Lady Katherine left in search of a headache cure. Sir William turned towards Mira again.

"I must apologize for her. With all this excitement from the party and the incident, she's even more prone to an active imagination. And she's been looking for excuses to stay here in London. My daughter has recently approved of a suitor, and with us leaving for the east, she can't exactly be available for pursuit, if you know what I mean."

"It's no trouble at all, Sir William. Any information concerning the investigation is welcome."

"You don't think it will take long for them to find the culprit, do you, Miss Blayse?"

Mira hesitated. Technically, they had found someone. Just the wrong someone.

"I'm sure they'll sort it out soon enough. Especially with Byro—Mr. Constantine here."

"It is lucky that he was here." Sir William's smile faltered for a moment. "Is it true that you both were hired to ensure my safety? I was only told that he was assigned to a case involving the treaty, but he's been acting more like a bodyguard than a detective."

"I'm afraid if he hasn't said anything, I'm not at liberty to say anything either."

"You've said enough for me to understand."

His mouth formed a grim line. Lady Katherine slipped her hand into the crook of his arm and slipped him a glass of brandy.

"At least we are safe," Sir William said.

"As safe as one can be with a killer about," Lady Katherine said, and her husband gave a weak chuckle.

Mira nodded. "I'm afraid I need to keep asking around. You'll let me know if you remember anything else or need something?"

"Oh, we'll let you know." Sir William patted his wife's arm.

Mira spoke with a few more people to no avail before she went in search of her brother. She found him hovering near Miss Renaldi. His distracted gaze told her everything she needed to know. She glided to his side and took his arm.

"There you are! I've been looking for you everywhere."

"Oh! Mira. I was just finishing my conversation with Miss Renaldi. Allow me to introduce you. Miss Elizabeth Renal—"

"Please," the young woman interrupted. "Call me Liza. And you're Samira Blayse, his fascinating sister?"

"Um. Yes." Mira smiled.

"I only say fascinating because rumor has it that you danced with the elusive Ambrose Sherard last night." Her eyes sparkled as she leaned forward with a whisper. "I heard he didn't dance with anyone else for the entire evening, and I'd love to know how you managed it."

Mira fidgeted with her sleeves as her face flushed with heat.

"You didn't tell me about that, Mira." Walker leaned closer and gave her a lopsided grin. "Do continue."

"I happen to be acquainted with his brother, and he introduced us."

Liza gave her a tightlipped smile. "How convenient."

"Yes, it was. Now if you'll excuse us." Mira tugged on Walker's sleeve and led him out of the dining room.

"I believe I owe you something for that save."

"Then you won't tell Uncle about Mr. Durant or Ambrose Sherard?"

"My lips are sealed. Although, you had best tell me the details."

"First, we need to find Byron. While I don't have evidence, I'm more certain than ever that our uncle saw someone leave that room. And there were most definitely two shots."

October 13, 1888:
Afternoon

"L ET ME MAKE SURE THAT I UNDERSTAND you," Byron said, pacing in the sitting room.

Mira and Walker sat on the couch as he marched to and fro.

"Lady Katherine thinks she saw a ghost, and you believe the ghost may be what your uncle saw last night?"

"Not a ghost. The man who came down the ivy. And I think the first shot my uncle heard is what woke her up."

"Very well. Let's play this out, then." Byron sat in an armchair across from them. "First, let's assume that the killer is someone that Mr. Sutherland knew. They come in to speak with him. At some point during the conversation, or perhaps before, they open the window. The killer locks the door behind them, leaving the key in the lock. Perhaps citing that their discussion mustn't be overheard."

He paused and glanced around. "Let's take this up to the study."

They traipsed up the stairs, following after the detective like ducklings. He opened the door and moved over to the desk.

"Walker, would you mind being Mr. Sutherland?"

Walker bit his lip in apprehension, then nodded and took a hesitant seat, avoiding the blood stain. Byron moved to the fireplace.

"We know the murderer was here because of the gunpowder. The locked door gives them time to escape out the window after the shot is fired. They remove a pistol from the display and—"

"Now hang on," Walker interrupted. "There is no way that they could have taken a pistol and loaded it without Mr. Sutherland noticing."

"Right you are." Byron tapped fingers on the mantel. "It is possible that they snuck away during the party and loaded the gun in preparation. So, whoever the killer is would have to be familiar with the layout of the house, and the study in particular. Otherwise, they wouldn't know where it was, or that there was a pistol available."

"Unfortunately, our uncle fits that description," Mira sighed and leaned against the wall.

"Let's continue. They take a pistol from the wall and shoot Mr. Sutherland." Byron paced to the window. "At that point, they exit the room in the only way possible and run around the side of the house to reenter the house by way of another window or door."

"Or they could have left the grounds entirely," Mira said.

"True. Although everyone from the party was still in the house when we gathered the guests together. The murderer would have had to come after the party. I suppose we can ask the butler about that."

"Just a moment, Byron," Mira said. "You mentioned before that the window must have been open before the shot, because there was no trace of gunpowder on the sill or frame."

"Yes?"

"But wouldn't the killer have had to use the sill to climb out of the window after shooting him?"

"Hm. You're right. I suppose the only logical explanation would be that they were wearing gloves, which they took off before leaving the room. Odd use of the precious time they had."

Byron moved back to the fireplace and crouched down again. "It's also odd that there is so much residue here. Normally, it's harder to see where a gun has been shot from."

"You think it was planted?" Walker asked.

"No. The scorch marks are too accurate to have been faked. Although . . ." He lay on his stomach just behind where the residue started and looked up at the desk. "Hm. These patterns would indicate that the shot came from the floor, not a standing position. But that would be impossible."

"What does that mean?" Mira moved over to him.

"Either that this is something else entirely, or that my knowledge of firearm discharge isn't perfect." Byron stood and dusted off his jacket. "Which is likely enough."

"And what about the second shot?" Walker asked. "Those pistols can only fire one bullet before reloading."

Byron released a slow breath and rubbed the back of his neck. "I can't answer that, either. And in looking around the room, I haven't seen any evidence of a second shot. That doesn't mean there wasn't one."

"Do you think, perhaps, that the second shot didn't come from the house? Maybe it was outside somewhere? That would explain why Uncle heard it, and I didn't," Mira said.

"Walker, go see if you can't ask the butler about any late-night visitors or early morning hunting parties in the area."

"You think someone was hunting at one in the morning?" Walker stood.

"It's worth looking into, at least." Byron shrugged.

Walker nodded and left the room.

"Mira, I told the Chief Inspector that I'd send you to him as soon as I saw you next. And seeing as I've just seen you," Byron's eyes twinkled, "I'm inclined to escort you to him myself."

He held his arm out to her and led her to the library. Mr. Durant was there already, with an official-looking gentleman who turned towards them as they entered.

"Ah. You must be Miss Blayse. I'm Chief Inspector Kramer. Please, sit down."

Mira did so, with Byron sitting beside her. Mr. Durant's gaze followed their movements.

"If you would, I'd like to hear what happened last night from your perspective," the inspector said.

"Well, I was talking with Mr. Durant in the conservatory when I heard a gunshot from upstairs."

"Might I ask what the two of you were discussing in the conservatory?" the inspector tapped his pen on his notepad.

"Oh. Erm." Mira looked between all three gentleman and took a calming breath. "He asked to speak to me during the party." She stalled for time. How was she supposed to explain their conversation?

"You see, we've met several times in Kensington Gardens, by chance. Although, last night was the first time we were intro-duced properly." She glanced at Byron. His brow furrowed as he appraised Mr. Durant. They seemed to be having a glaring contest. Mira turned back to the inspector.

"He asked me to meet him in the conservatory after the party. While I wasn't certain why, I was curious."

"And what did you discuss?" The inspector turned to Mr. Durant, who flushed.

"Well, I . . . er . . . I wished to know if she was courting anyone."

Mira's breath caught in her throat. "I didn't realize that was what you were asking!"

"I hadn't gotten to it by the time the gun went off! And besides, we hadn't started off on the right foot. I wanted to make amends first."

Byron cleared his throat. "Shall we continue?"

The inspector nodded. "Please, start where you left off."

Mira told the rest of her side, with Alexander pitching in with details here and there. Byron sat back as the story unfolded, eyes flicking back and forth between the two of them with keen scrutiny. Mira fidgeted in her seat as the inspector scrawled out the last of his notes.

"Thank you for your honesty. You're free to go."

Mr. Durant nodded and left the room. Byron stood as well, but Mira hesitated.

"Inspector Kramer, have you spoken with my uncle yet?"

"Not yet, but I heard his account of things from Officer Evans."

"What are your thoughts on the two shots?"

"I haven't talked with everyone, but so far only one shot was heard."

"Speak with Lady Katherine White. Her account might shed some light on the subject."

"I intend to talk with everyone before I allow them to leave, but thank you for the tip."

Mira nodded to him, then joined Byron as he moved to the door and opened it for her. She strode into the hallway and bumped headlong into Dr. Kelley. The force knocked his brief-case from one hand and his suitcase from the other. The brief-case clasps came undone, and a slew of papers spread across the wood floor.

"I'm so sorry!" Mira bent to help retrieve them, Byron following suit.

"No harm done!" the doctor replied, stacking them as quick as he could.

Mira handed the last of the papers she collected over, then

turned to Byron who had gone bone white. He stared at a pamphlet in his hands. Dr. Kelley shuffled the papers back into his briefcase as Mira peeked over Byron's shoulder. Her eyes widened, recognizing the emblem of the Cobden Club. Byron shook his head and handed the pamphlet over with a smile.

"Are you on your way out?" he asked.

"Indeed I am! The inspector has grilled me thoroughly and given me clearance to leave. And with the medical examiner on the premises, you surely don't need me."

"Safe travels, then." Mira smiled.

The doctor nodded to her, grabbed his suitcase, and hurried down the hall. Once he was out of sight, she turned to Byron.

"What's the Cobden Club?"

Byron froze. He glanced at the ceiling before taking her hand and pulling her into the closest sitting room. He turned to her after ensuring the door was closed and locked.

"Are you certain you want to know?"

"Is it as bad as The Pit?" Mira shivered. She hoped there would never be a time that she returned to a place like The Pit again. The name alone brought disgusting imagery to her mind.

"No. But it is in the same realm. While The Pit is a meeting place for all members of Circe, the Cobden Club is for more elite members."

Mira's eyes widened. "You mean, Dr. Kelley is a member of Circe?"

"Er, not necessarily. You see, the club is open anyone, with sufficient funds and status, of course. One doesn't need to be aware of Circe to be a member. It helps Circe to keep a low profile, and it gives them the perfect opportunity to make connections with businessmen and nobility alike. Dr. Kelley could simply be a member of the club with no connection to Circe." Byron cocked his head to one side and sucked in a breath.

"But?" Mira prompted.

"It is quite the coincidence. I'd like to look round his room before the maids clean anything up."

A quick walk and a stop for directions led them to Dr. Kelley's previous room. It was located on the first floor on the opposite end of the house from the conservatory and front entry. A large, curtained window gave a gorgeous view of the green. Byron, of course, paid no attention to the view, and went straight to work, prodding anything that looked remotely suspicious. After surveying the room, he joined her in her sightseeing.

"Not much to go off of, I'm afraid." He opened the window and leaned out. "Although, this is where we found the stray bits of ivy."

"Really?" Mira leaned out, keeping herself steady by gripping the sill.

"It could be another coincidence, but it is possible that he was the one who climbed down the trellis."

Mira pulled back and clasped her hands together. "Then he would be the one who shot Mr. Sutherland!" She frowned, finding a brown, oily substance on her fingers. "Do they oil windowsills?"

"Maybe the hinges, but never the sills. Let me see."

He took her hand in his and looked it over, face pensive. Mira bit her lip and looked away.

"Looks to be shoe polish." He moved to the sill and found the source with a grin. "I think it's entirely possible that Dr. Kelley went for a stroll last night."

"And, he has the same build and hair color as Mr. Sutherland! No wonder, Uncle mistook the doctor for him!"

"There's only one question left." Byron sat on the bed and Mira sat next to him.

"Yes?"

"What was the motive?"

"Oh dear. That is an issue, isn't it?"

"I'll go inform the inspector of what we've found. It could be enough to get your uncle off the hook."

She nodded and Byron stood. As he approached the door, he stopped and turned back.

"Mira?"

"Yes?"

"If Mr. Durant had managed to ask you if you were courting someone, what would you have said?"

She took pause at that. "Knowing what I know about Mr. Durant, I think I'd say that I wasn't interested."

"And what do you know about Mr. Durant?"

"He's . . . suspicious. He's given me several warnings from Circe, actually."

Byron's eyes widened before narrowing. He moved back over to her.

"Have we talked about him before?"

"I've mentioned him. He's the one who gave me the letter after we caught Molly Bridges."

Byron's hand trailed to his satchel. "So, he is the mysterious gentleman you painted a picture of?"

"Yes, although I didn't know his name until yesterday evening."

"And yet, you met with him, alone, in the middle of the night?"

"When you put it that way, it sounds awful." She crossed her arms. "I was curious!"

"And what did he tell you?" Byron's jaw tightened.

"That he had no idea what Circe was. Apparently, he received an anonymous letter telling him about me and to deliver some messages. They paid him for his work, but he thought it was an elaborate prank."

Byron's posture relaxed as he paced to the window. "Hmm. That does sound like something Circe would do. Then there would be no direct connection to the Order. If the messenger gets caught, then . . ." He stopped his deductions and turned back to her. "But there's always the possibility that he is lying."

"I know that. Of course, I do."

He shook his head. "I don't like this. You need to stay away from him until we can figure this all out."

Mira studied his face. His expression flipped between worry, fear, and an emotion she didn't quite recognize.

"Why, Mr. Constantine, you aren't jealous, are you?"

"What?! No. Not at all. I-I," he stammered. "He could be dangerous."

"Right." Mira stood and smoothed out her skirts. "Well, I'm going to see what Walker found out from the butler. And weren't you going to speak with the inspector about what we found?"

Byron nodded, opened his mouth to say something, then closed it again. He turned and left the room.

Mira took a deep breath. Of course, it wouldn't be that simple. It had taken weeks for them to solve the Pennington case. If Circe was involved, the truth was bound to be complicated. She went in search of her brother.

Unfortunately, Miss Renaldi found her first.

"Oh! Miss Blayse, how fortunate that I ran into you!"

Liza latched onto Mira's arm, stopping her in the hall, and spoke in a low voice.

"I need your help."

"Oh?"

"I've been trying everything to catch your brother's attention. Everything! But he kept giving me confusing signals last night, and today I can't even talk to him!"

"How do you mean?"

"Well, I kept on opening my fan so I could shut it again, but he didn't seem to notice that at all."

"Pardon?"

"You know, shutting my fan meant I wanted to talk with

him. In private. So, when that didn't work, I forewent the fan and moved on to my gloves. But I accidentally dropped both of them before I could do anything. I was grateful he was looking away then, because otherwise I would have been mortified. But he picked them up again, so that means that he loves me?"

Mira stared at her. What was she on about? Liza continued.

"But then, he took a handkerchief out of his pocket and dabbed at his forehead, and I don't know what that even means! And then, of course, he twirled it in his left hand and replaced it in his pocket. I'm so confused."

"What does picking up gloves have to do with love?"

"Oh, well, dropping them both is a signal that means 'I love you.' I would assume if he picked them up it means the same?"

Mira blinked at her. "You can't possibly mean that all that you just told me is a system of communication."

"You aren't aware of it? Oh bother. That means your brother probably had no idea?"

"No."

"Well, that's a relief." She huffed a laugh. "And here I was all worried that I made a fool of myself. But you simply must learn about signal flirtation! It's the best way to communicate without speaking. I have a book all about it, and I'll lend it to you if you like."

"That would be kind of you." Mira didn't fancy learning an entirely new language just to flirt. Perhaps she and Byron could create their own signals for silent communication during cases. Although, what good would it do her when Byron would forget the system overnight? As she thought about it, it would be good to know what to avoid in case some other gentleman, like Mr. Durant, took her fan and glove usage the wrong way.

"But how am I to know if your brother is interested in me at all?" Liza lamented.

Mira stifled a laugh. "He isn't likely to be if you're smothering him. Do you know where he is now?"

"He said he was going to go pack, and I didn't think it proper to follow him to his rooms."

"Wise plan."

"Speaking of which, I just saw Mr. Sherard leaving that room you just came from."

"And?"

Liza shook with mirth. "I can't believe it! You aren't even the least bit concerned with how that looks?"

Mira's cheeks burned. "I-I didn't think about it."

"Are you courting, then?"

Mira swallowed and searched for a method of escape. "Well, he hasn't exactly asked me, and my uncle hasn't, well . . ."

"Say no more! I understand. Family can be quite the issue. Although I can't imagine your uncle not approving of you marrying the brother of the soon to be Baron Sherard."

"He's more than that." Mira spoke before she realized what she was saying.

Liza grinned. "You're even in love with him! How fortunate is that!"

Mira's voice rose a few octaves. "Well! I ought to go pack as well! Nice talking with you Liza!"

How could she be thinking about Byron, and love, and courting and flirting while her uncle was wrongfully imprisoned? Goodness, Mr. Sutherland's body wasn't even cold, and here she was feeling faint over nothing at all! Mira shoved the last of her clothes into her suitcase and sat on it. Dash it all. There was Alexander, too. Idiotic Alexander, who could very well be working with Circe, but who very well could not. And he remembered her. Actually remembered her, and—

No. That wasn't fair. Byron loved her. Despite it all, he loved her. If his expression from earlier was anything to go by, he loved her almost as much as she loved him. And didn't that count for something? Except, did he actually love her, or were those feelings fabricated, orchestrated, made up from whatever he wrote in his journal? And did she actually love him? What were these emotions anyway?

She growled and latched the suitcase, pushing her feelings down as far as they could go. Pushing as hard as she pushed on her suitcase. There. That ought to keep them in check until . . . well, until they solved the mystery. But there would always be another mystery. Would she have to push her feelings back every time? For how long? And would he ever actually remember her?

She caught up with her brother in the front entry hall as he replaced the phone receiver.

"Just talked with the stationmaster. The last train leaves at ten tonight if we need to stay here longer. Most of the other guests have already left," he twitched, "save a few."

"Yes, I just talked with Miss Renaldi. She's intent on getting me onto her side."

Walker looked scandalized.

Mira laughed. "Don't worry. She hasn't succeeded. Yet. But she is nice."

"And incredibly forward."

"Sometimes you're too much in the past, like our uncle. She likes you, Walker."

"And I'm terrified of that. I hardly know her!"

"Good thing there is a remedy for that," she teased. "Did you find anything out from the butler?"

"Quentin is incredibly thorough, that much is sure. He had lists of every individual who has been at the estate in the past few months, and their reasons for being there. As far as he can tell, there were no late-night visitors to Mr. Sutherland, and there were no hunting parties approved on the grounds. Especially at that 'god-forsaken hour,' as he put it." He ran both hands over his face. "Took me forty-five minutes to be free of his charts and papers. Forty-five minutes!"

Mira ignored her brother's plight. "Then the murderer must

have been in the house already, and there has to be an explanation for the other shot."

"Perhaps Uncle heard wrong?"

"That doesn't bode well for him then." Byron strode up to them. "I've spoken with Inspector Kramer. He's going to look into Dr. Kelley, but I'm afraid your uncle is still the only suspect with motive."

"What's the plan, then?" Walker leaned against the wall and crossed his arms.

"There's not much more we can do here, especially with everyone leaving. I've pulled some strings, and the inspector has agreed to move your uncle to Scotland Yard and to transfer the case there as well."

"Will that cause any issues for the trial?" Mira asked.

"I don't think so. Most of Sutherland's business associates live and work in London, as well as most of the guests from the party. All our suspects will be close at hand." Byron yawned.

"How long have you been up?" Mira moved to his side.

Dark circles resided beneath his eyes, but he offered her a small smile.

"Oh, since just after the murder occurred. I will certainly sleep well tonight."

"Are you staying here or heading back to Palace Court?" Walker replaced the telephone directory in the drawer.

"It would be best if I returned to familiar territory. I trust you're returning to London as well?"

Mira nodded. "Have you made arrangements yet?"

"If you haven't, you are more than welcome to come with us." Walker smiled.

"Are you discussing travel plans?" Liza came down the stairs.

Walker's face drooped before he stuck on a fake smile and turned to greet her.

"Yes, we are. Are you traveling back tonight as well?"

"Oh, I had better. My parents expected me this morning. Although, I didn't say precisely when I was coming back, so it should be alright."

"Why don't we all go together?" Mira gave a sly smile to Walker, who stiffened.

"What a wonderful idea! I'll go gather my things!" Liza sang as she retreated up the stairs again.

"I thought you weren't taking her side, Mira." Between Walker's pout and his folded arms, he looked like a petulant child.

"Who's taking sides? I just thought it would be safer to travel in greater numbers. Are you coming with us, Byron?"

"I suppose I will. I'm not sure what Castel's plans were, but I'd rather ride with you."

"What about the ambassador?" Walker asked.

"I was mostly worried about something happening at the party. He should be safe to travel back to London, and I'll check up on him tomorrow."

❧❀☙

MIRA TOOK COMFORT IN HOLDING TIGHT TO Byron's arm as they walked through the train station. She could tell that Miss Renaldi enjoyed the proximity to her brother. Perhaps she shouldn't have pushed them together after all. She chuckled and looked away.

"I'll go get the tickets," Walker said, extracting his arm from Miss Renaldi's grip. "Constantine, why don't you see about the luggage, and you ladies can stay here?"

Miss Renaldi looked sorry to let him go, but she recovered quickly and latched onto Mira next.

"Why did he call Mr. Sherard, Constantine? And weren't you calling him Byron earlier?"

Mira bit her lip. "It's complicated. And it isn't exactly my secret."

Liza raised her left hand and covered her heart with the other. "I swear I won't tell a soul."

People were likely to gossip anyway, weren't they? Mira took a deep breath.

"Well, he's both. Ambrose Sherard, and Byron Constantine."

Mira paused, realizing that she didn't precisely know which was his proper name. Didn't Castel call him Byron? But then . . . no, she wasn't quite certain. She shook her head.

"It's complicated. He's a private investigator."

"You don't mean to say that he's *the* Detective Constantine?"

"Yes. He is."

Liza's mouth gaped open, and Mira was reminded of how young she was. Barely nineteen. It surprised Mira that her parents allowed her to go to such a gathering alone. Granted, Mira had managed to convince her uncle, strict as he was, to let her do all sorts of things that weren't strictly proper. Liza broke out in a grin.

"How did you meet him? As Ambrose Sherard, or Byron Constantine?"

"I met him as Byron," Mira said wistfully.

Liza leaned in to tease. "And how did you fall in love with him? As the baron's brother, or as the dashing detective?"

Mira blushed and pushed her away. "Does it matter?"

"I see you two are getting along well," Walker said, approaching them with tickets.

He gave Mira a look, and she shrugged. Liza beamed at Walker and took out her fan, before thinking better of it and putting it away. Byron returned just then, and Mira was more than happy to return to his side.

"Shall we?"

They found a small compartment and situated themselves with Byron and Mira on one side and Walker and Liza on the other. A still exhaustion spread over the group, and it wasn't long before the swaying of the train brought them all close to sleep. Byron nodded off first, and Mira smiled at how relaxed his features became. Without the worries of the world, he seemed so young. Walker was next. Liza motioned for Mira to lean forward, and she placed her flirtation book in her hands. Mira rolled her eyes but welcomed the diversion, reading about ways to flirt with handkerchiefs, gloves, fans, hats, and even walking sticks.

About an hour later, the train jostled Byron awake. He blinked around at his surroundings, confused. For a moment, Mira worried he had forgotten everything again, but he smiled at her and fell back to sleep. She sighed and turned to the window. Every time he slept was a gamble of how much he forgot. A short nap was usually safe, but never guaranteed. At least this time he still remembered her.

Soon enough, they were back in London. Liza gave Walker a calling card before she left to find a hansom cab to take her home.

"I'd better call one as well. Do you want me to find you one too, Constantine?" Walker glanced over the calling card before slipping it in his pocket.

"That would be brilliant."

Walker nodded and walked into the mist. The station clock struck nine.

"I meant to ask, which is your real name?" Mira looked up at Byron.

"They're all real to me. But I suppose you mean the one my parents gave me?"

Mira nodded.

"Byron Ambrose Sherard. But in social settings, my family generally called me Ambrose." Red crept up around his ears. "It's a family name."

"Why Constantine?"

"I liked the way it sounded."

She hummed in response. He tipped his head to the side.

"I meant to ask you something as well."

"Yes?"

"Well, when we were speaking about Mr. Durant and whether you would court him . . . "

"Yes?"

"I was just wondering—"

"Mira! Constantine! The cabs are ready!" Walker ran up. He plucked up his and Mira's suitcases.

"Can we have a minute, Walker?"

"Oh, did I interrupt something?"

Byron rubbed the back of his neck. "Not at all. It wasn't important. Shall I see you tomorrow?"

"After the service. Unless you'd like to come?"

"I'd be honored to."

Mira smiled. "See you tomorrow then."

She moved with Walker to the cab and glanced back before entering it. Byron stood under a streetlight, staring after them, before he turned and stepped up into another hansom cab. Mira sighed and settled next to her brother. It was then that she realized that she still had Liza's book.

October 14, 1888

A STRANGE SILENCE SETTLED OVER THE DINING ROOM the next morning. Landon took the news quite well, considering everything. Yet the palpable loss from Cyrus' absence left a gloomy cloud. Mira poked at her eggs. Nero rubbed around her feet.

"It will all work out, Mouse." Walker ate another piece of toast.

Mira glanced up at him. "I know that. It's just—"

The front door buzzed, and Landon left the room to answer it.

"It's a bit early for Byron to come, isn't it?" Walker turned towards the door.

"I wouldn't expect that he's even read his journal yet."

The door opened, and Professor Edward Burke swept into the room, his usual amiable grin spread across his features.

"How are my favorite twins?"

Mira couldn't help her smile. "Professor! We weren't expecting you!"

"Well, I was in the area, and I don't really have anything planned today so I thought I'd come see Walker. After all, I haven't seen him in well over a year."

He ruffled Walker's hair and sat down. After a glance at the head of the table, he frowned.

"Where is your uncle?"

Mira traded a look with Walker. "I'm afraid we have some unfortunate news."

"What happened?" The professor's face darkened.

"Someone shot Mr. Sutherland at the party," Walker said. "They arrested our uncle as the main suspect."

Burke's mouth fell open as his eyes widened with shock. "What do you mean?"

As Mira recounted the story once again, she realized how surreal the situation was. On a normal morning, her uncle would sit at the head of the table, rustling a newspaper as he turned the page. Everything was wrong.

"I can't believe it." The professor held his head in his hands. "Why on earth would they think your uncle was involved?" He sat up straight, expression tightening as a glint of fury passed over his eyes. "He was in the wrong place at the wrong time, but that doesn't mean that he's a murderer!"

"We know that, and you know that, but until the police or Detective Constantine find some evidence to free our uncle, I'm afraid there isn't much we can do." Walker leaned back in his chair.

The professor's eyebrows shot up, and his shoulders relaxed. "Detective Constantine? Has he taken the case?"

"He happened to be at Sutherland's gala." Mira nibbled at a piece of toast.

"How fortunate! He'll solve it for certain." The professor nodded and shifted back in his chair, glancing at Mira. His hopeful expression fell, seeing her fiddling with her silverware.

"And how are the two of you holding up?"

"I don't think it's set in yet. It's not quite real." Mira gave up on eating anything and pushed her plate away.

"I'm so sorry, Mira."

The professor leaned over and gave her hand a squeeze. She gave him a tightlipped smile in return.

"I think, overall, we're doing as well as we can," Walker said. "And we're going to keep going about business as usual."

"That's the best anyone could do under the circumstances." The professor nodded again. His face twitched in thought as he drummed his fingers on the table. After a moment, he took a deep breath. "I think I have some errands to run after all. I'll come check up on the two of you tomorrow."

"We aren't five, professor." Mira rolled her eyes.

"Oh, and you have Landon looking after you. How could I forget? You'll be fine!" he called over his shoulder.

"He's going to the police station, isn't he?" Walker said, once the professor was gone.

Mira shook her head. "I do not envy the earful that the constables are going to get." She folded her napkin. "I'm going to get ready for today's service. Are you coming?"

"Er, actually, I was planning to meet with Miss Renaldi today." Walker turned a lovely shade of pink.

Mira smirked. "So, you do like her."

"I don't know yet! I just thought I'd give it a shot. And besides, I'm sure that you want to spend some time alone with Mr. Constantine."

Mira flushed but couldn't find her words.

"I'll take that for a win." Walker winked. "Now, I presume you haven't stolen my best suit?"

"Of course not."

"Good." Walker kissed her forehead and left the room, humming. Mira ran to catch up with him.

"Would you mind returning a book she lent to me?"

THE AUTUMN WINDS WHIPPED AROUND HER AS Mira strolled through Kensington. Her dress stood out against the wet leaves and pavement, making her look like the only flower in the park. If it weren't for the cold, bees would have been buzzing around the lilac details on her lavender gown. She walked with purpose past the duck ponds and the palace. As she rounded the bend that would take her straight to Palace Court, Alexander Durant fell into step beside her.

"Good morning, Miss Blayse. I had hoped I'd find you here."

"Do you just loiter about in Kensington Gardens, waiting for me?" Her gaze flicked up to his.

"If I think you'll be here."

"Well, I'm afraid I have places to be." She sped up.

"With Mr. Constantine?"

"Yes. Although it is none of your business," Mira huffed.

"Without a chaperone?"

"How presumptuous of you to think that we need one." She kept walking, but he matched her step for step.

"It's just terribly improper for a young lady such as yourself to be alone with a bachelor."

"I didn't realize you were married, Mr. Durant!" Mira feigned surprise.

Alexander froze. "What?"

Mira turned around to face him, taking a step backwards. "Well, if it is improper for me to be alone with a bachelor, I'm sure it is equally so for a bachelor to be alone with me. And here we are without a chaperone." She faked a gasp and covered her mouth with one of her hands. "But what will your wife think?"

Alexander laughed. "I see your point."

She turned back on her course, and he continued to escort her. They approached the fence that marked the edge of the gardens, and he stepped in front of the opening. He made for an effective blockade.

"Are you trapping me here, then?" She crossed her arms and tried to pass him again.

"Well, if I'm going to be disappointing my wife, I might as well make a story of it." He leaned in close, and she felt his breath on her lips.

Mira's eyes widened as she stepped back, and Alexander laughed harder.

"You always think the worst of me, don't you?" He took a breath and glanced down, hands in his coat pockets. "I'd wish that I'd never agreed to deliver those messages, but then I don't think I'd have met you." His gaze snapped back to hers and he smirked.

Mira fought the smile that tugged at her lips. "You're a terrible flirt, Mr. Durant. May I pass?"

"I'm afraid there's a toll at this gate."

"And what's the price?"

"Your respect?"

"That's a bit steep, don't you think?" She tried to sidestep him but he followed her every move.

"It's all I ask."

"Very well. You have my respect."

Mr. Durant smiled and stepped to the side. She walked past him. "For today."

She crossed the street to enter Palace Court, half-expecting him to follow her. But as she looked over her shoulder, Alexander tipped his hat and disappeared back into the gardens.

Shrugging, she continued her journey to number 27 and pulled out her key. She stepped inside, a piano melody greeting her as she came in. Bracing herself, she moved to the sitting room.

Byron didn't look up from the piano, engrossed in the music. His right hand picked out a simple melody as the left moved back and forth to strike the proper chords for the harmony. Mira set her things on the couch. The movement caused Byron to falter as he looked up at her, confusion crossing his face.

"Have you read your journal?" she asked.

"Finished it about forty minutes ago." His scrutinizing stare traveled her person and settled on her eyes. "You're Mira."

It wasn't even a question, and Mira broke out in a smile, her heart fit to burst.

"Yes. I am."

He shot her a grin. "I knew it had to be you. My journal is particular about certain details. And your self-portrait certainly helped as well."

"Did some of those details include going to church?"

He shot up to his feet. "Yes, it did. Are you ready to go?"

She nodded.

"Let me get my hat."

He moved up the stairs and disappeared into his room. She stood at the base of the steps and adjusted her gloves. Byron popped out of his room again and offered his arm as they left Palace Court and made their way towards the church.

They arrived during the pastor's reading of the lectionary. They slipped into an empty pew and sat next to an elderly couple. The pastor read the last verse of the section and the organ warmed up for the first hymn of praise. Byron's deep baritone caught Mira by surprise as they sang.

Around the second verse, Byron stopped singing. Mira glanced up at him from the hymnal. His gaze settled on something, or someone, a few rows ahead of them. She followed the line of his vision and found the back of a woman's head, her blonde hair piled up on top of it.

As she focused back on the third verse, Byron jolted. She whipped her head up as the young woman made her way down the aisle as if to leave the church. Her own eyes widened as she recognized her. Grace Trimbell. Byron shared a glance with Mira as Grace passed them.

Mira nodded, and they both rose to follow her, gaining a few dirty looks from the surrounding members of the parish. Mira shot them an apologetic look before catching the door as it shut behind Byron.

She dashed after him, hat askew, as he caught up with the young woman.

"Miss Trimbell!" he called. She turned about and went quite pale, but she didn't run.

"D-do I know you?"

Byron stopped, dumbfounded. "I, er, you are Grace Trimbell?"

She swallowed. "Well, yes, I suppose I am."

"You came to me for help once."

"Did I?" She fidgeted with her gloves, eyes searching for an escape.

"Yes? About four years ago."

"Oh, that was a rather long time ago. So easy to forget things like that. What was your name?"

"Byron Constantine."

"I remember now. Yes. You-you're the detective." She looked like she would rather be doing anything else.

"Yes! And it would seem I'm in need of your help now."

"O-oh?" she stammered.

Byron ran a hand through his hair. "Why don't we talk about it over an early lunch? Do you have the time?"

"Well, I . . ." She looked up at him through her lashes and averted her eyes. "I suppose I can't say no to you."

Byron grinned. "Splendid." He turned to Mira. "This is my secretary, Miss Blayse. I think she knows the best cafés in the area?"

"Of course," Mira managed.

She ended up leading them to a small tea shop a few blocks away. Her and Byron's café was closer, but she didn't feel like sharing everything with Grace just yet. She bit down the twinge of jealousy that settled in her gut and ordered something light. And then decided she wanted cake for this conversation.

They arranged themselves around a table, teetering on their own wire legged chairs. Grace seemed much more at ease sipping at some tea.

"I can't believe you recognized me. It's been so long!"

Byron chuckled. "It surprised me as well, you see—well I happen to have a memory problem nowadays."

"R-really? What kind of problem?"

A sigh gave way to a grimace. "For the past four years, every day I've woken up and thought it was still February 1884."

"Goodness. That's quite terrible!"

Mira sipped at her tea.

"Yes, well, I've managed."

Byron shot Mira a meaningful look, and she focused harder on her teacup.

Grace tucked a strand of hair behind her ear, hand shaking. "Y-you mentioned that you needed help? How could I help?"

"It's quite extraordinary. I didn't remember you at all. Not a scrap of memory about you, I assume because we must have met after the accident. But when I bumped into you, I had all these memories come rushing back!"

"All of them?"

"Well, not all of them. But a few. More than I had ever remembered before. And your name came to mind. And since then, I've been remembering bits and pieces of each day. I might not remember it all immediately, but I certainly remember it before I read my journal."

"I see." Grace sipped at her tea.

"I'm wondering if you can tell me anything about the case I

worked for you or what happened during that time. If we can piece together what happened, maybe my memory will heal."

His earnest face would have anyone scrambling to help him. Or at least, that's what Mira thought. She finished her cake and wished she had another piece.

"I'm not sure if I can really help you with that," Grace said, lip quivering. She placed her hand on her throat, rubbing it a bit.

"Anything you can tell me would help." Byron leaned forward, desperate.

Grace looked down.

"I asked you for help in finding my brother. He had been missing for a few weeks and you tracked him down to," she faltered before whispering, "to an opium den."

Byron frowned. "Hm."

"I'm afraid I don't remember any of the details, but does that help?"

He drummed his fingers on the table. "No more than it did before. Perhaps I just need time to think on it."

Mira stiffened as Grace reached over and took his hand.

"Please forgive me," she whispered.

Byron glanced down at their hands and then back at Grace. "For what?"

She pursed her lips and shook her head. "For not having more information."

Byron gave her a half-smile. "It's perfectly alright, Miss Trimbell. You've given me more than just about anyone to work off of."

Grace let out a breath and smiled, pulling her hand back.

"I'm afraid that I must be going. But it was so nice to see you again, Eli—er—Byron. Perhaps we can run into one another some other time?" she giggled.

Mira readjusted her posture with a poorly hidden frown.

"I'll be certain not to knock your packages astray the next time." He smirked at her. He actually smirked!

Mira folded her napkin and placed it on the table, giving a forced chuckle along with the two long-lost friends.

"Oh, and it was so nice to meet you, Miss Blayse." Grace smiled like sunshine and Mira felt obliged to return it.

"It was a pleasure to meet you as well, Miss Trimbell."

Quiet followed Grace's departure. Mira wasn't sure what to say, and based on Byron's expression, his cogs were mulling things over. She refused to be jealous. Except, here she was, completely and totally jealous of a woman who had barely had any contact with Byron. Although she did seem awfully familiar with using his first name. Why would she do that? Unless, of course, she did exactly the same thing and helped Byron with her own case. That would be an awful lot of contact. And she looked so young! She couldn't be more than twenty! She frowned. Alright, twenty wasn't *that* young. If Mira's uncle wanted her married off by eighteen—and what a disappointment she must be, unmarried at twenty-two and dangerously close to spinsterhood—then Grace wasn't young at all.

Where was she going with this?

Oh, yes. Something about Grace wasn't adding up. Or was that the jealousy speaking? But what if the green vengeance was right and there was something wrong? She couldn't shake the feeling that Grace was lying about something. But what could she do about it anyhow? If Byron wanted to up and go off with her, what was she supposed to do? Especially if just bumping into Grace had brought back some of his memory? Being in constant contact was bound to do something to help. So, it didn't matter what Mira wanted, regardless of the fact that she loved him.

And what an easy thought that was. How strange to accept it so quickly, so absolutely? Samira Rose Blayse was hopelessly in love with Byron Ambrose Sherard Whatever His Name Was Constantine! She glanced over at him and was surprised to find him looking her over with confusion and worry.

"You're going to bite your lip clean off with the way you're worrying it. Whatever is the matter?"

Mira gave a nervous laugh. "Oh, well, I was just puzzling out what Miss Trimbell said. And more particularly how she said it." She chastised herself. She should have actually been thinking about what Grace had said, instead of wondering about her relationship with Byron.

"You noticed, too?"

"Er, tell me what you noticed." She leaned against the table.

Byron numbered each item on his fingers. "She fidgeted quite a bit, repeated herself, stuttered, and didn't maintain eye contact until she apologized. I feel like she was lying."

"That's exactly what I thought!"

"I'm not sure if there is a way for us to determine what the truth actually is, or even if it's important. But her story didn't bring anything up for me at all. Not like when I bumped into her or picked up that pamphlet at Mr. Sutherland's."

Mira's eyes widened. "I thought you had disappeared for a moment when you were looking at it! Why didn't you tell me it brought back memories?"

"There were more pressing things happening at the time. We had just found a new suspect and needed to investigate quickly."

"What memories did it spark?"

"I knew the club had connections to Circe. I had uncovered the connection through some codes sent in the newspaper. The last I remember, I was planning on going to check out the Cobden Club. Then I woke up, weeks later, with no recollection of what happened."

Mira nodded for him to continue.

"After bumping into Grace, I had more memories surface. And I'm positive they were from before the accident, but I didn't remember them before. I had gone to the Cobden Club several times. I remember that the pamphlets that they distribute have another sort of code in them. And, well, I have some foggy memories of Grace again that could be in an opium den. But it also could be in the Pit. I'm not exactly certain."

Mira swallowed a jealous spike as a spark of dark hope sprung within her. "You mean she might be connected to Circe?"

"I . . ." He ran a hand through his hair. "I really don't know. I hope not. She doesn't seem the type."

"Neither did Molly Bridges."

"Was that the one in the last case? The Shadow?"

Mira nodded.

"You're right, of course." He sighed and rubbed at his temples. "But at the same time, she could be innocent."

"Wasn't she lying though?"

"We don't know that for certain, and even if we did, we don't know what she was lying about."

Mira sighed. Byron sat up and cocked his head as he looked at her.

"But I do know one thing."

"What's that?"

"Your body language suggested that you were jealous."

"What? Me?" Blast, she hadn't been stoic enough.

His gaze narrowed. "Why didn't we go to the Rose and Crown, then? It's closer."

"I . . . er . . . well."

He laughed. "What a pair we make."

He leaned on the table again and fiddled with his fountain pen. She blushed and glanced away.

"We do need to make a game plan of how to free your uncle, though." He uncapped the pen and opened his journal.

"Wouldn't the Cobden Club be the best place to start? After all, our main suspect has quite the connection there."

"That's what I was thinking, too. I'll go there tomorrow." Byron made a note in his journal.

"Don't you mean that *we'll* be going there tomorrow?"

"Don't be ridiculous. It's a gentleman's club. And besides, it's one of the main hubs for Circe. It's dangerous there."

"Oh, and it's not dangerous for you?" She folded her arms.

"I'll go in disguise. Don't worry."

"I'll always worry."

He caught her gaze and softened.

"Tell you what, we'll meet back at Palace Court by five tomorrow. If I don't make it on time, then you can," he waved his hand in a circle, thinking of the word, "send the police after me or something."

"Because that wouldn't be suspicious or anything." She rolled her eyes.

"Of course it won't, because I'll be back before five." He set his fountain pen down.

"Fine. But you had better tell me everything."

"I'll be sure not to leave anything out."

Mira bit her lip. "Where is the Cobden Club, anyway?"

"Good question. We ought to figure that out before tomorrow."

He looked out to the street and motioned for Mira to stay as he walked off. Soon enough, he returned with a newspaper.

"The Cobden Club is more secretive about things, for obvious reasons. So, their location changes month to month. Usually, it will say in the advertisements." He flicked the paper open and spread it out on the table. He circled a code in the advertisements, and created a grid in the margin, decoding the secret message.

"Ah. Here it is. The Cobden Club is meeting at number 73, Chancery Lane this month."

"Then I'll know precisely where to send the police if you don't come back."

"Of course." His eyes twinkled.

"I ought to get back to my uncle's house." Mira picked up

the paper and folded it under her arm. "Walker should be home soon enough, and I'd rather not miss him."

"I had nearly forgotten about him. Where was he this morning?"

"Visiting Miss Liza Renaldi. I'm hoping it went well."

"Miss Renaldi?"

"She was at the party?"

"Ah." He glanced at his journal and nodded. "Yes, they would work together, wouldn't they? I won't keep you then."

He stood and offered her a hand to help her up. Then he kissed the back of it.

"Shall I walk you back?"

"If you'd like."

His proffered arm suggested his preference, and she smiled as they moved back towards Swan Walk.

After a few minutes, Byron cleared his throat.

"You know, jealousy doesn't suit you."

"It doesn't suit you either."

"Well, there is a simple way to remedy the situation."

"Oh?"

"If we were actually courting."

Mira's cheeks flushed, and her heart raced. Byron continued to ramble in her silence.

"According to my journal, I actually meant to ask you the other day. Mr. Durant asking you about it . . . well it struck a nerve. Reading over that entry this morning caused my insides to churn. You can't imagine my relief when I read that you would have told him no."

She took a deep breath. "I'd love to, Byron. Of course, I would. But if we're going to do it, I'd like to do it properly. Unfortunately, we'll need my uncle's permission, and that's harder to ask for at the moment."

"Say no more. My heart is content in knowing that you are willing to take a chance with me, memory loss and all."

"I'd say it has its charms." She smirked. "Besides, I think Uncle will be more impressed with you if you manage to prove that he's innocent."

"Being a Sherard isn't impressive enough for him?"

"Oh, he doesn't know that yet."

Byron grinned. "Then I can win him over by my own merits. Brilliant."

They stopped outside of Swan Walk and they both suppressed a sigh.

"I'll see you tomorrow? After your escapades at the Cobden Club?"

"Of course."

"I'm looking forward to it."

She reached up on her tiptoes and kissed his cheek. His eyes widened, and he dropped his hat in surprise.

"Goodnight, Byron," she said as he fumbled with his hat.

"Goodnight, Mira." He caught his hat, touching his cheek. She smiled at him before walking up the stairs and into the house.

She found Walker in the sitting room reading and sat on the arm of his chair.

"How would you like to help me break into male society?" she said, setting the newspaper on his lap.

October 15, 1888

"You had better not ruin these," Walker said as he adjusted Mira's collar. Or, more precisely, the collar of his shirt that Mira now wore.

She cocked her head to the side. "Why? It's not like you'll be using them again."

The last time she raided her brother's closet, she didn't know about his hoard of clothes from his younger years. Had she known, it would have been a much simpler affair, with less hemming, to be sure.

"They still have sentimental value." He cleared his throat. "And I'm afraid that they don't suit you all that well. You still look decidedly female."

"Well, I am wearing my corset right now. And I have some plans to ensure that no one will be the wiser. After all, this time around I'll have to be even more convincing."

She looked herself over in the mirror. His older clothes fit her much better, and he even had old shoes that fit her. She twisted her face. How would she hide her hair if they asked her to take off her hat?

"I'm going to *really* get ready," she said as she moved out of Walker's room.

A jolt of worry passed through her at the thought that her uncle might see her, and then the pang of reality hit her. She quickened her pace to her room and stripped out of Walker's clothes to take care of her curves.

Removing the corset did most of the work. Then it was a simple job of binding up her chest with a large strip of fabric and changing back into his old clothes. From the neck down, she looked the part. Now to do something about the hair.

She pulled and teased her hair, trying to find something that would work without cutting anything. She ended up pulling it up high on her head, fastening it, then letting some of it hang down the back. With her brother's bowler hat over the top, you couldn't tell that it normally went down to her waist.

Grabbing her sketchbook, she sat down at the mirror again. She flipped to several portraits of men to compare facial features and ended up sighing at the mirror. There wasn't much she could do about it. The shape was rounder, her nose too slender, and her brows much too thin to pass as a man. Perhaps a boy. Would they allow boys into gentlemen's clubs? Looking at her drawings again, an idea struck her.

She moved to her desk and pulled out a stick of charcoal and applied it to her brows to darken them and make them fuller. Chewing on her lip, she roughly sketched some of the charcoal near her ears to simulate sideburns. After finding some scissors, she took some fake hair pieces that matched her coloring and cut the tiniest bit off the ends, creating a mound of short hairs. She applied a bit of glue to the sides of her face, and carefully positioned the bits of hair on her face. Her face prickled and stretched from the action. She gave herself a once over when the glue had dried and shrugged. Not exactly ideal, but passable. Now to find a judge.

She skipped down to Walker's room and entered without knocking.

"How's this?"

She turned around to give him the full picture. His mouth gaped open. She laughed.

"Come on, Walker. If Viola could impersonate Sebastian, I'm certain I could impersonate you."

"First of all, generally Viola is played by a man, so visually it works better. Second of all, how did you manage all that?"

"Is it convincing enough, do you think?"

"Not when you're talking like that."

She moved over to his mirror, and he stepped beside her.

"We could be twins," he said with a smirk.

She pushed into him with her shoulder. "We are twins, you idiot."

"Well Sam, are you ready to head out?"

Mira gave a grimace at the name and nodded. "I'll need to lower my voice, huh?"

She demonstrated, and Walker laughed.

"Maybe I should do the talking?"

"You wouldn't know what to ask!"

"Let's just play it by ear."

THEY TOOK A HANSOM CAB TO CHANCERY Lane and walked the rest of the way to number 73. Walker paused outside, turning to Mira.

"And what if they don't let us in?"

"Then we'll think of something else," she said, deepening her voice.

He shrugged, and they entered the club. A steward with round spectacles and a dashing black beard sat behind a desk. Spectacles would have been brilliant. Why hadn't she thought of that?

"May I see your club cards?" he asked.

Mira stepped forward and lowered her voice. "We've been invited here by Ambrose Sherard. He should be on your books."

The clerk gave her a quizzical once over before opening a black book and running his fingers along the lists.

"Ah, yes. Mr. Sherard. He must have come before my shift, but he is in attendance today. Only recently became a member. I'm surprised he's invited guests so quickly. May I have your names for the books?"

Walker stepped up. "Yes, I'm Walker Blayse and this is my brother Samuel."

The steward made note of that and gestured for them to enter. Mira smirked at Walker as they were about to pass through. Then the steward stopped.

"May I take your hats and coats?"

Mira stiffened then shook her head. "We'll be leaving soon enough."

Surprisingly, the steward only inclined his head and allowed them to pass through. They'd made it into the club! Mira turned back to him.

"I believe another friend of ours may be here today as well. Dr. Lorenzo Kelley?"

The steward took a quick glance at the book and shook his head.

"I'm afraid he isn't in today, sir."

She nodded and continued with Walker up the stairs.

"Why did you use your real name?" Mira hissed to him as they passed through a library.

"I didn't have time to think of an alias." He shrugged.

"Well, before we leave here, we need to take a look at that book." She glanced back over her shoulder. "See if there are any other names that seem familiar."

"How are we supposed to manage that when the steward is there?"

"I suppose we'll have to find a distraction or something. He can't stand there all day."

They passed by the billiards room without seeing anyone of interest.

"Why exactly are we here again?" Walker fiddled with his cuffs.

"I wasn't about to let Byron go alone. And if all goes well, we might learn something new about Dr. Kelley. We need proof that he was the one who murdered Mr. Sutherland."

"So, we need to find Byron?"

"I'd rather not have anyone recognize me just yet."

"That's assuming that he remembers what you look like."

"Well, his memory has been impro—"

"Walker, is that you?" Professor Burke broke off from a conversation and approached the duo.

Mira swallowed. Of course, not every member of the Cobden Club would be a member of Circe, would they? Byron was a member, after all.

"Oh! Professor Burke!" Walker said. "I didn't know you were a member of this club!"

"I could say the same for you!"

"Oh, a friend invited me as their guest."

"Who is it? Perhaps I know them?"

"Oh-er . . . "

Walker glanced at Mira which brought the professor's attention to her. Burke fumbled with his drink.

"Please tell me that isn't who I think it is," he hissed.

Mira sighed. "Hello, professor."

The professor looked heavenward, set his drink on a nearby table, and grabbed them both by the arm, tugging them into an empty side room. Once inside he released his grip, closed the door, and paced in front of the dim fireplace.

"My word, child! What have you done?"

"I've done what I had to do to get into the club." Mira slumped into a nearby armchair, the faint trace of a headache settling behind her eyes.

"Yes. But why? What in blazes were you thinking?"

He looked between the two twins. Walker only shrugged and pointed to his sister.

"I'm sorry, Professor, but I can't explain it to you." She rubbed at her temples.

"Can't or won't?" He stood over her and tapped his foot.

"It's complicated."

The professor fidgeted with his ring and paced again. "Complicated doesn't cut it. Do you know how complicated this will be to explain this to your uncle? Let alone," he trailed off with a sigh. "Why can't you leave well enough alone, Mira?"

"I'm afraid that I'm here because of my uncle." She sat up and stared him straight in the eyes. "So even if he does hear about this, I hope he is wise enough to forgive me for such a breach in propriety. And really, this isn't the worst thing I could be doing."

"This is for the case?" The professor stopped pacing to look at the twins.

"Yes, sir," Walker said, sitting down. "We have reason to believe our suspect is a member of this club."

"Really?" The professor sat down next. "A murderer? Here? In the club?"

"Not at the moment. The steward said he wasn't here today." Walker leaned back.

Mira bit her lip. If Byron were correct about the Cobden Club, it was likely there were quite a few killers in attendance. She stayed quiet for the moment.

"That still doesn't explain why you're here, Mira. And dressed li-like that." The professor looked the two of them over. "It's like I'm seeing double. Other than the height, of course." He rubbed at his eyes.

"I'm sorry if you don't approve, but I'm not leaving until we find something that we can use."

The professor sighed. "Alright. I know better than to argue when your mind is made up. Who exactly is your suspect?"

"Dr. Kelley," Walker said.

The professor blinked several times, eyes widening. "Lorenzo? Really?" He frowned and stood to pace again. "I've only known him a short time, but I couldn't imagine . . ." His brow furrowed even more.

"Well, it isn't him for certain. That's why we're here," Mira said.

"Maybe you can help us, seeing as you know the club so well." Walker added.

"I'm not sure what I can do."

Mira paused a moment. "Could you possibly distract the steward so we can borrow the guest ledger?"

"What do you need that for?" he asked.

"I'd like to see who is on it and see who might be in contact with Dr. Kelley."

"Oh, that was replaced this week. It would be much simpler to misplace one of the old ones for a while. It's back in the storage room."

The professor stood and made his way to the door. "I'll go grab it. You two stay here. It will look more suspicious for all of us to go, since the two of you aren't members of the club."

"What are the odds of meeting him here?" Walker leaned against the armrest.

"Slim," Mira said.

The more important question in her mind was how many members of the club were involved with Circe. Her mind brushed over every interaction with the professor up to that point and couldn't fathom him being involved with anything so sinister. Then again, there were plenty of people who don't seem suspicious whatsoever but have a nasty disposition hiding underneath.

"You don't think he's part of Circe, do you?" She drew her gaze from the fire to her brother.

"The professor? Impossible."

"Is it?"

Walker frowned and leaned forward, steepling his fingers.

"You really think between his travels and teaching and looking after us he even has time to be involved in a secret evil society? And aside from that, he was dad's best friend. Our godfather. Do you really think he'd be involved with the organization that murdered our parents?"

"Well, no, but—"

"But nothing, Mira. Did you see how surprised he was that Dr. Kelley was involved at all? And how quickly he decided to help us? The whole point of this club is to be a cover for Circe, yes?"

Mira nodded.

"Well then, it stands to reason that part of that cover means that other people might become members as well." Walker leaned back.

Mira smiled. "I've been rather silly, haven't I?"

"I wouldn't say that. I didn't expect him to be here either. But did you see his face when he realized who you were?" Walker laughed and Mira suppressed a giggle.

The professor walked back in, black book in hand.

"That was easier than I anticipated." He handed it off to Walker. "Now the two of you need to leave before anyone suspects anything."

"You'll let us know if you hear anything suspicious?" Mira asked.

"I'll do anything I can to help you clear your uncle." The professor softened. "I'll come by Swan Walk as soon as I have any news."

Mira resisted the urge to hug him and followed Walker out of the room. As they came around the bend that passed the library, she bumped straight into another gentleman. Her head shot up to apologize, but she found herself speechless as she stared up into deep blue eyes.

"Sorry about that." Byron smiled at her before knitting his brow together.

He opened his mouth to say something but Mira latched onto Walker's arm and marched straight outside, not bothering to look back.

Halfway down the block Walker burst into laughter.

"I thought the professor's face was good, but yours is even better! It's still red!"

"Shut up, Walker."

HALF AN HOUR LATER, MIRA FINALLY PEELED the binding from around her torso. She let out a sigh of relief as her aching chest and back were able to relax. Her corset had never looked so comfortable. Bits of sideburn resisted her scrubbing as she worked to remove the glue keeping the hair in place.

By the end, she looked almost presentable, minus not having her hair up. She ignored it—her hair had been through enough as it was—and left her room to head to Palace Court.

"You clean up well, Mira," Walker snickered as she passed by his room.

"Well, at least I look far better as a man than you would ever look as a woman."

"No contest there, seeing as I'll never have the opportunity."

"Never say never," she said as she dashed down the stairs.

She needed to make it back to Palace Court before Byron. Maybe if she made them some sort of lunch, he'd never know that she had been to the club in the first place. Of course, how was she supposed to explain how she got the ledger?

In her haste to create an alibi, Mira almost ran into Landon in the front entry hall.

"Miss Mira, Mr. Constantine is waiting for you in the sitting room."

"Oh! He is?"

"Yes. Would you like me to bring any refreshments up?"

Mira paused a moment. "Could we have some sandwiches, please?"

Landon nodded and retreated through the dining room door. Mira turned towards the sitting room. Of course, Byron would ruin her plan by coming straight to Swan Walk. She smoothed out her dress, checked her hair in a mirror in the hall, and entered the sitting room. Byron was leaning against the mantelpiece. He looked up, locked eyes with her, and grinned.

"Hello Mira."

"Hello Byron. I wasn't expecting you to come here."

"I thought I'd surprise you." He stepped towards her. "How was your morning?"

Mira set her bag in one of the armchairs and moved to the window. "Uneventful. Did you find anything out at the club?"

"Well, I did learn that I shouldn't trust you to stay behind." Byron followed her and tried to catch her expression.

Mira's cheeks burned. "You recognized me?"

"I didn't fully put the pieces together until you walked in just now, but yes. Although your disguise was quite well done. I'm sure no one else noticed anything amiss, especially with your brother next to you."

"I rather enjoyed figuring out how to pull it off." A small smile graced her lips.

"I'm still upset that you went, even though I told you it was dangerous." He rubbed a hand over his face.

She turned towards him. "I wasn't about to let you go alone."

"You could have at least said sorry for bumping into me

or told me who you were." His gaze flicked up to hers, and he raised an eyebrow. "I suppose I'll forgive you if you tell me what you found."

Mira nodded and retrieved the ledger from her bag. "This is one of the guest ledgers. It has the names of all the members of the club, and the people who have come to visit them at one point or another."

"Where'd you get this?" He trailed a finger over the names.

"Professor Burke is a friend of the family and happens to be a member of the club. Walker and I didn't know that, of course, until we bumped into him. He offered to retrieve this and keep an ear out for anything odd."

"You trust him?" He glanced up from the ledger.

"Of course."

"Hm. Well, this is better than anything I found out. I mostly loitered around people and listened in on their conversations. Nothing too profound. I hoped I could catch Dr. Kelley and ask him a few questions."

"That is unfortunate. But at least we have this to start with?"

"It will have to do for now. Can you fetch some paper and be my scribe to write down who's come to visit Dr. Kelley?"

Mira nodded and left the room to grab some paper. When she returned, Landon was setting down a tray of sandwiches and tea.

"Thank you, Landon."

"Of course, Miss. Let me know if you need anything else."

Byron gave her a questioning glance as the butler left the room.

"I thought you might be hungry. I certainly am."

She punctuated this by picking up half a sandwich for herself and taking a bite. Byron shrugged and grabbed one of his own, handing a fountain pen to her. He took a bite of his sandwich and opened the ledger to look at names. As he would find a name, he'd read it out, along with the date to Mira, and she'd write it down. Once they got to the end of the ledger, and the end of the sandwiches, Byron leaned back.

"He certainly had a lot of visitors during those two months."

"Twenty-three to be exact." Mira counted them up. "Mr. Harding visited him three times and Mr. Rowley visited him twice."

"Hm. Tomorrow we ought to make a visit to your uncle. See if he knows anyone on that list."

"Why not go now?"

Byron glanced up at the clock above the mantle. "It's just after four now. Visiting hours are generally earlier. Besides, I don't think you want to show up to visit your uncle when you've still got a bit of sideburn stuck to your face."

Mira stiffened and scrubbed at the sides of her face with both hands. The hair and glue pricked at her skin. Byron smiled.

"I had an inkling that it was you when I bumped into you. In the future, when you need a disguise, we ought to find a way to hide your eyes. They are a dead giveaway for anyone who knows you."

"Ah, but even with the self-portrait that I gave you, you still didn't fully recognize me."

"Memory loss does make it trickier. I'm still sorry I didn't wake up remembering you today." He glared at his journal.

"Did you remember anything from yesterday, though?"

"I remembered talking with Grace. Nothing about going to church though." He leaned forward. "I'd never have forgiven myself if something had happened to you this morning."

"Honestly, Byron, that was one of the least dangerous things I've ever done while working with you. No guns, or knives, or prison cells."

"But I didn't know that going in. It's been years since I looked into the Cobden Club. For all we knew, it could have been just like the Pit, and even then . . ." His eyes glazed over.

"Byron?"

He shook his head and placed a hand to his temple. "Just another memory. Nothing to worry about."

"What was it?"

"There were two gentlemen that I talked to when I went to the Cobden Club that last time. I'm almost positive they were with Circe." He focused on her again. "I think I remember their names. I'll have to check my files and see if I have anything on them."

"This is great. You're getting things back!"

"Only in bits and pieces. And it doesn't make sense half of the time."

"It's still progress."

"At this point, I don't care what happened then. I'd be happy just to remember what's happening now."

"Byron, we need to know what happened to you."

"I know. I know." He sighed and stood. "I ought to go. I promised Castel that I'd come to dinner, and you really ought to clean up a bit more before tomorrow."

She led him back to the front entry, and he slipped on his hat and coat again. He turned towards her and took her hand, kissing the back of it.

"I'll come by first thing in the morning," she said.

He tipped his hat. "I'll be waiting, and hopefully, I'll remember."

October 16, 1888

MIRA DRESSED IN A FLASH THE NEXT morning, not wanting to waste a minute.

Opening the door, she ran straight into Mr. Durant. He caught her and grabbed hold of the railing with his free hand, stopping them from careening down the steps together.

"You're in a hurry," he said, laughing.

Her face flushed, and she stepped away from him. "What are you doing here?"

"I've come to pick up your brother. I'm taking him on a tour of the company I'm apprenticed to."

"Oh, I see."

She opened the door again, Mr. Durant following her. Walker met them in the entry hall.

"Durant! You're early! Did you want some breakfast?"

Mr. Durant smiled. "That would be splendid!"

Walker looked Mira over. "Where are you off to?"

"Palace Court. We're going to visit Uncle Cyrus."

"Why didn't you tell me?" Walker groused.

"It didn't cross my mind."

She looked between Mr. Durant and her brother. Did she really trust Alexander enough to leave them alone?

"You'll have to tell me everything when you get back. Maybe I'll stop by later today to visit him." Walker turned towards the dining room.

Mira gave Mr. Durant one more suspicious glance before turning to leave.

"I'll see you tonight!"

Mira bounced on her toes as she pulled out the key to Palace Court and slipped it into the lock. The smell of bacon struck her as she entered. Byron's head popped out from the doorway to the sitting room, halfway through a bite of toast. He swallowed and cocked his head at her.

"Who are you again? I haven't quite finished reading."

"Mira Blayse," she answered as she hung up her coat.

Byron's eyes widened, a red tinge staining his cheeks.

"Right. Right. Come on in then and have something to eat."

She soon settled on the couch with her plate and teacup as Byron read his journal. He kept sneaking glances at Mira, which she noticed as she peered up at him between bites of breakfast.

Byron closed his journal and set it on the side table next to a white notebook. "Sorry for forgetting again. But I did remember that we were going to Scotland Yard today and most of the dinner with Castel! So, it seems I am continuing the trend of retaining memories from day to day."

"You don't need to apologize, Byron," Mira said, setting her plate on a side table. "I'm glad that you remember something."

"Let me grab that list of individuals who contacted Dr. Kelley. I think I left it in my room."

"Oh! I have it!" She pulled the sheet from her sketchbook.

"I suppose my memory isn't as good as I thought it was," he chuckled. "Shall we go then?"

SCOTLAND YARD WASN'T PARTICULARLY BUSY WHEN THEY arrived. A constable that Mira didn't recognize manned the front desk. After arranging for her uncle to come up from the cells, Byron and Mira made their way to the interrogation rooms.

"Did Walker not want to come?" Byron said.

"I'm sure he did, but he had already made plans with a mutual . . . er . . . acquaintance of ours. Mr. Durant, actually."

Byron furrowed his brow a moment, then nodded. "I think I read about him."

"I'd be surprised if you didn't."

The door opened, and her uncle walked in, accompanied by two constables. Mira jumped up and hugged him tight, not thinking. He hugged back as well as he could.

"I've missed you," she whispered.

Byron gave a gentle tug on her arm, and she stepped back. The constables led Cyrus to the table, cuffing him to it. Mira sat across from him. His eyes drooped with exhaustion, and he seemed far more withered than she remembered him. He'd aged a few years in the short time that had passed.

"I'm glad you came, Mira, although I'm sorry you have to see me like this."

"As if I wouldn't come. Walker would have been here too, but he's looking into an apprenticeship."

"Good lad." He leaned on the table. "I assume the two of you are looking into what actually happened that night?"

"Yes, sir." Byron uncapped his fountain pen. "And we have some questions for you."

"I'll help you in any way that I can."

Byron nodded. "At the moment, we are most suspicious of Dr. Kelley. We found pieces of ivy outside his window, and shoe polish on the sill, which would suggest that he climbed in or out of the window that night. You mentioned you saw someone outside while you were on your walk?"

"Yes. At first, I thought it looked like Mr. Sutherland. Obviously, it wasn't. I was a good distance away from him and couldn't make out his features clearly. But the moon was half full that night, so I got a good look at his clothes. He wasn't wearing a jacket, just a white shirt, dark trousers, and I think a red cravat or something of the kind. I would have followed him, but then I heard the second shot."

"Hmm." Byron wrote everything down. "How long had you and Mr. Sutherland been in discussions about merging your two companies?"

"The process has taken about a year, but we've tried to keep it secret, in case things didn't work out. Would have been joint business partners. I'm not sure what's going to happen to either company now."

"Can you think of any enemies that Mr. Sutherland may have had?"

Cyrus shook his head. "None whatsoever. Vince and I have been friends since we were boys, and he was always well-liked."

Mira pulled out the list from the Cobden Club and slid it over to Cyrus.

"Do you recognize any of these names, Uncle?"

He picked up the paper and read over it.

"Elijah Harding is the head manager over shipping at Sutherland's company." He passed the list back. "What's the significance of the list?"

"They are people who have visited Dr. Kelley in the past few months," Byron said, eyes focused on his journal.

"I haven't worked with Harding much. He's one of the few people who knew of the merger, although I'm not sure he knew the full extent."

Byron nodded and made a final note. "Is there anything else you can tell us?"

Cyrus shook his head. "If I can think of anything else, I'll be sure to let you know. Or I suppose, I'll let one of the constables know."

Mira bit the inside of her cheek. "Is there anything I can do for you?"

"Keep investigating. I never thought I'd be grateful for this 'hobby' of yours, but I am." He looked at Byron. "But I expect you to take care of her while I'm in here."

Byron glanced at Mira with a soft smile. "I'd do that either way."

They stopped at the chief inspector's office on the way out of the Yard.

"Good morning, Mr. Constantine! And you too, Miss Blayse," Juliet greeted them with far more enthusiasm than usual.

"Good morning, Miss Chickering." Byron's gaze flicked to the nameplate. "You seem chipper."

"It's a beautiful day, is all. The chief inspector is in if you want to speak with him."

Byron knocked on the door before entering.

"Ah, Constantine! I had expected you this morning. Officer Donley mentioned you had gone to talk with Cyrus Griffon."

"We did. And we have a new suspect for you."

"Oh?"

"Dr. Kelley."

"The man who initially examined the body? Why on earth would he have anything to do with this?"

"We're still investigating the matter, but Mr. Elijah Harding, Sutherland's second in command, so to speak, was in contact with Dr. Kelley before the party. Mr. Griffon saw an individual climbing down the ivy that night, and we found traces of ivy and shoe polish near Dr. Kelley's window."

"That is interesting, and quite the coincidence if he didn't have anything to do with it. We haven't talked with Mr. Harding yet." Thatcher shuffled through a stack of papers before retrieving one and handing it over. "Here's the address of the company. Go check it out."

THE EMORIA-SUTHERLAND TRADING COMPANY WAS FOUNDED WELL before Mira was born. Uncle Cyrus' company worked with them on multiple occasions, and Mira remembered going to the main building several times as a child.

The crumbling brick stood as proof of the company's longevity as a construction crew bustled about on scaffolding. Byron and Mira slipped beneath the crew's work on the exterior and entered the building. They approached the main desk together, where a man tapped away at a typewriter. He glanced up at them.

"May I help you?"

"Would you point us towards Elijah Harding's office, please?" Byron leaned on the desk.

"Normally you would need an appointment." The man eyed them and shrugged. "Third floor, down the right hall. Second door on your left, just next to Mr. Sutherland's old office."

Following the man's directions through the building, they approached the office door. It hung open by an inch. Voices came from within. Byron motioned for Mira to stick close to the wall and stay silent.

"I'm not sure what to tell you, Poole. I'm just trying to keep the business together."

"Yet you are ignoring the very reason they've placed you here," came the terse reply.

"How can you expect me to open up a new branch when everything is up in the air? We don't even know if I'll be the one in charge. Sutherland's new partner could be cleared, and then I wouldn't be able to manage it."

"Then we have to hope that doesn't happen."

Mira glanced up at Byron, eyes wide. He put a finger to his lips and leaned closer.

The first man sighed with the shuffling of papers. "Is there anything else I can do for you? Or did you just come to berate me?"

"Actually, there was one other thing. Since things didn't go according to plan, we're going to need to try a different approach with the Byzantium project. For that, we need access to one of the warehouses."

"Fine. I'll send someone to look into it."

"Keep me informed." The legs of a chair scraped against the floor.

"Of course, Mr. Poole," Harding seethed.

Byron pulled Mira a few steps back down the hall and then pretended to walk the length of the hallway again. A lean man with an unfortunate gargoylesque face removed himself from the office, tipping his hat as he passed them.

Byron glanced at Mira, one brow raised, before knocking on the door.

"Come in!" The gruff voice from before commanded. Byron eased the door open and pushed inside.

"Good afternoon, Mr. Harding. My name is Byron Const—"

"Not interested! I'm sorry, but we are not interested in any inventions at the moment, and we certainly aren't hiring. Check back in a few months," Mr. Harding said without looking up.

"You misunderstand my intentions. I'm Byron Constantine and this is my secretary, Miss Blayse."

Mr. Harding's eyes shot up, giving Mira a once over, glancing at Byron, then settling back on her again. She swallowed, shoulders tightening.

"Oh, I'm so sorry. Please take a seat. What can I do for the both of you?" His smile seemed to get wider by the second as he clasped his hands on top of his desk.

"I'm a private detective working with Scotland Yard on the Sutherland case."

Harding's smile vanished. "It was quite the shock to hear of Vince's death. How can I help with the investigation?"

"We have a few questions." Byron pulled out his journal and readied his pen. "When did you find out about the merger between the Emoria-Sutherland and Griffon trading companies?"

"I've only known about it for a week. Mr. Sutherland didn't deem it necessary for me to know." He sat back. Mira caught the bitterness in his tone. "I had told him before that the company wasn't ready for a merger, but it seems he didn't listen and went behind my back. Several of the lawyers on both sides knew, of course. If I had known, I would have made Sutherland's gathering more of a priority. I can't help but think if I had been there, that maybe none of this would have happened."

"Why weren't you able to attend?"

"I had promised my wife a night at the opera. Sutherland has social gatherings every month, and I didn't want to disappoint my wife."

Byron nodded and pulled out a sheet of paper from his journal, passing it over.

"Do you recognize any of the names on this list?"

Harding picked up the sheet of paper and looked it over. He shook his head. "Should I?"

"Not necessarily. They are just individuals who attended

Sutherland's party that we haven't been able to contact. If you had known any of them, I would have asked for their addresses."

"Sorry I couldn't be of more help."

"It's quite alright. Thank you for your time, Mr. Harding."

Byron was grinning by the time they got to the stairs.

"I didn't realize you had a guest list," Mira said.

"I didn't. I wrote a list of random individuals and included Dr. Kelley's name to gauge recognition."

"And he didn't recognize the name . . ." Mira's lips curled into a smile as well.

"Oh, he did. Didn't you notice the way his fingers twitched as he read over the list? He read over it a few times, trying to figure out exactly how to respond so we wouldn't know he was lying."

"This doesn't prove that Dr. Kelley did it though."

"No, it doesn't. But it does prove that there is something going on there."

They turned the corner, narrowly dodging a collision with a familiar head of blonde hair. Byron froze.

"Grace? What are you doing here?"

"I work here. And I could ask you the same thing." Grace crossed her arms, tense and holding some files close to her chest.

"We were talking with Mr. Harding about Mr. Sutherland's death," Mira said. "It must have been quite the shock for the company."

"Yes, well . . . it was." Grace gazed at the floor and took a breath. "I'm afraid I must be going. Accounting needs these files." She gestured with the folders in her arms. "It was nice to see the both of you!"

She rushed past them, and Byron stared after her.

Mira waved a hand in front of his unfocused gaze. "Byron?"

When he didn't respond, she sighed as she looped an arm through his and lead him out of the building.

Of course, every time they met with Grace, he remembered

something from before! Shouldn't she be happy about this development? She nodded to the man at the front desk as they passed, but didn't stop until they were on the pavement. By that point, Byron refocused on his surroundings and glanced around.

"When did we get out here?"

"Just now. I led you out here while you were having your flashback. Did you remember anything important?"

He shook his head. "Vague details and colors. Nothing particularly useful."

"Alright then. Where to?"

"I need to think on this. You go on home, and we'll continue the investigation tomorrow."

"You're sure?"

"Positive. I need to write this down while it's fresh."

She nodded and let go of his arm. "Take care of yourself, Byron."

He gave her a half-smile over his shoulder as he headed towards Palace Court. "You as well, Mira."

Mira called for a hansom cab, not wanting to be alone with her feelings for longer than necessary. They already swirled with streaks of jealousy and confusion. If her eyes could be greener, they would be. She clenched and unclenched her fists to diffuse the energy. Why was she so upset? Wasn't it a good thing for Byron to remember things? Did it matter that he only remembered things when in proximity with Grace?

She marched up the steps to Swan Walk and slammed the door shut behind her. Landon popped out of the dining room.

"Is everything alright, Miss?"

"Just grand, Landon." She walked past him to go up to her room.

"Do you want to talk about it? I can make some tea."

She whirled around on the steps. "What is there to talk about? There's nothing wrong whatsoever! Byron's getting his memory back. Isn't that great?" She spread her hands out in front of her wildly.

". . . yes?" Landon set his duster down on the side table.

Mira took a deep breath and let it out, the fire behind her words dying down. Tears pricked at the corners of her eyes.

"Then why am I so upset about it?"

Landon's eyes softened, and he held out a hand to her. "Come here."

She came down the stairs, and he pulled her into a hug. A sob racked through her body as he led her into the sitting room to sit down. A storm brewed inside her chest, trying to get out. Landon held her while she cried, and handed her a handkerchief when she calmed down.

"Will you tell me what happened?"

He rubbed her back. Mira swallowed and dabbed at a few remaining tears.

"He's retaining his memory more each day. And he keeps having flashbacks to memories that he's lost. It's been happening because he's been running into a woman he helped just after the accident."

Landon stayed quiet, and Mira took a breath before continuing.

"I've been with him practically every day since September. He's said that he's in love with me, even if he can't remember me. But that's the problem. He doesn't remember me."

She stood and moved over to the fireplace. "Even as he remembers things from yesterday or two days before, for some reason he never remembers me." Her voice cracked. "But he remembers her. He remembers pieces of the case." She crossed her arms and turned back to Landon. "We've talked about courting, but how can we make that work?" Her eyes teared up again, and she looked at the ceiling, blinking them back.

"I should be happy, Landon. He's healing."

"It's okay that you aren't, Mira. You have been holding up incredibly well, considering everything."

"What do you mean?"

"Aside from the issue of Byron's memory, you witnessed a gruesome murder, and your guardian was arrested for it. Have you recovered from that?"

She worried her lip between her teeth and sat down. "No. I suppose I haven't."

"I can't imagine what it's like for the person you love to never remember you. I would think it would be frustrating. And then to have him remember someone else? That would be painful. I don't blame you for being jealous."

She gave a weak chuckle and folded the handkerchief in her lap. "I suppose my eyes needed to live up to their jade hue at some point."

"Have you talked to him about how you feel?"

"No. It isn't fair to him. After all, it isn't his fault that he doesn't remember me. And I am happy that he's regaining his memories. It just . . . it hurts, too."

He nodded. "Understandably so. Do you feel any better?"

"A bit."

"You ought to consider talking to him about it. If you keep this to yourself, it will only hurt both of you."

"Even if I told him, would it make a difference? He'd forget again."

"Miss Mira, I should hope tha—"

They both turned as the front door opened and closed. Mira straightened and wiped the remaining tears away before Walker came in, all smiles.

"I'm in love!"

He flopped into an armchair. Mira laughed, the tension bleeding out of her.

"The tour went that well?" She cocked an eyebrow at him.

He sat up. "Oh! Was that today? So much has happened since then."

"Well, go on then." Mira leaned forward.

"The tour went splendidly. Afterwards, Alexander and I were talking, and the topic of eligible women came up."

"Why am I not surprised?"

"Actually," Walker cleared his throat, "the conversation came up because he asked me about you."

Mira flushed. "Me?"

"He wanted to know what your favorite type of flower was. Of course, I didn't know. I really should, seeing as I've known you for most of my life, barring five minutes. I told him roses were probably fine."

"I like roses well enough. Although my favorite flowers are pink camellias."

"Of course, you would go for something difficult to find. Anyway, that's beside the point. He asked me if I had my eye on anyone. So of course, the conversation turned to Miss Renaldi."

"Naturally." Landon nodded in agreement as Mira laughed.

"By the end of the conversation, I decided I ought to visit her again."

"And now you're in love?"

"Well . . . I do have something to confess. I didn't return the book to her like you asked me to. I thought that maybe I should get familiar with the signs myself. And I must say, that sitting in a room with a chaperone and conversing without them being aware of it is quite fun."

Landon cleared his throat. "Do I need to read this book in case I'm ever the unlucky chaperone?"

"Not at all, Landon. I'm sure it would be quite boring," Walker said, eyes shining with mischief. "The bottom line is, I don't think I've had this much fun in a long time. She's a bit like you, Mira. Not nearly as stuffy and proper as other girls. I thought she was being forward, but I suppose she was just taking initiative."

He hopped up and moved to the door. "We arranged to take an outing tomorrow, so I ought to figure out what to wear!"

Mira shook her head and looked at Landon. "At least someone is happy and in love."

He smirked. "Falling in love is easy. Landing on your feet is another matter."

October 17, 1888

*T*HE SUN TRICKLED ONTO MIRA'S FACE, BUT she turned away, pulling the covers tight around her. Nero growled at the movement and jumped off the bed.

"Mira, are you up yet?" Walker called through the door.

She groaned as he opened it and stepped inside.

"You aren't ill, are you?" He moved over to her and set a hand against her forehead.

She mumbled into her pillow.

"Come on, Mouse. Get up and tell me what you think of my outfit." He pulled the covers off of her, and the chill of the room brought gooseflesh to her arms.

"Walker!" She attempted to steal them back.

"I'm only trying to help you! You usually head off to Byron's in half an hour, don't you?"

He let go of the blanket as she pulled on it, and she fell back in a heap.

She grumbled and sat up. "That doesn't mean that you can come in here and steal my blankets."

"I'll be out of your hair as soon as you give me an opinion." He turned in a slow circle to show off his outfit.

"Okay. I think you're an idiot." She blew some hair from her face.

"On the clothing if you will." He leveled a glare at her and turned again.

She gave his blue suit and red cravat ensemble a once over and shrugged.

"You look nice. I'm sure Miss Renaldi cares more about you than what you are wearing."

He nodded and appraised himself in the mirror. "I hope you're right."

"Now get out of my room so I can get dressed!"

WALKER HAD BEEN RIGHT, AND MIRA WAS running late. Not ridiculously late, mind you, but late enough that she called a Hansom Cab to take her to Palace Court. After paying the driver, she headed up the steps to meet Byron again. Her heart sunk, but she took a deep breath and opened the door.

"Byron?" she called as she hung up her coat in the hallway.

Silence met her as she entered the sitting room and glanced around. After checking the kitchen, she headed up the stairs. The door to his bedroom was open, so she peeked in, but found no trace of him.

"Byron? Where are you?"

Moving further up the stairs, she pushed open the door to his office. Mira took in the disheveled state of the room, from the papers and files that overran the desk to the overfilled bookshelves. Her brows knit together at Byron's absence once again.

She moved to the desk and glanced over the papers. One file caught her eye. *Victoria, Queen.* She pulled it away from the rest and glanced at the door. Still no sign of Byron. She flicked it open. This file was in shorthand but contained a few letters similar to the one Castel had delivered. The first page read "*Assassination Attempts*" with a list of names, dates, and methods.

Edward Oxford, June 10, 1840, Pistol
John Francis, May 29, 1842, and May 30, 1842, Pistol
John William Bean, July 3, 1842, Pistol
William Hamilton, June 19, 1849, Pistol
Robert Pate, June 27, 1850, Cane
Arthur O'Connor, February 29, 1872, Pistol
Roderick Maclean, March 2, 1882, Pistol

Mira stared at the list. So many assassination attempts. At the bottom of the file was the note, "*See Newspaper Code.*" She set the file down and rifled through the rest of the papers on the desk, before stopping on a thin booklet. Opening it, she found Byron's neat handwriting.

> *July 8, 1884. In another attempt to regain my memories, Dr. Laherty has suggested that I write down as much as I can remember from my most recent case. That is the purpose of this document, and the file related to it.*

Mira swallowed and closed the booklet. She always wanted to know the particulars of the case that led to the accident. But this seemed like an invasion of privacy. Then again, here it was out in the open on the desk. In his private office. She sighed. Didn't she need to know about these details if she was to help him regain his memories?

Castel delivered a request from the Queen in early November 1883. The case related to the increase in anarchist threats and the explosions in the Underground that injured at least 70 individuals last October. I was to look into the Irish Republican Brotherhood, who were responsible for most of the bombings that have occurred in the last few years. The main question revolved around whether the IRB had a connection to the assassination attempts on Her Majesty. However, they also wished for me to find ties to the anarchist threats. The letter included the contact information of Chief Constable Adolphus Williamson of Scotland Yard's special branch.

After meeting with him, I found he didn't have any specific leads on the matter. I decided it would be prudent to determine where each of the "assassins" of the Queen were and see if I couldn't ask them about their motives. Most of the individuals were either dead, banished, or in asylums. However, I discovered that Arthur O'Connor had returned from his banishment in New South Wales. He was living in London under the name 'Arthur Connors.'

After tracking him to his workplace and gaining his trust, I asked him what led up to his assassination attempt. I learned he was the great-nephew of Feargus O'Connor, and that he had grown up hearing of the United Irishmen and the political exploits of his uncle. While he wasn't particularly interested in the movement to begin with, a man approached him while he was away at school and asked him if he wanted to help the Fenian movement. He invited O'Connor to the Cobden Club and showed him how to determine its location through a code in the newspaper.

When he arrived, they led him to a back room, wherein members of the Fenians (and Circe as I later found out) met to discuss their plan of action. He was swept in with the fervor and convinced that if he could threaten Queen Victoria, that perhaps she would release the Fenian prisoners. Part of his reasoning behind it was to live up to his heritage and to make a major difference in the movement. O'Connor was 18 at the time of his attempt.

When I revealed I was a detective investigating on the behalf of the Queen, he practically begged me not to reveal his location or that he had returned from New South Wales. I promised, as long as he told me any other information that he had about the Cobden Club. He agreed and proceeded to explain the newspaper code to me so I could monitor the communications. I also found out about the Cobden Club's publications for its members. I decided at that point that it was time to visit the Cobden Club for myself. That is as far as my memory serves me.

Mira let out a slow breath. She had hoped that the narrative wouldn't end there. While it was new information to her, it didn't give much insight into how to help Byron. Of course, he never did remember the day of the accident, did he?

They must have caught him when he went to investigate the Cobden Club. But how had they discovered him? After all, she, Walker, and Byron himself had infiltrated the club with no issue earlier in the week. She turned the page out of habit and found a new set of writing. She recognized it as Byron's by the hand, but the letters shone out in blue ink instead of black. It seemed fresher than the rest.

Some of my memory has returned, and I had best write it down before I lose it again.

I tracked down the club's location and went in disguise to join it. I used the name Elliot Thorne as an alias and attended the club a few times a week in the hopes of finding some kind of connection. After three weeks, I overheard a startling conversation relating to the trial of the Glasgow bombers from earlier that year. The two gentlemen discussed how they might avoid getting caught, should their plan for another bombing succeed.

Mira swallowed. She remembered the bombings, of course. Most of them had happened while she was at finishing school, so she didn't know the details. She blew some hair out of her face and continued to read, anxiety gnawing at her stomach.

At this point, they noticed I was eavesdropping on their conversation. One went to speak, and I held a hand up, telling them I had heard that the club was a front for the Fenians and had hoped I could join.

Mira's jaw dropped. She had been expecting the narrative to end there, for him to have been caught and—well she wasn't sure what she expected.

I found out their names were Damian Sharpe and Sean Walsh. Gaining their trust was a slow and arduous process. I could tell that they were planning something big, but for the first month they didn't do much. I caught whispers through doors, but never anything concrete. Eventually, they explained another group was involved, and while they wanted to let me work with them, they had to wait for their approval. I knew I was in over my head from the mo-

ment they mentioned Circe. Unfortunately, I didn't have the evidence I needed for the police yet. While I knew Thatcher would believe me, there wouldn't be much he could do. So, I watched and gathered as much information as I could. I subscribed to the club's publication and kept an eye on the coded messages sent through it.

From what I could tell, the members who were in on the underground network were stockpiling gunpowder and explosive compounds. Sharpe approached me on February 20th and asked if I would be interested in helping them with a job on February 26th. He promised that after the job, he'd introduce me to the owners of the Cobden Club. I agreed. I spent the next few days preparing for the job and compiling any evidence I had for the police. I intended to give it to Inspector Thatcher on the 27th. Although they didn't give me any indication for what the job would entail, I surmised it would probably be another bombing. The last thing I remember is going to bed on the 25th of February, and I have yet to find my file of evidence for the police.

Mira rubbed at her temples, absorbing the new information. Byron had actually worked with Circe for a time. She closed the booklet and set the rest of the documents exactly how she found them. It occurred to her that Byron had still not made an appearance.

She called out for him again as she went back into the sitting room, with no response. Pinned to the wall above the fireplace was a note.

Meeting with Ambassador White. Ten o'clock.

So that was where he left to. Odd that he hadn't let her know about the meeting. She glanced at the clock. It was noon and Byron still hadn't returned. Perhaps if she came back after lunch, she'd catch him.

LANDON GREETED HER AS SHE CAME INTO the front hall at Swan Walk.

"Professor Burke is here to see you, Miss. He's in the sitting room with your brother," he said as he helped her out of her coat.

"Thank you, Landon." She turned in that direction, pausing at the door as the conversation within became heated.

"This is serious, Professor," Walker said.

"I know. Which is why we must do something immediately."

"Even if we were to go to Palace Court, they won't be there. They'll have gone to investigate something or other."

"Then I'll wait here."

"I can always pass on the message when she gets back."

Mira pushed the door open. "Or you could tell me right now."

She stepped into the room. Both men stood.

"You're back early," Walker said

"As are you. Did Miss Renaldi not like your outfit as well as you hoped?"

"We rescheduled for this afternoon. Something came up." He glanced at the professor, and she followed his gaze.

She had never seen the professor so nervous, clothes rumpled, and hair sticking out in every direction. He ran a hand through his hair and brought his empty glass over to the decanter on the side table. Walker cleared his throat.

"I probably ought to go now if I'm to make our new appointment."

He pressed a kiss to her forehead, gave her hand a squeeze and retreated from the room.

"You were right."

The professor poured himself another drink. Mira moved to an armchair as the professor slumped over again. "I've been a member of that club for years, and never even knew what happened behind closed doors." He took a long swallow.

"Do continue, Professor."

"I've been keeping an ear out for anything suspicious. For the last few days, things have been business as usual. But I've spent all my free time at the club in hopes of seeing or hearing something about Dr. Kelley. This morning, I went into one of the libraries to procure a book. I figured it would be best to appear busy if anyone were to suspect I was listening in. This library is attached to an inner office, and it just so happened that the door hadn't latched. It was enough that I could hear the conversation happening within."

Mira leaned forward as the professor took another swallow of gin.

"I recognized one of the voices as Dr. Kelley's. He was speaking to another man about one of his patients. At first, I thought nothing of it, but I continued to listen just in case. At one point his friend thanked him for everything that Kelley had done for his great-uncle. Dr. Kelley responded saying that it was his job and asked about the funeral arrangements. Neither of them seemed remorseful. It could have been that they weren't close to the deceased. However, as their conversation continued, it became clear this wasn't the first time that one of Dr. Kelley's patients has died under his care."

"That is hardly surprising in his line of work. I assume you mean more have died than is usual?"

"Exactly. The way they discussed it, it sounded like it was a pattern. As if the people who visit Dr. Kelley at the club seek him out in order to ask him to . . . well, kill off their wealthy relatives."

The professor's hands shook, and he set the glass down. "I wouldn't believe it if I hadn't heard it myself. I always thought Dr. Kelley was a pleasant man, but—"

"Well, we still don't have proof, but this is certainly something to look into." Mira bit her lip.

"How are you so calm?" He looked up at her. "We're talking about murder, potentially dozens of them, and you aren't even the least bit disturbed?"

Mira's mind tread back to the ghastly sight of Mr. Sutherland. She shook her head.

"I would be, except that this could be the key to freeing Uncle Cyrus. Do you remember the name of his friend?"

"I checked the ledger on my way out. His name was Derek Rowley."

"He's visited Dr. Kelley before then." She stood and paced over to the fireplace. "We'll have to check the rest of the individuals who have visited him at the club. See if any of their relatives have died under mysterious circumstances."

She turned back towards the professor. He held his head in his hands. The glass beside him held more air than liquor again. She sat next to him.

"Are you alright, Professor?"

He shook his head. "Is this what you do every day?"

Mira pulled her gaze away, steeling herself for another lecture on the dangers of detective work.

The professor swallowed. "Towards the end of their conversation, a gentleman I knew came into the library and called out my name rather loudly. At that point, Kelley and Rowley went silent. I'm sure that they noticed the door was ajar. I've never known such terror before in my life, and I've faced down tigers with your uncle, and greedy investors with your father. I don't think they know I was listening, but what if they did?"

"Don't worry, professor. We'll get to the bottom of this. I'd just stay away from the club for the time being."

"I'm canceling my membership, actually. I don't know if I could trust anyone there again. That's the thing, Mira. I never even knew. And I wasn't really in any danger until I went searching for it. That's what worries me the most."

The professor took her hand in his, eyes wet. "You do this sort of thing every day. I can't begin to imagine what kinds of things you've seen or experienced. But you quite literally go out of your way to learn about these terrible things and interact wi-with murderers. I know I'm not family—"

"But you are." Mira swallowed thickly. "In everything but blood."

He shook his head. "I can't bear the thought of something happening to you, especially now that I've seen it myself. You must be tired of hearing this from your uncle, and I've avoided saying much up until now but," he took a shaky breath, eyes watery, "your parents' deaths still haunt me—your father's especially—and I'm not certain I'll ever get over it." He looked away, composing himself. "Mira, so much happens without us knowing, and I don't know if anyone is trustworthy."

Mira thought of Alexander. About his story of why he "threatened" her. Was it just a story? Did he actually work for Circe? She took a deep breath.

"I've seen much in the past few months that I wish I could forget, Professor. The world is quite a bit darker than I thought it was. But that only makes the bright sparks burn brighter. And while what I do is dangerous, certainly, it is important that I do it. How could I do otherwise?"

"I understand why you are continuing to do this now. It is imperative that we clear your uncle. But what of life afterwards? I know that someone has to do this kind of work, but do you have to be the one to do it?"

Her smile wavered, and she looked down. "I suppose not,

however," she trailed off with a sigh, "I want to help people. People like Uncle Cyrus who are innocent and wrongfully imprisoned. Stopping deaths or thefts before they happen. Trying to make the world a place where more children can grow up with their parents."

The professor winced at that, and his eyes darkened. "I can see why this is important to you. I just don't want to see you hurt. These people are dangerous."

"Do you trust me?"

"What?"

"Can you trust me to take care of myself?"

He swallowed and his eyes roved over her face for a moment. Then he nodded and gave her a tight-lipped smile.

"I can."

She leaned over and gave him a hug. He stiffened, then tightened his hold on her.

"You stay safe, too. Stay away from the Cobden club. Keep in touch. And try not to worry," she said before pulling away. "I don't know if I've ever told you how much you mean to me, to all of us, really. You've practically helped Uncle to raise us, yet I don't think you recognize how much we need you."

"You have that the wrong way around. It is I who needs you. You help me remember to live."

AFTER A QUICK LUNCH AND PARTING WAYS with the professor, Mira headed off to Palace Court. Byron needed the professor's information sooner rather than later. Despite that, she opted to take the shortcut through Kensington Gardens, rather than call a Hansom Cab. It was just after two when she left Swan Walk, so Byron would almost certainly be back at Palace Court by the time she reached it. Hopefully.

As she was passing the pond, she felt a familiar presence.

She glanced to the side and found Alexander Durant walking next to her.

"Good afternoon, Miss Blayse."

"Mr. Durant, how is it you always find me?"

He laughed. "I must confess that most of the time it is purely by chance, I assure you. Today, I was off early from my apprenticeship, so I took a walk and saw you. Often, I'll see you as I am on my way to work or leaving."

She narrowed her eyes. "Forgive me if I don't trust that."

"Ask your brother! He'll confirm not only when I come and go from the apprenticeship, but also that Kensington is the fastest route between my rooms and work."

"I suppose I'll have to give you a pass until I see him next."

"Ah yes, he's with Miss Renaldi, is he not?"

"Something to that effect."

"I wish him well. I think they would be a good fit."

"You're a matchmaker now?"

He shrugged. "I dabble."

She scoffed and walked faster. While on any other day she might needle more information out of him, she really needed to deliver her news to Byron. Alexander caught up to her as she exited the gardens. But this time, he continued to follow her across the street.

"To be honest, you surprised me. Usually, I don't find you in Kensington until later in the evening. And you're walking towards Palace Court, not away from it."

"Trying your hand at deduction now?" She raised an eyebrow at him.

He ignored her. "Has something happened?"

"Byron had an appointment this morning."

"Ah, I see. Is he remembering well enough on his own, then?"

"He's regaining some memories, yes."

As they came down the street, her eyes caught the door to

number 27 opening. So, Byron was at home after all! Her heart fell into her gut as Grace Trimbell walked out. Mira could just make out Byron standing in the doorway, finishing their conversation. Mira swallowed, shifted to the other side of Alexander, and grabbed his arm. As Byron's door closed and Grace came down the street, Mira used Alexander as a shield, passing number 27 entirely. She ignored the pink tinge to Grace's cheeks. Or at least, she tried to.

"What are you—" Alexander started to say.

"Shh!"

They rounded the corner, and she let go of his arm. Alexander rocked on his feet with an amused expression.

"Now, what could that have been about?"

"I don't know what you mean." Mira's chest tightened.

"A new client, perhaps? Of course, if she was, you wouldn't be so upset about it."

Mira couldn't quite fathom it either. Her brows furrowed. Perhaps if she knew why Grace was there, it wouldn't be so painful. That was it. She just needed to talk to Byron. He would explain everything, wouldn't he?

"Thank you very much for escorting me, Mr. Durant, but I'm afraid I must be going."

She went to pass him, and he placed a hand on her arm, giving it a gentle tug.

"Wait a moment, you shouldn't go talk to the love of your life in such a state."

"Now you're just teasing me." Mira's cheeks heated.

"You're right. It's entirely possible to fall in love twice. How silly of me." He leaned closer.

"You're ridiculous." She pushed him away.

"That's better than suspicious."

"What do you want?"

"For you to smile, and it seems as if it's working."

Mira laughed despite everything. "Is that all?"

His smile faltered. "For now, that should be enough. I hate seeing you upset, especially when I can't do anything about it."

She paused and studied his face. His eyes, especially, were deep and dark and sad. Greyer than his usual golden hazel. She bit her lip.

"She's someone he used to know. Someone he remembers," she whispered.

"I'm sorry. I know his memory is a sore spot for you."

"It is. But I really do need to go to him. I've received some new information that could help free my uncle."

"Then, by all means, get along to him. I'm sure we'll see each other again."

"That's almost a certainty."

"You know where to find me."

Mr. Durant tipped his hat and headed in the opposite direction as Mira headed back to number 27.

She found the door unlocked and entered, shrugging off her coat. Byron's footsteps echoed from the sitting room.

"Who are you?"

Mira froze as she placed her hat on a hook. "You don't know?"

She looked up at him. His blue eyes held no recognition in them. Her heart dropped.

"I'm supposed to remember you, aren't I?" He furrowed his brow and took a step closer to her.

She swallowed. "D-did you not read your journal this morning?"

He cocked his head, gaze flicking from one bit of clothing to the next. Sure signs of his making deductions based on her appearance.

"I didn't think I needed to. I remembered enough to get on with the day."

She folded her arms, muscles quivering. "I suppose you remembered your meeting with Ambassador White?"

"How do you know about that?"

A look of genuine surprise crossed his face, and she turned away, fingernails digging into her arm.

"Did you remember the journal when you woke up this morning?" She kept her voice level.

"Of course, I've remembered it for the past four days at least." He stepped to the side, trying to catch her gaze again.

"Then you would know how important it is!" She brought a hand up to her mouth, surprised at her volume. He took a step back.

Her gaze met his beautiful blue eyes, and her voice cracked. "Why did you think you didn't need it?"

She paced past him into the sitting room, heartbeat pounding. Tears pricked in her eyes.

"Would you just tell me who you are?" he snapped.

"Even if I told you, you wouldn't know."

She shook her head, and Byron threw his hands in the air.

"A name would be more than eno—"

"I could tell you my name, and you wouldn't have any idea of who I am!" Her voice rose again as the first tears fell.

Byron's hands balled into fists, and she turned from him, shaking.

"Then let me read the blasted thing. I thought I could try living a day without it! And I managed that perfectly fine until now." His voice shook.

Mira kept her back to him, not wanting to see the pained look on his face. He shifted behind her, and she recognized the sounds of leather and paper. He had retrieved his journal. Her anger froze into resignation. She squeezed her eyes shut and took a breath.

"Don't read it." Her voice lowered to a whisper. A prayer.

"What?"

She turned and caught his startled expression, journal in his hands.

"Don't read it," she said. "If you wanted a day without the journal, then take it."

He narrowed his eyes. "I thought you wanted me to remember you."

"Not today." The "not like this," left unsaid.

He shuffled from one foot to the other. She stepped closer to him, unsure of what to say. In lieu of further conversation, she moved back into the entry hall to retrieve her things. He ran a hand through his hair and followed.

"You're leaving then? Just like that?"

"You don't need me today." She kept her gaze on the floor.

Silence pooled between them, and after a moment, her eyes trailed back to him. His pained expression made her hesitate.

"Just one more question," she said.

He nodded for her to continue.

"Who was it that just left from here? A new client?"

His cheeks flushed. "Erm . . . no. Her name is Grace. She's an old friend. She's been helping me with my memory."

Mira clenched her fists but managed a tight smile as she opened the door and stepped out.

"Oh, of course. How could I forget?"

October 18, 1888

*M*IRA TOOK EXTRA CARE IN GETTING READY the next morning. She chose one of her nicer burgundy gowns and ensured that every hair remained in the style atop her head. If her exterior appearance seemed to be styled to perfection, perhaps Byron wouldn't notice how torn up she was inside. She could pretend that she hadn't yelled at him the day before.

She could forget.

Her fingers shook as she unlocked the door at Palace Court, but she entered as if nothing had happened the day before. She placed her coat on the hook, ignoring the gnawing anxiety in her stomach. Taking a deep breath, she hoped with futile desperation that he hadn't remembered their argument. For once, she counted on his memory being like a sieve, and hoped their dispute was small enough to slip through the delicate cracks.

"Byron?" she called out, stepping into the sitting room.

He looked up at her from his seat in the armchair. His journal sat in his lap, along with a white notebook. The tension left Mira's shoulders. He furrowed his brow, and she froze in the doorway.

"Aren't you early?"

She glanced at the clock on the mantel. Eight-thirty. It was a bit soon for her to be at Palace Court. Even with her focus on acting as normal as possible, she hadn't checked the time before leaving Swan Walk. It must have been nerves about him forgetting again.

"Only by a bit. How much more do you have to read?"

"Not much."

He gestured for her to sit down, which she did. After studying her for a moment, he returned to his reading. The silence settled around them as Mira pulled out her sketchbook. If it were a normal morning, she would sketch while he read. Her pencil hovered over the page, but she couldn't bring herself to sketch anything.

Of course, did it even matter if she did things as she "normally" did? Would Byron even notice? She flipped through the pages and studied her sketches instead. Byron cleared his throat, and she glanced up at him.

"How are you?" He leaned forward, eyes searching her face.

Her shoulders tightened. "Quite well. Perhaps a bit tired."

He opened his mouth, then closed it, cocking his head.

"And you?" she asked, closing her sketchbook.

"What?" He shook his head and refocused on her, setting his journal and notebook aside.

"Are you well?"

"Enough, yes. Just baffled." He stood and moved over to the window, running a hand through his hair.

"How so?" She focused on tracing her fingers over an ink stain on the cover of her sketchbook.

"I seem to have decided not to write anything down yesterday, and I can't for the life of me remember most of what happened." His gaze flicked over to her.

Relief flooded Mira's chest, pushing the anxiety back. So, he hadn't written it down after all!

"I remember waking up and going to meet with the ambassador, although that is rather fuzzy, and I remember coming home. Everything else is a blur." He sat next to her, and her eyes rose to meet his. "Care to fill me in? I must have had a reason not to write anything down."

She swallowed. Did she dare to tell him the truth?

"From what you told me yesterday afternoon, you wanted to have a day relying only on your memory. To see what you could remember without your journal. I had some errands to run in the morning while you were with the ambassador, so I'm afraid I can't fill in too many of the gaps."

Byron leaned forward and fiddled with his fingertips. "I see. There was nothing else?"

"Nothing of importance." Had the carpet always been so interesting?

He sighed and moved back over to his journal. He picked up a piece of loose-leaf paper sitting next to it, glanced it over, then looked to her again. Tucking the paper between the pages, he sat down and leaned back.

"Well, I suppose we can't do anything about yesterday. Might as well further the case today. Any ideas of where we should take the investigation next?"

Mira bit down the thought that after the case was over, he wouldn't need her anymore, and chose instead to focus on her news.

"I actually have some new information to add to our evidence," she said. "It was part of my errands yesterday."

Byron sat down and readied his fountain pen and journal. "Please, go on."

"I've mentioned Professor Burke before, but I don't know if

you have anything written about him. He's an old friend of the family, and Walker and I bumped into him at the Cobden Club when we were investigating."

Byron's brow furrowed. "Has he been a member long?"

"A few years, I believe. But I can vouch for his character, especially considering what he found out for us."

He leaned in closer and nodded.

"He agreed to keep an eye on things there and let us know if he saw anything suspicious. Yesterday, he overheard Dr. Kelley and Mr. Rowley discussing the death of Mr. Rowley's great-uncle. According to the professor, it sounded as if Dr. Kelley seemed to be involved in the death somehow, and not in the way a normal physician is. Based on that evidence, I think it would be wise to investigate our list of individuals who have met with Dr. Kelley. See if any of their relatives have died recently under suspicious circumstances."

"You're thinking that we have another killer, like the Ripper, on our hands?"

"Potentially. Although I'd say it's a single person behind all of them. Likely, Dr. Kelley."

"It's worth looking into, but I'm not sure how it will connect Kelley with the murder."

Mira chewed on her lower lip. "I can see two ways of approaching this. First, Mr. Harding is the one with the motive, and we know he met with Dr. Kelley before the murder. His name on the ledger should be proof enough of that, even if Mr. Harding denies it. Although without proof of an exchange of money, I'm not sure if we can do anything on that front."

"That is a tricky point. What was the second approach?"

"Mr. Durant was the one who fetched Dr. Kelley on the night of the murder. If we ask him, he might know if Dr. Kelley was out of breath when he opened the door. After all, he wouldn't have had much time to climb down the ivy and run around the house before Mr. Durant came looking for him. Would that be enough evidence?"

"Not alone, no. But we have the ivy and shoe polish as well. And if your friend is correct about Kelley being involved in other murders, then that should be enough for the police to arrest him, at least. I'd say that our first stop needs to be Scotland Yard to get them on that lead."

Mira nodded and packed away her sketchbook as Byron readied himself to leave. The tension in her shoulders lessened as her anxiety dispersed. One argument could hardly ruin their rapport, could it? Her mind turned fully to the case, and she paused as she slipped into her coat and stepped out the door.

"Wouldn't we have heard about these supposed murders, though?" she said. "You'd think that they would all be traced back to Kelley if he was present for all of them. Murder is a messy business, after all."

Byron cocked his head as he signaled for a hansom cab to stop, and they both nestled in.

"Well, suppose that these individuals are older. For instance, Mr. Rowley's relative was his great-uncle. He was bound to be getting on a bit. It could be like Mr. Graham, where the police thought it was natural causes and didn't look closer at the situation."

Mira nodded, silent as guilt washed over her. If they hadn't questioned Mr. Graham, would he still be alive? It was her fault that Circe knew he was a witness, after all. A hand atop hers pulled her from her thoughts. She glanced up at Byron's sad smile.

"Thinking like that won't help anyone. It wasn't your fault." He squeezed her hand.

She shook her head. "How could you know what I'm thinking?" she attempted to tease.

"Just observant, I suppose. I'm sorry for bringing it up."

They rode in silence the rest of the way to Scotland Yard,

and he kept his hand on hers for most of it. For comfort, or for something else, Mira wasn't sure.

Once he helped her down from the hansom cab, he kept a distance between them as they entered the police station.

Fred wasn't at the front desk, so they continued up the stairs and stopped in front of Juliet Chickering.

"Good morning, Mr. Constantine, Miss Blayse," Juliet said in earnest.

Mira's eyes widened. Since when was Juliet happy to see her?

"You're in good spirits." Byron pressed forward on his toes. "Does it have anything to do with that bouquet of flowers on your desk?"

Juliet bit her lip and looked down as Mira noticed a vase of pink dianthus flowers. One red rose stood in the middle of them.

"Observant as always, Mr. Constantine," Juliet said with a grin. "I met him about a week ago, and he's already told me he loves me."

"Those flowers are rather serious," Byron teased. "And what do you think of him?"

"I was planning on giving him a pink camellia when I see him next. Unless that would be too forward?"

"I'd say it is the perfect response to these flowers. Is Thatcher in?"

"He's finishing up some paperwork. Let me see if he's up for a distraction."

Mira turned to Byron as Juliet disappeared into the office.

"Flowers are serious? What is that supposed to mean?"

"Pink dianthus are a declaration of love and passion. A single red rose means love at first sight. I'd say you can't get more serious than that. Are you not familiar with the language of flowers?"

"I knew it existed, but I've never studied it myself."

She eyed the flowers again and thought back on previous bouquets she'd been gifted. Had they held secret messages too?

"My mother kept a flower dictionary next to her bible. I read through it once when I was bored, and somehow still remember it. Funny what random things stay in your brain while important things sift out of it."

"You are remembering more, Byron."

He gave her a wan smile. "Not what's most important."

Juliet exited the office, leaving the door open behind her. "He's waiting for you."

Byron led the way into the office. Mira gave one last suspicious glance at the bouquet before following him.

"We've got a lead for you, Thatcher," he said, pulling out a chair for Mira.

The chief inspector looked up from his desk. "Is it a good one?"

"The best. Mira, why don't you fill him in?"

Mira settled into her seat and relayed the professor's information. Byron handed him the list of people who had met with Kelley. Thatcher leaned back after hearing the explanation.

"So, we check over each of these names," he tapped the paper with the back of his hand, "and see if there are any deaths associated with them?"

"Exactly. The most recent name to check for is Derek Rowley. His great-uncle recently passed on. Do an autopsy and check for drugs or poison," Byron said.

Chief Inspector Thatcher made a note on his pad. "We'll get on that right away. In the meantime, we need to link Kelley to Sutherland's death. If Mr. Harding hired him, we need evidence of that."

"Would proof of payment be enough?" Byron asked.

"Just about, I'd say. See if the bank has anything to say on the matter. Take Wensley with you in case they don't answer your questions and let me know what you find."

THEY FOUND FRED MULLING ABOUT NEAR THE records room. Byron clapped him on the shoulder.

"Want to do some real investigating?" he said with a grin.

Fred rolled his eyes. "Why do you think I went into the police force?" He turned towards them and set his files down. "What kind of investigating?"

"How does murder sound?"

"Dreadful, but count me in. Where are we going?"

Mira stood back while Byron filled Fred in. How would it be for Byron to remember her fully every morning? She followed them out to the street, where they all piled into a hansom cab with Byron in the middle. Byron and Fred continued to jab each other with subtle banter as they moved along. The closer they got to the bank, the more she felt like she didn't need to be there.

"What do you think, Mira?" Byron leaned a shoulder into her.

"What?"

"We were just discussing who Thatcher likes best. Me or Fred."

"It's not fair to bring her into it," Fred said. "Obviously, she's his favorite."

A smile spread across Mira's face. "Why can't we all be his favorite?"

"Ah, that goes against the very definition of the word! But I suppose if it keeps the peace, we'll have to settle for that." Fred winked.

"I think that both of you are ridiculous."

"And I think we're here." Byron gestured for Fred to get out. "Why don't you see who we need to talk to while we pay the driver?"

Fred nodded and headed up the steps. Byron helped Mira off

from the carriage and paid the driver. As the cab drove off and Mira turned to enter the bank as well, Byron grabbed her hand.

"Just a moment."

She turned back towards him with a questioning glance as he dropped her hand.

"Is it normal for you to be so quiet?" Byron asked. "Based on my journal accounts, I imagined you to be quite talkative."

"Depends on the day, I suppose." She rubbed at her arms. "And who we're with. I could listen to you and Fred all day."

Byron frowned. "Except you weren't paying attention." He faltered and looked away. "Is this about yesterday?"

Mira's stomach dropped. "What about yesterday?"

He ran a hand through his hair. "I woke up this morning with a loose sheet of paper on top of my journal. It mentioned that a young lady had come to my rooms yesterday. A young lady who was rather upset at me for not reading my journal."

He glanced back at her. She kept her expression neutral. He took a deep breath.

"After reading my journal, I would have thought that the young lady would be you, Mira."

The start of a headache pinched the back of her skull. "Why didn't you say anything this morning?"

"I wanted to be certain it was you. Why didn't you?"

She crossed her arms and stepped back. "I thought you had forgotten about it."

"Usually you fill me in on what I forget." Byron fought to catch her gaze.

"You have the general idea of what happened. No need to rehash it again."

As she turned to walk up the stairs, he pivoted around her, so he was in front of her, stopping her in her tracks.

"Except I think we need to. Evidently, this is upsetting you, and I need to know what happened so we can avoid it in the future."

Mira glanced at the other people moving about in the street. "Byron, this is neither the time nor the place to have this conversation."

"Can I at least apologize?"

"Byron, Fred is—"

"Right here!" Fred bounced onto the step next to her. "Unfortunately, we can't access the records without a warrant, even with me here."

"Dash it all. We'll have to find some other way of getting the proof, then." Byron turned away from them both, getting that deductive gleam in his eye.

Mira relaxed. Maybe they could avoid the conversation after all.

"Do you think Harding keeps a copy of his accounts at Emoria-Sutherland?" Fred asked.

"It's possible. But how would we get access to them?" Byron paced on the step.

Mira sighed and rubbed at her temples. "When we were there last, we ran into Grace Trimbell. She mentioned something about accounting. Perhaps we could speak with her about it?"

"Good thinking!" Fred signaled for another hansom cab to stop.

Byron moved to her side and offered an arm, which she took. He led her down the steps and leaned close to her ear.

"Don't think I've forgotten. We are going to discuss yesterday when we get back to Palace Court," he whispered.

SOON, THEY FOUND THEMSELVES IN FRONT OF the main desk at Emoria-Sutherland. The same man typed away at his typewriter but glanced up at the trio as they entered.

"Back again? I'm afraid this time you need an appointment."

"Actually, we need to talk with a worker. Grace Trimbell," Byron said.

The secretary gave them all a suspicious glance, then sighed. "Follow that hallway to the end and you'll find a staircase. Fourth door on your left."

Following his instructions, they found the door without issue. Fred knocked on it before entering.

Grace stopped shelving ledgers to look up at them. She blushed at seeing Byron. Mira fought back the jealousy in her throat.

"Elliot? Oh, sorry. Mr. Constantine, Miss Blayse, what a surprise. Who's this with you?"

"Frederick Wensley at your service," he gave a slight bow and a cheeky grin. "But you can call me Fred. Everyone does."

Grace gave a light laugh. "I'd offer you all seats, but I'm afraid there's only the one. What are you doing here?"

Byron ducked his head into the hallway before pulling back in and closing the door. He lowered his voice to a low whisper.

"We were wondering if you happened to have access to some of the account books for Mr. Harding,"

"I do." She furrowed her brow. "Please tell me this is hypothetical."

"I'm afraid not. We need to see his personal ledgers for the past few weeks. Specifically, to see if he's exchanged any money with Dr. Lorenzo Kelley." Byron gave a cursory glance over the room.

Grace paled. "Are you wanting me to lose my job?"

"This is a life-or-death situation, Grace."

Grace took a deep breath and released it. "Fine! Fine."

She set the ledgers in her arms down on the table and opened a drawer, taking out a key.

Mira caught a muttered, "But this is the last time I'm saving you, Constantine," as Grace unlocked a door and disappeared inside.

"Grace, eh? You know each other from before the accident?" Fred asked.

Mira stood taller and examined the bookshelves.

"Something like that," Byron responded.

Mira could feel his eyes following her. Grace reappeared in
the doorway and deposited an armful of ledgers on the desk.
She handed one to each of them and took one for herself.
"These are from the last couple of months. The names of the
individuals are on the right side.

Mira opened her ledger and followed the line with her
finger. They worked in silence, aside from the occasional flip of
a page until Mira found a familiar name.

"Here it is! Dr. Lorenzo Kelley! Harding paid him ten
pounds for medical services."

"That's a bit steep, isn't it?" Fred asked, peering over her
shoulder. "Most doctors rarely charge half a pound for a house
call."

"And it proves that Harding knows who Kelley is, even if
he denies it," Byron said. "Fred, you go let the chief inspector
know and get hold of a warrant. They'll want these records at
the trial."

Fred nodded and left.

"Trial?" Grace asked, sitting down.

"We believe Mr. Harding hired Kelley to kill off Mr. Sutherland." Byron placed his ledger on the desk.

"Oh, dear." Grace swallowed. "Well, I hope you get to the
bottom of it." She gave them both a tight smile. "I'm afraid I
need to get these back to records before anyone misses them. It
was nice seeing you both."

She picked up the ledgers again and disappeared into the
back room. Byron opened the door and gestured for Mira to
leave.

✦

As they strolled down the street, Byron kept a firm but gentle grip on her arm. Soon enough, they were walking through St. James' Park. The leaves glittered in gold and amber hues, the sheen reflecting off of the water. Byron pulled her over to a bench and sat down. Silence settled over them, with the exception of some squawking pelicans.

"I'm sorry, Mira," he whispered, and thumbed circles over the back of her hand, gaze set across the pond. "I can't even remember the details of our conversation to know what went wrong."

"It isn't your fault."

"You were upset yesterday because I didn't remember you. Isn't it my blasted memory that is causing all the trouble?"

"You can't help your memory, Byron."

"But I could have read my journal. Until I remember you, I cannot allow myself the luxury of being without it."

She shook her head. "I understand why you did it though. You're confined by leather and paper, trying to live a normal life." She averted her gaze as she continued. "It's my fault that I'm feeling this way. I should have explained who I was the moment I knew you hadn't read your journal."

"I'm afraid that wouldn't have made much of a difference. I would have had to read my journal to confirm your story." He rubbed at his temples.

Mira shook her head and huffed a laugh, pushing her own feelings further down. It really wasn't his fault that he had forgotten her.

She fiddled with a strand of hair that escaped from under her hat. "You've been doing so well remembering everything else, though. I think Grace is really helping you."

Byron's eyes widened. "I didn't realize that you knew about that."

Mira pulled her other arm free and adjusted her hat, attempting a teasing tone. "Did you mean to keep it a secret?"

"Not necessarily. I just know that my memory has been returning as I've spent time with her."

"Soon enough, you'll remember all the facts of each case without writing anything down at all." She smiled at him. "Then you won't have to worry about the journal anymore."

"Won't that be the day?" He chuckled, and his gaze softened.

He reached over and tucked the wayward strand of hair behind her ear. She pulled away.

"Well, I think we've made enough progress on the case for today. I ought to get back to Swan Walk. After all, it needs to be spick and span before my uncle comes home." She stood, and he followed.

"May I walk you home?"

"I know the way. Good afternoon, Mr. Constantine."

His smile wavered, and he nodded. "Until tomorrow, Mira."

She sped up as she left him clustered in the autumnal shade of the scarlet oaks. He was too good, trying to put things to rights, and she hated leaving him like that. But she couldn't trust herself not to burst with jealousy or bitterness about him remembering Grace while forgetting her. It wasn't fair of her to take it out on him at all. She couldn't help him the way Grace could. It was better to leave and parse things out on her own. She pushed his pained expression to the back of her mind and willed the tears to subside until she reached the safety of Swan Walk.

October 19, 1888

*M*IRA GLANCED UP FROM HER BREAKFAST AS her whirlwind of a brother came into the dining room. He placed a kiss on her cheek and served himself a plate.

"Good morning, dearest sister! Seems I haven't run into you in a few days."

"Perhaps we would have crossed paths if you weren't with Miss Renaldi so often. My, my. What will Uncle Cyrus say when he gets home?" She smirked.

Walker placed a hand to his chest, faking offense.

"I'll have you know that we have had a chaperone for the entirety of our visits together, aside from a short escape into Hampstead Heath. Unlike you and your beloved who go wherever with whoever you wish."

"That is a different matter entirely, and you know it. We aren't even courting." If a bit of bitterness slid through her tone, Walker didn't notice.

"Well, when Uncle Cyrus gets—" He stopped. "Wait, Uncle is coming home?"

"Considering the fact that we found evidence condemning Dr. Kelley, I'd say that it is a fair assessment."

Walker grinned. "Brilliant as ever, Mouse."

"Don't act so surprised." She cleaned off her plate and set it to the side. "Let me know how things go with Liza today. I'm off to Palace Court!"

"Don't have too much fun!"

Mira stepped outside and took a deep breath of the swirling chill wind. Another day away from the argument, and she felt much better. Looking at her feelings from a distance, it was evident that her frustrations stemmed from Grace, not Byron.

It always stung each time she knocked at Palace Court only to find that he had forgotten again. But in this case, what bothered her most wasn't Byron's memory, but that he remembered Grace. And since she couldn't change that Grace was a part of Byron's life, well, she'd have to push forward.

She took the shortcut through Kensington Gardens, hoping to run into Mr. Durant. A strange hope indeed, after all her suspicions. But he would have the final nail in the coffin for Dr. Kelley.

As she traced a path around the pond, she caught sight of him. He set his pace at a brisk walk, not seeing her. She laughed under her breath and decided to catch him by surprise.

"Busy today, Mr. Durant?" she said, coming up beside him.

Alexander jolted and turned to her with a smile.

"I'm running a bit late, is all. But I have a moment if you wanted to talk."

"It's only a quick question, nothing more."

Alexander nodded for her to continue.

"When you found Dr. Kelley, was he out of breath?"

"That's a strange question." He stopped walking and furrowed his brow. "I'm not sure I remember. I believe he was. Why do you ask?"

She shook her head and turned to leave. "Just something for the case. Thank you!"

"Wait, Miss Blayse." He ran to catch up with her. "You can't just show up out of nowhere, ask a question and disappear."

"You do it all the time."

"Well, it's a nasty habit that I'm trying to break. And what I'm meaning to say is," he rubbed the back of his neck, "I would like to spend more than a few fleeting moments getting to know one another."

Her eyes narrowed, and he held his hands up.

"How can you ever learn to trust me if you don't get to know me?"

She paused. "You really are in earnest?"

"I am."

"Well, perhaps. But first I've got to get my uncle out from under police suspicion."

"I can wait."

"It shouldn't be too long of a wait now." She smiled at him. "Now, weren't you going to be late?"

"A pleasure as always to talk with you, Miss Blayse." He kissed the back of her hand before turning back towards his destination.

She paused outside of Palace Court, trying to decide whether to knock or use the key. Byron made her choice for her when he opened the door and stepped out, stopping before he knocked her over.

"I was just coming to find you. Thatcher sent me a telegram telling us to come to Scotland Yard as soon as possible."

"Let's not keep him waiting, then."

WHEN THEY ARRIVED AT THATCHER'S OFFICE, THE man busied himself with organizing stacks of papers and files. He glanced up at them when they entered.

"There you are! You've stirred up a nest of devils here at the Yard."

"Is that a good thing?" Mira asked, sitting down.

"Well, yes and no. No, because now we've got a barrel of deaths that were actually murder. Yes, because that means we can bring the murderer and his accomplices to justice," Thatcher said.

"So, you found something in the autopsy report?" Byron sat beside her.

"Mr. Rowley's great-uncle was poisoned, and it seems that Dr. Kelley took great care to make it look like old age and illness. In questioning the family members of some of the other individuals on your list, we've found that every person so far has had a relative die under Dr. Kelley's watchful eye."

"I'm glad we stirred things up then." Byron leaned back in his chair.

"I'll be heading over with some constables to talk with him shortly. We'll stop by Harding's with our warrant to get his ledger and then make the arrest. I think that with the evidence we have, we can pin Sutherland's death on the two of them."

"I also spoke with Mr. Durant this morning. He said that Dr. Kelley was out of breath, likely from running around the house. I know it's circumstantial but with everything else," Mira trailed off.

"We have more than enough to clear your uncle. Especially since Harding has more of a motive." Thatcher set the last report in the stack down. "Would the two of you want to tag along and see this to the end? This was more your case than mine."

Byron shared a look with Mira then nodded. "We'll come along."

AFTER A QUICK STOP AT EMORIA-SUTHERLAND'S TO get the ledger from a reluctant Mr. Harding, they headed straight for Dr. Kelley's practice. Chief Inspector Thatcher rapped on the door, which opened a few moments later.

"May I help you?" Dr. Kelley glanced over the group, tensing as his gaze fell on the constables in uniform.

"May we come in?" Thatcher asked.

Kelley swallowed, then nodded, leading the way into a small sitting room.

"I gave my statement back at the Sutherland estate, if that is what this visit is about," Kelley said, fidgeting with his ring.

"We have some additional questions," Byron said, moving over to the fireplace.

Mira sat in an armchair.

"Had you met Mr. Sutherland before coming to his estate last week?" Thatcher said, opening the ledger.

"No. I was invited by his business partner, Mr. Harding. Unfortunately, Elijah had some other business come up, and he was not able to make it."

"Interesting." Byron straightened his cuffs. "What is your usual rate for house calls?"

"Depends on the severity of the case." Kelley side eyed Byron. "Most calls I charge a crown for."

"What was the severity of Elijah Harding's case?" Thatcher asked.

"Beg pardon?" Kelley pressed his lips into a hard line.

"Well, according to this ledger, he paid you ten pounds for medical services. That's forty times what you normally charge." Thatcher closed the ledger.

"It was an incredibly severe case, and he gave me extra for my trouble." He shuffled from one foot to the other.

"And if we spoke with Harding's wife, would she remember such a case?" Thatcher stepped closer.

"I-er," Kelley stuttered.

"Dr. Lorenzo Kelley, you are under arrest for the murder of Vincent Sutherland and Matthias Rowley. Although I'm sure a few others are bound to come up."

"You must be joking."

"I'm afraid not." Thatcher gestured for a constable to restrain him.

"What evidence do you have against me?"

"We have an eyewitness that saw a man of your build climb down the ivy. Based on the shoe polish on your window, the ivy outside, and this proof of payment, we believe that you killed Sutherland at the behest of Elijah Harding. Along with the evidence that you helped Derek Rowley kill his great-uncle, I'd say that warrants an arrest," Thatcher said.

Kelley laughed as a feral expression took over his features. "Done in by a shoe. Who would have thought? Well, that was a good run. I'm surprised they let me get caught."

"Who?" Mira asked.

"As if you don't know, Samira Blayse."

Kelley's voice grated on her ears as a chill ran down her spine. Byron placed a hand on her shoulder.

The constables escorted Kelley out to the police wagon. Thatcher stood on the steps with Byron and Mira.

"I've got a bit of paperwork left to do, but we should be able to release your uncle tomorrow, Miss Blayse."

"Thank you, Chief Inspector."

"It's my pleasure." He tipped his hat to her and went to join his constables.

"Well, there's another case set to rights." Byron slipped his arm through hers and led her down the steps. "Now we only need to worry about the ambassador getting to Constantinople in one piece."

"I had completely forgotten about that!" Mira looked up at him.

"No worries. My journal hadn't," he joked, and she rolled her eyes. "I've checked in on him several times and we've confirmed his travel plans. I'll be escorting him to the station the day after tomorrow."

"Then I suppose it's back on the trail of Circe. Although, our lead has evaporated."

"What about your mysterious gentleman? Mr. Durant?"

"I'm convinced he has nothing to do with Circe."

"That you know of."

Mira paused. "Well, yes. But there's evidence that Circe only used him as a messenger, nothing more."

"I'd still like to keep an eye on him, just to be sure."

"I suppose we do have several members of Circe already locked up. Do you think that Chief Inspector Thatcher will let us talk with them?"

"I highly doubt any of them would be talkative. But we can always try. It could keep us occupied until the next case."

"Right." Mira looked down.

"Is something the matter?"

"Not at all." She shook her head and forced a smile. "It just occurred to me you might solve the next case without your journal. Seeing as you're remembering things so well."

Byron shook his head. "I think I'll still use it to document the most important things. It wouldn't do for me to forget a major clue. Unless, of course, I can guarantee that you'll remember it."

He patted her arm. "Granted, I can't do that until I remember you."

Her smile wavered, and he called for a hansom cab to stop for them.

"Tomorrow you should meet me at Scotland Yard. Then you can bring your uncle home with you and spend the rest of the day celebrating and resting. It's been a hectic week."

"That sounds lovely."

Once Byron had dropped her off at Swan Walk, Mira rushed inside to tell Walker the good news. She found him, Miss Renaldi, and Landon in the sitting room. Walker beamed at her as she came in.

"Hello, Mouse! Look who's here!"

Miss Renaldi ducked her head in embarrassment and stood to hand Mira a piece of paper.

"I only stopped in for a moment."

Mira glanced down at the bright white paper and gold lettering. An invitation of some sort.

"My parents asked me to invite the two of you to our garden party this Sunday." Liza's eyes flicked back to Walker for a moment. "It will likely be the last one of the season before we move back to our estate in Yorkshire for the winter. I know the last party you attended went awry, but I promise it will be fun! You are more than welcome to invite Mr. Constantine as well."

"Oh!" Mira blinked back her surprise. "How nice!"

She glanced at Walker who nodded his head behind Liza.

Mira smiled. "We'd love to come. Please thank your parents for the invitation."

"Oh, splendid! It's at three o'clock this Sunday. Of course, all the details are on the invitation."

"Is it possible to invite one additional person?" Mira bit back a smirk.

"Who did you have in mind?" Liza responded.

"Well, seeing as our Uncle Cyrus is coming home tomorrow . . ."

Walker jumped up and hugged her.

"Everything is working out just fine," she whispered to him as she hugged him tight.

October 20, 1888

Mira and Walker entered Scotland Yard together the next morning. She waved to Fred and kept an eye out for Byron. She caught his eye as he came down the steps from Chief Inspector Thatcher's office.

"They're finishing up the paperwork. Your uncle will be out any moment now."

"Thank you, Byron." Mira smiled up at him.

"Of course." Byron turned to Walker. "Just making sure. You're Walker, yes?"

"Actually I'm . . . not clever enough to come up with another alias." Walker laughed. "It's good to see you again Constantine."

Byron shook his hand, but Mira kept her eyes on the staircase. The moment her uncle's face appeared, she ran to meet him, crushing him in a hug.

"I'm happy to see you too, my dear." Cyrus laughed into

the hug. "Might we celebrate at home? I feel ridiculous wearing party clothes in the middle of the day."

"Oh, I've missed you." She gave him one last squeeze, then let go, leading him down the stairs.

Walker jumped in for a hug once he reached the bottom.

"Glad to see you, old man."

"And I you." Cyrus pulled away from the hug and offered a hand to Byron.

"I owe you a great debt, Detective Constantine."

"The pleasure was all mine. And besides, your niece had just as much to do with your release as myself."

Cyrus looked between the twins, and his eyes welled up with tears. "Let's go home."

October 21, 1888

"Mew."

NERO KNEADED AT MIRA'S SHOULDERS BEFORE plopping down on her face. Mira squeezed her eyes shut and turned the cat, so he was more on her chest.

"Good morning, kitten. Hungry?"

Nero responded by flicking his tail in her face.

"I see."

Mira eased Nero off of her, stroking his soft fur, and sat up. She pulled the curtains aside and let the sunshine wash over her. Taking a deep breath, she stood and dressed herself for the day.

She slid down the main bannister and bounced into the dining room, feeling like a child again. Her uncle and brother already sat at the table conversing. She moved to her uncle's side first, placing a kiss on his forehead, then ruffled her brother's hair and sat down.

"Good morning, all!" she said, humming to herself.

"A good morning indeed! I don't know if I've slept better." Her uncle stretched his back. "Those cell beds were nothing short of horrific."

"I can imagine, Uncle." Walker took a sip of tea. "Do you feel up to coming to the garden party?"

"Well, I don't know. On the one hand, the last party ended poorly. On the other, I'd like to meet Miss Renaldi again, especially since you two seem to have gotten close since I last saw you."

"I never knew that she was so interesting, Uncle." Walker gave a lovesick sigh, and Mira shook her head. "We've been going to these galas together for years, and I never knew her."

"She is a promising young lady, that is certain. And what about you, Mira? Have you heard anything more from Ambrose Sherard?"

Mira's cheeks heated. "Yes, actually."

"Splendid!" Cyrus set his newspaper down. "I may have both of you married in another year!"

"Oh, I see how it is. You won't get rid of us that easy." Walker wielded his fork in a faux-threatening manner.

"I just want both of you to be happy and settled. That's all." Their uncle glanced between the two of them. "Nothing would make me happier."

"All in good time," Walker said around a mouthful of toast.

Cyrus grimaced but made no comment, instead turning back to Mira.

"What did Mr. Sherard say?"

That he didn't know who she was. That he loved her. That he remembered everything but her. That he was sorry.

"It's kind of hard to narrow it down." She nibbled on a bit of bacon. "Would you like to meet him?"

"Of course I would!"

"He should be at the Renaldi garden party today."

"In that case, I will come for certain. What was the address again, Walker?"

"Westfield Park, Chelsea."

"So not that far then."

Mira set her teacup down and stood. "I'd best get ready for the service."

AFTER CHURCH, MIRA ESCAPED FROM HER UNCLE and brother with the excuse of walking through Kensington Gardens. While that was true, she turned her steps towards Palace Court, hoping to find Byron at home and give him the invitation. With all the excitement from the day before, she had entirely forgotten to invite him before he had left her to celebrate with her family. And even if her emotions were all muddled, she couldn't help but be curious about how her uncle would respond to his title.

She walked through Kensington Gardens without running into Mr. Durant. Oddly enough, she missed his banter.

Byron sat at the piano again when she entered his rooms. She placed her coat up on the hook and peered into the sitting room. He nodded to her as she came in, but continued playing. A glance at his side table showed he had read his journal without her interference. After the final notes rang out, he smiled at her.

"Mira?"

"Yes, Byron?" She couldn't help the hope in her tone. Had he remembered her?

"Your self-portrait does you a disservice."

She sighed. Forgotten once again. At least he had her sketches to remind him.

He cocked his head. "Isn't Sunday your day off?"

"Officially, yes. But I come bearing an invitation."

"Oh?" He stood and moved over to her. "What kind of invitation?"

"Miss Liza Renaldi has invited my family and you to a garden party. It starts at three."

"A garden party? Me?"

"It's not as if you haven't been to one before, Mr. Sherard." Mira teased.

Byron's eyebrows shot up. "I told you about that?"

"Didn't you write it down?"

She glanced at his journal. It sat on top of a white notebook on his side table.

"I suppose I didn't, or I missed that part."

"Well, my uncle is very interested in meeting you. He isn't aware of your dual identity. That is, if you are up to it."

"Your uncle is the one dead set in traditions?"

He paced over to the armchair and picked up his journal. He flipped it open and made a note, before setting it back on the white notebook.

"Very much so."

"So, meeting him as Ambrose Sherard is likely to impress him more than my skills as a detective?"

"I think he's already impressed by your skills. After all, you saved him from the gallows."

"We did that."

"Yet he's indebted to *you*. So. Are you coming?"

"I'll have to leave from there to drop off the ambassador at the station, but I'd love to come."

"He's leaving today?"

Byron nodded.

"Do I need to come with you?"

"No. You should stay with your family."

She cocked her head at him and nodded. "Very well. Here's the address." Mira handed him the invitation. "I'd best get back now before they realize I'm missing."

"I'll see you in a few hours, then." Byron set the invitation on his journal and kissed the back of her hand. "What color dress will you be wearing?"

"Dark blue with rose-colored flowers and all the frills. And a ridiculous hat."

"I happen to like ridiculous hats." He leaned closer, and she caught a whiff of sandalwood.

"Well, I'll make it all the more ridiculous for you then."

He smiled at her, then straightened his jacket. "I suppose I'd better get dressed in something more suitable."

AFTER FUSSING AND PREENING IN FRONT OF the mirror for over an hour, Mira once again looked presentable. She braided and curled her hair, intertwining it with fake hair pieces. Dozens of pins kept it all in place, aside from a few curls that trailed down the back of her neck. Her gown had several skirts, with the top layer of dark blue gathered up on both sides, revealing a blue skirt with pink flowers and ruffles beneath. It cinched at the waist, with a large bustle on the back. The top part of the dress was mostly white and lacy, save for the sleeves, which showed off the floral pattern with lace at the cuffs. Her last accessary was the ridiculous hat, which had a spray of silk flowers to match the dress, and a fluffy feather. This she pinned to her hair with two large hat pins.

She descended the staircase in a much more graceful fashion than she had that morning, meeting her brother at the base.

"Do I look proper enough, do you think?"

"It's certainly a change from when you stole my clothes." Walker teased.

"What was that?" Cyrus said, coming down the stairs behind them.

"Just a joke, Uncle." Walker laughed. "Shall we go?"

Iт was not as small an affair as Mira expected, in part because of the size of Westfield. Mira hadn't been there since she was a little girl. Sprawling grass, countless trees, and the weather was simply perfect. Liza's parents must have pulled some strings to allow for them to use it for such a gathering. A large tent was set up on the near side of the park, with a table filled to the brim with refreshments. Blankets and umbrellas were positioned about at a comfortable distance for conversations.

Liza Renaldi approached them wearing a gorgeous white dress with cool-colored flowers scattered over the fabric. She rushed up to Mira and took both of her hands in hers.

"I'm so pleased you all could come!"

"Wouldn't miss it for anything." Walker grinned. "Might I introduce my Uncle Cyrus?"

Liza let go of Mira and moved next to Walker. "Oh, I've met you once before, but it's good to see you again! I'm so glad everything worked out."

"As am I. Beautiful weather for a garden party. Quite odd for October."

"We just wanted to do one last hurrah before we move back to the country for the season. And seeing as it's stayed so warm these last few days, we thought it would be nice to do it outside."

"Well, it's splendid." Mira turned about to see if she could catch a glimpse of Byron. So far, she didn't recognize any of the guests other than themselves.

"Go ahead and mingle. I'm afraid I'm playing hostess, but I'll come over as soon as I can." Liza turned to welcome a new batch of guests, and Walker led the way towards a blanket just past the tent.

"Such a lovely girl," Cyrus said, settling down on the blanket. "Now where's your Mr. Sherard, Mira?"

"I'm sure he'll be here, Uncle." Mira positioned her skirts around her.

Walker stayed standing. "Shall I grab some refreshments?"

"Please," Mira said.

Cyrus let out a happy sigh and leaned back. "It's good to be in the sun again."

"I thought you hated the outdoors," Mira chuckled.

"I like it on my own terms."

"It is nice today." Mira leaned back, feeling the sun on her face. It was uncommonly warm and simply brilliant.

"We ought to get that umbrella over you. Wouldn't want you to freckle." Walker set down a spread of refreshments. "Oh wait, it's too late for that."

"Let her be, Walker. Everyone should be able to enjoy this sun," Cyrus said, eyes closed.

Walker and Mira shared a glance.

"Are you feeling alright, old man?" Walker sat next to Mira.

"Perfectly. I've just come to a realization."

The twins waited expectantly as Cyrus continued. "I think I've placed too many expectations on the two of you. To think of all the times I've gotten after the two of you for breaches in propriety and yet," he paused, sitting up and looking straight at the two of them, "sitting in that cell, I wasn't thinking about those times. I was thinking of how I wanted you two to be happy. Yes, I want the best for you, but perhaps I don't know what that is."

Mira's mouth dropped open in surprise as he went on, eyes a bit wet. "I think I've been so caught up in the past, that I haven't realized the treasures I have in front of me in the present."

꧁⚜꧂

AFTER TALKING SOME MORE AND NIBBLING ON the refreshments, Mira pulled out her sketchbook and watercolors to pass the time. Walker went off to find Miss Renaldi, and Cyrus continued to enjoy the sun and the social atmosphere. After Mira had captured a view of the park, Walker returned with a familiar face.

"Look who I found!" Walker startled Cyrus out of his daze.

"Why, Mr. Constantine! This is a pleasant surprise." Her uncle stood to greet the detective.

"I had a promise to keep." Byron shifted his gaze to Mira.

She stood and smoothed out her skirts, noticing that his tie matched what she was wearing. She smiled and took his arm.

"Uncle, may I introduce you to Byron Ambrose Sherard, brother of Castel Sherard."

She stepped back with a mischievous glint in her eye as Cyrus choked on his spit.

"Sherard?!"

"I've been told it's a family name," Byron joked, shoulders tense.

"But how?"

"I decided to use a pseudonym to protect the family name while still becoming a detective. And while my family sometimes questions my decision, I like to think they are proud of me."

"As well they should be!" Cyrus clapped a hand on his back and led him over to the blanket. "My dear boy, I was under the impression you were two separate people! I had no idea."

"Most people don't." He rubbed the back of his neck and escaped from Cyrus' grip. "I'm afraid I can only stop in for a moment, though. I need to escort Sir William to Victoria station, and I'd rather not leave him waiting."

Mira crouched down to pack up her supplies, and Byron moved next to her.

"No, Mira. I can handle this one on my own. Stay and enjoy the last of the sunshine. I'll see you tomorrow?"

"Of course."

He helped her back to her feet, kissed the back of her hand, and turned to walk away. Cyrus stood next to Mira.

"You know, I always thought he was a good sort."

Mira rolled her eyes. "The first time you met him, you called him a charlatan."

"I was right, wasn't I? He lied about who he was."

She turned her gaze to Byron's retreating form. "No. He didn't. Not really."

AFTER A BEAUTIFUL AFTERNOON, THE SMALL FAMILY returned to Swan Walk in excellent spirits. Cyrus excused himself to his office to take care of some business affairs, and Mira found herself sitting with her brother in the parlor.

"Do you think they would approve of Liza?" Walker glanced up at their parents' portrait.

"While I know them as well as you do, I'd venture to guess that they would. After all, I like her, and I have impeccable taste." Mira took her turn at draughts, taking two of his pieces.

"And an impeccable strategy it would seem." He leaned forward, tapping the top of the board. "You are absolutely devastating me at this."

"You're distracted."

"I'm thinking of asking her father if I could court her. I mean, we've been beating about the bush for the past we—"

Mira interrupted, looking up at him in surprise. "You've seen each other almost every day. How are you not courting?"

"It's not official! And it's all happening so fast."

"Do her parents like you?"

"They give every indication that they do."

"Do you like her?"

"Honestly?" Walker sighed. "I think I'm actually in love."

Mira looked up at him from the board. "Well then, you need to find out if she loves you. She certainly likes you, but—"

"I know. I just don't know if I'm ready to breach that topic."

Mira paused a moment, stood, and went to a shelf, shuffling through the titles until she found what she was looking for.

"What would you want to tell her if you could?" She flopped into the armchair again.

"That I've fallen for her so hopelessly, and I can only wish she loves me in return."

Walker fell into a wistful daze. Mira gave him a critical eye.

"Can you not be serious?"

"Mira, I'm not sure if I could be more serious."

"I had no idea you could be so moved." Mira flipped through the book. "According to this, you should give her a bouquet of red carnations, daffodils, and daisies. That combination should be enough to get the message across. Although most of those aren't in season."

He stood and snatched the book from her hands. "Let me see that!" He flipped through a few pages and glanced up at Mira.

"Do you think she'll know what it means?"

"Based on her use of the flirtation handbook—"

"Oh! I completely forgot to use that today! What if I did something wrong?"

"You can remedy it with flowers, I'm sure." Mira tapped her piece across the board, claiming several more of Walker's pieces.

Walker perused the book a few moments more and sat across from her again. He leaned forward and made his move on the board.

"What about you and Byron?"

"What about us?"

"Well, if things are serious between me and Miss Renaldi after a week, what does a month say about the two of you?"

"Things are complicated." Mira leaned back in her chair.

"Do you love him?"

Mira swallowed and looked down. Did she? If all the emotions of the past week were anything to go off of, she was quite possibly as far gone as her brother. She gave him a small smile.

"I think I do."

"And it's obvious how he feels for you."

She shook her head and shifted another piece on the board. "It's more nuanced than that. I'm not sure if he is capable of loving me yet."

"I saw the way he looked at you. You can't say that wasn't love."

"But was it? Walker, he doesn't remember me. Every day he forgets me. He falls in love with the idea of me, and that is entirely based on what he's written. That version of me isn't real, is it?"

Walker went quiet for a moment, hesitating in making his move. He set the piece down and looked at her.

"I see what you mean. But isn't he remembering more nowadays?"

"Yes." Mira's voice softened. "But never me."

October 22, 1888

MIRA WOKE CLUTCHING HER CHEST, TRYING TO breathe. Somewhere within the dreams of drowning in fabric and enormous platters of sandwiches, the strange mixture of topics from the day before morphed into shadowy figures. Hat pins turned into knives and the sunshine into a smoldering fire and ash.

Sitting up, she pushed the curtain aside, noting that the sun hadn't yet graced the sky with even a drop of sunlight. Street lamps flickered in the darkness. Nero curled into her side, and she dropped back onto her pillow with a sigh, not feeling tired enough to fall back to sleep.

Yet, it was much too early to go to Byron's. She rubbed a hand over her face, trying to decipher the last tendrils of the nightmare as it slipped away. Shaking her head, she rose to dress for the day. She watered her mums, fed the cat, and climbed up to the roof to bask in the sunrise over London. In the distance, the Thames sparkled with the early morning light. Satisfied, she went downstairs to see if anyone else was up, and to find some breakfast for herself.

Her uncle sat at the dining table, Walker standing over him. They spoke in hushed tones, staring at the newspaper in her uncle's hand. When she entered, they quieted further, and Cyrus hurriedly folded the newspaper.

"Good morning, Samira!" Cyrus forced out.

Mira frowned, folding her arms.

"What are you two up to?" She narrowed her eyes.

"Just reading the news!" Walker stumbled over his words. His panicked eyes suggested it wasn't good news.

"May I see the paper?" She stepped forward and extended her hand.

Cyrus and Walker shared a look before her uncle slumped in his seat and handed it over.

Mira unfolded it and flicked it out. Front and center, the headline read, *"Attack at Victoria Station."* The first line continued, *"An unknown group attacked passengers at Victoria station. Police are still looking into the matter."*

She dropped the paper on the table.

"We were trying to figure out the best way to tell you," Cyrus said.

Mira ignored him and ran to the entryway. Walker followed after her.

"They would have mentioned it if it were him."

"I have to make sure he's alright." She slipped on her coat.

Walker sighed and handed over her hat. "Alright." He kissed the top of her head. "Be careful."

"You sound like our uncle."

He rolled his eyes and opened the door. "Maybe he's right about some things."

After paying the hansom cab driver, Mira ran up the steps of Palace Court, pulled out her key and burst inside. Coming into the sitting room, she half expected Byron to be standing there, alarmed. But he wasn't there. Without bothering to take off her coat, she checked for notes, then checked the bedroom and the office, with no trace of Byron.

She came back into the sitting room and shook her hands out, pacing. There had to be a different explanation. Walker was right. They would have mentioned who it was that disappeared if it were Byron. Or Ambassador White, for goodness' sake! Her eyes darted across the room again, looking for any notes she may have missed.

A knock at the door startled her out of her thoughts. She shook her head, took a deep breath, and moved to the entry hall, easing the door open. Grace Trimbell stood on the step and Mira stopped herself from flinching back.

"Is Byron here?"

Loose wisps of hair framed Grace's face, and Mira noted that the buttons on her bodice were misaligned by one.

"He's not."

"May I come in?" Grace took a step forward.

Mira relented and stepped back, closing the door behind Grace, and following her to the sitting room.

"What are you doing here?"

"I saw the newspaper. That's why you're here, isn't it?" Grace said, settling onto the couch and living up to her name.

Mira took a calming breath and sat beside her. "Yes."

"Then you thought exactly the same as I did. I wanted to make sure he wasn't involved."

They sat in silence for a few moments, Mira worrying at her lip. She kept glancing at Grace, trying to determine if that was all she was here for.

"What do we do now?" Grace asked.

"What do you mean?" Mira crossed her arms.

"If Byron were here and someone had gone missing, how would you proceed?"

"We don't know for certain that he's missing." She fiddled with a loose thread on the end of her coat.

"So, you suggest we wait here until he returns?"

Mira looked her over, brow furrowed. Grace leaned back and gave a sharp laugh.

"You don't trust me."

"How very observant of you."

"Miss Blayse, every interaction I've had with you has been cold." Grace looked her up and down. "It doesn't take much observation to deduce that much."

"I have no reason to trust you."

"But do you have a reason to distrust me?"

Mira stood and paced over to the mantel. "He remembers you."

"He remembers plenty of people," she scoffed.

"But only from before his accident." Mira whirled back around. "You didn't meet until afterwards."

"Actually, we met before." Grace studied her gloves, adjusting the fingers.

"That's not what he told me."

"You trust Byron's memory?" Her gaze flicked up to Mira.

Mira sucked in a deep breath. "What is it that you want?"

"The same thing that you do. You care about Byron, don't you?"

"I . . ." Mira swallowed.

"Answer me. Honestly."

Grace's brown doe eyes locked with hers, and Mira faltered. "Yes. I do."

"So do I. Can't we work together until he is safe? Afterwards I will happily go back to being jealous of you, but for the moment we have to set that aside."

"Jealous of me?" Mira's eyes widened.

"That's beside the point." Grace stood and offered her hand. "Temporary truce?"

Mira narrowed her gaze, then relaxed and shook Grace's hand. "Alright."

Another knock rapped at the door. Mira dropped Grace's hand and ran to the entryway. A telegram boy stood on the step.

"Telegram for Miss Samira Blayse?" He offered her the envelope.

"Thank you." She snatched it up, and the boy tipped his hat, walking away.

Mira moved back into the sitting room and retrieved the letter opener from Byron's side table. She slid it along the top and pulled out the telegram.

> *Number 12 Bolton Street, Westminster. Come now.*
> *Castel Sherard.*

"What is it?" Grace moved to take the telegram from her.

Mira kept hold of it. "It's Byron's brother. He's asked to meet."

"Let's go, then."

Mira hesitated. Did she really want Grace coming with? Then again, perhaps it would be better to keep an eye on her. She nodded and set the envelope on the side table.

BOLTON STREET WAS SIMILAR IN DESIGN TO Palace Court, with red brick buildings and white trim. Grace and Mira walked down to number 12 in silence, a sense of foreboding settling over them.

"Have you met his brother before?" Mira broke the tension.

"No. Have you?" Grace straightened.

"Twice. He's . . . nice enough."

Mira rapped the knocker twice and stepped back to be in line with Grace again. The door opened and a well-dressed man looked them over.

"May I help you?"

"My name is Samira Blayse, and this is Grace Trimbell. Mr. Sherard should be expecting us."

The man nodded and gestured for them to come in. After taking their coats and hats, he escorted them to a library. Castel sat behind a desk looking over papers. Her eyes grazed over the room, taking in the books, a side table with a decanter of ghastly green liquor, and the dull light coming through the curtains. Castel glanced up at them as they entered.

"Ah, Miss Blayse. And who is this?"

"I'm Grace Trimbell."

Castel raised an eyebrow. "I'm afraid I only asked for Miss Blayse to come."

"This is about Byron, yes?"

Castel's mustache twitched. "It is. But it does not concern you."

"If Byron is involved, then it concerns me. Please continue." Grace sat in one of the armchairs. Castel cleared his throat.

"I suppose we don't have time to argue the point." He turned to Mira. "Byron and the ambassador were captured last night. We aren't entirely sure who orchestrated it, but we are certain that they intend to disrupt the treaty signing. The ambassador's wife was traveling separately and was not involved."

Mira swallowed and lowered herself into the remaining armchair. She fought to keep her hands still in her lap.

"Her Majesty assigned Byron to look for potential threats. Had you found anything in your investigation?"

Mira shook her head. "There weren't any leads that I was aware of. Byron met with the ambassador without me often enough, so he might have known more."

Castel rubbed at his temples. "If we can't locate the

ambassador before the twenty-fifth, he won't make it to Constantinople in time. We have less than three days and no idea of where to start."

"Why didn't the paper discuss any of these details?" Grace asked.

Castel huffed. "Tensions between the signing countries are high as it is. If word got out that our ambassador was missing, it would only be worse for us."

"Have the police found anything?" Mira asked.

"They've only been able to identify who was taken by talking with witnesses. They couldn't identify the assailants, and no one has come forward with demands."

"Well then, we have our work cut out for us." Mira stood.

Castel's eyes widened. "Miss Blayse, forgive me for giving you the wrong impression. I asked you here to find out if you were aware of any leads that Byron was following and to inform you of what happened. That is all."

"And I thank you for informing me. But if we only have three days, then we need to get on the case immediately."

Castel scoffed. "Go home, Miss Blayse. Leave this to the men."

Mira took a deep breath and left the room, Grace directly behind her. The butler helped them recover their things and soon enough, they were on the street.

Mira clenched her fists and pushed back the urge to scream in frustration.

"The nerve of him to call us halfway across London and suggest we couldn't do anything!"

"He could go smother a parrot all day for all I care." Grace sidled up beside her.

Mira burst out with a laugh. "Smother a parrot?"

"Didn't you see the absinthe on the side table? Why is it that most men try to solve their problems with alcohol?"

"I haven't the faintest idea."

They walked farther down the street, coming up on Piccadilly. "You aren't going home, are you?" Grace asked.

"Heavens, no!"

"Good. Because I think I may have some idea of where to look."

"You do?"

Grace looked away and rubbed at her hands. "Let's go back to Palace Court. It should be safe there."

GRACE REFUSED TO TALK ABOUT THE CASE until they had made up a pot of tea. The two women settled in the sitting room of Palace Court, finally free of their coats. Mira stirred some milk and sugar into her cup. Grace cleared her throat, closed her eyes, and took a deep breath.

"What do you know about Circe?"

Mira choked on a sip of tea and set the cup down, spluttering. "Circe?"

"So, you are aware of them." Grace opened her eyes and sat forward. "Good. That makes this easier."

Mira tensed, expecting Grace to pull out a revolver or something. Instead, she picked up her own teacup and took a sip.

"You work with Circe?" Mira narrowed her eyes at her teacup. If Grace had poisoned it, would she be able to tell?

"I don't have a choice," Grace bit out, eyes hard.

"Does Byron know?"

"More or less, yes." She averted her gaze.

"I don't understand."

Grace set her teacup down and fiddled with the hems of her sleeves. "My mother died the night after I was born. Heaven knows who my father was. I was taken in by a couple who helped my mother give birth." She fidgeted, picking the tea up again to take a sip before continuing. "They named me Grace, because by the grace of God, I survived. When I was four, they died from cholera, and I was alone."

Grace held her teacup closer to herself, cupping the warmth. Mira narrowed her eyes, trying to see if she was lying, but not seeing any kind of tell.

"I don't remember how it happened," Grace huffed a laugh. "I was wandering the streets in one moment and being warm and held close to someone in the next. They called me Trimbell because I trembled so much, and they taught me how to steal. Being so small, it was easy to go unnoticed and pick the pockets of people around me. It became second nature."

"You didn't know it was wrong?"

"You have no right to judge me," Grace snapped. "I was young when they took me. I had no idea what was right or wrong. All I knew was I was hungry, and stealing gave me food and warmth and a place to sleep. Maybe they didn't treat me as well as they could, but we were family."

"I'm sorry."

Grace shook her head. "You couldn't know. You may not be an aristocrat, but you haven't had to work a day in your life."

Mira glanced away. "What does this have to do with Byron?"

"I met him when I was sixteen, although he went by Elliot Thorne at the time. I was in charge of sewing inconspicuous pockets into men's clothing so they could carry explosives without anyone noticing."

Grace smiled for the first time, gaze far away.

"It was his first job with Circe, and he was so full of light and life. He was kinder to me than anyone I had ever worked with before. He joked, but it was never in bad taste, and he would get after the other men for talking down to me. He made me laugh."

Grace turned to Mira again. "You know how easy it is to

fall in love with him. He introduced me to a different world, made me think that maybe, just maybe, I could live a different life. One night, we both sat on the edge of a dock, looking up at the night sky. He asked me why I was with Circe, and I told him it was all I'd ever known. He asked what I wanted to do with my life, as if I had a choice in the matter. And it really made me think.

"It was only a few weeks, but he changed my life. The day before they planned on setting the explosives, he told me that if I wanted to have a different life, that I needed to stay clear of the Cobden Club, Circe, and the dynamite plot for three days. He gave me some money and suggested a place for me to stay. I did as he said and disappeared for a few days. But I kept up with the news and found out that the police had disarmed almost all the explosives. The only one they missed was at Victoria station. Someone had told the police about the campaign beforehand, and I knew it had to be Elliot. Why else would he tell me to leave?

"When the papers didn't mention anyone being arrested, I came back to the Cobden Club. I found out through whispers that a traitor had been caught in the explosion at Victoria station and was being held by Circe. I found out where they took him and convinced those in charge of him to let me take care of him. He was unconscious. They told me they had set the explosives, but he saw a mother and her child going into the luggage compartment and he ran back to warn them. They got out, but he caught the brunt of the explosion. The others knew he must have tipped off the police, so they brought him back to find out exactly what he told them.

He stayed unconscious for a week and was disoriented and unable to sit up for another week after that. I nursed him back to health and helped him make sense of things. He didn't even remember who he was at the beginning. Then his memory cleared more and more. I tried to get him to tell me about his life before. Orders came from the Big Three to interrogate him by any means necessary. Every night they would bring me back, and I'd clean up the blood and try to patch him back together. They had some sense, as they avoided his head, but . . ." She shivered, paling.

"One day I heard they couldn't get anything out of him because of his memory, and that if he didn't give them something that night, they would kill him. I couldn't let that happen. So, I sneaked him out. I brought him to the docks, away from where anyone could see. He was so delirious. Kept calling me an angel from heaven. It killed me to leave him there, but I remembered him talking about Inspector Thatcher when he was more lucid. I sent a telegram and rushed back to Circe. They suspected I had something to do with it, but I convinced them otherwise.

"A year later, I asked if I could retire from Circe. I was tired. But once they have you, you can never leave. Not really. They set me up with Mr. Harding in Emoria-Sutherland as a secretary. I make enough money to support myself and do rather well. In exchange, I keep quiet about other dealings that might go on there."

Mira sat in silence for a few moments, taking the story in. Her heart twisted in pain, thinking of what Byron had gone through. She swallowed and turned her thoughts back to the case, mind sticking on the shipping company. Mr. Sutherland hadn't been a member of the Order, had he?

"You mean to say that Emoria-Sutherland is part of Circe?"

"Not entirely. You see, Circe tends to work its way up the more profitable businesses, doing its work in the shadows. Mr. Harding was planted there initially, along with a few others. He worked his way up until he was over certain areas of shipping. He was already setting up a new smuggling operation when you and Byron shut down Vaporidge. Circe needed it set up faster, but the only way to do that would be to put a member of Circe in charge. If your uncle hadn't merged his company with Emoria-Sutherland when he did, Mr. Harding would have stepped up and Circe would have been able to do whatever they wished."

Mira sat back, feeling quite sick.

"When I ran into the two of you on my way back from shopping, I could barely breathe. I hadn't seen Byron in over four years, even if I'd kept up with his cases. It would be too risky to even be seen with him."

"But he recognized you."

"Exactly. And then again on that Sunday. He knew I was lying about him helping my brother. He found me again, and asked for the real story, and I could never say no to him. I've been helping him remember what happened, in hopes that he'll recover everything."

Grace took a deep breath and sipped at the last of her tea. Mira processed the new information as a myriad of emotions burned her insides.

"Thank you for telling me." She settled on gratitude.

"I needed you to trust me, and the best way of doing that is telling the truth." Grace shrugged.

"But you mentioned you have some idea of where they took them?"

"Yes." Grace leaned forward and set down her cup. "It was one of the last things that Mr. Harding took care of before he was arrested. He had some of the men who were working on the Emoria-Sutherland facade go down to our warehouses at Butler's Wharf and see if they couldn't find a room or two suitable for staying in. He said he was planning on surprising the workers with an inspection first thing in the morning. Having never done an inspection before, I can't help but wonder if this has something to do with Byron."

"You may be right. But why would Harding be involved with the ambassador?"

"I'm not sure. All I know is that Circe uses whatever resources they can, and we have access to the warehouses."

"Well then. Let's not waste any time."

It was half-past two when they left Palace Court for a second time, Grace leading the way. Mira trailed behind, trying to determine if this was a trick. Everything about Grace screamed that she was in earnest, but what if she wasn't?

"First, we need to stop at Emoria-Sutherland. I can get access to Harding's files. Maybe they have more information about which warehouse we need to go to." Grace slowed so she was by Mira's side again.

"Good idea." Mira's mind whirled, trying to determine the best course of action. Her gut told her Grace couldn't be trusted. She reminded her too much of the Shadow. Why would she just offer up the information that she had worked with Circe before? Unless, of course, she really loved Byron. Her stomach churned. This was the only lead to him, wasn't it? She continued this internal argument all the way to Emoria-Sutherland, following Grace up to the main office.

"Wait here a moment while I retrieve the files." Grace grabbed a key and disappeared into the back. Mira swept her gaze across the room and leaned up against the desk. Was there even any proof of Grace's story being true? Aside from Byron recognizing her, of course.

Her fingers brushed up against a book on the desk. She turned and picked it up, recognizing it as the same type of flirtation manual that Miss Renaldi had lent her. She rolled her eyes and flicked it open. Grace couldn't possibly ascribe to secret fan signals, could she? However, as she glanced down the page, she noted some entries were crossed out with annotations next to them.

Hat Flirtations

Running the finger around the crown- ~~*I love you*~~ *We are all present.*

Inclined towards the nose-We are watched.

Putting it behind you- ~~*I am married.*~~ *The deal is off.*

Putting it in front of you- ~~*I am single.*~~ *The deal is on.*

Touching the rim to the lips- ~~*Does he accompany you?*~~ *I have a message.*

Holding the hat in one hand and tapping it with the other- ~~*Can we meet again?*~~ *Number of taps is the time of meeting.*

As she flipped through the pages, she found more of these secret signals for hats, canes, fans, gloves, even napkins if you were at a dinner party. Every type had annotations of alternative signals. Mira jolted as Grace dropped a pile of records in front of her.

"A bit of light reading?" She raised an eyebrow at Mira.

"I'm sorry! I just have a friend that has this same book and—"

"I'd hope it isn't exactly the same," Grace said, picking up the first file and sifting through it.

"Well, hers doesn't have anything written in it. Why did you cross the original meanings out? Wouldn't it make it difficult to communicate if you're the only one who knows the signals?"

"It would if I were the only one. Go to page forty-three."

Mira did as she instructed and found the page on dinner party flirtations.

Setting glass in front of you- ~~I'm yours~~ **We are not alone.**

Swirling the glass, one sip- ~~Are you single?~~ **Change the subject.**

Dropping a utensil- ~~Don't talk to me.~~ **Understood.**

Folding napkin into a triangle- ~~Meet me after.~~ **I'm with Circe.**

She stopped reading. "These are for Circe?"

"It's rarely used. Generally, the two parties agree on what system they are using before they infiltrate somewhere. It can be useful if you are trying to convince someone that you are a member of Circe. And of course, it's good for silent communication."

"But anyone could accidentally use a signal!"

"That's true. But there are multiple stages of signals to ensure that only those in the know are aware of the conversation."

"How on earth do you memorize all these?" Mira set the book down and picked up a file for herself.

"I never could. It's like a separate language. Hence why I keep a copy with me just in case. I don't like it when people are talking silently while I'm in the room. Granted, most everyone else would just see it and think I was trying to court someone."

Mira nodded and focused on the files. They passed the time in silence, rustling papers here and there, until Grace found what she was looking for.

"Here it is! This is the order that he sent with the workers. They said a backroom in warehouse eight was available."

"So, if Byron is anywhere, it will be there?"

"Precisely!"

Mira glanced out the window. The sun was working its way to the horizon at this point.

"Would it be better to go under cover of night or in the morning do you think?"

Grace sat down. "I'm not sure. During the day, there will be workers. But at night, everyone we meet would definitely be part of Circe."

Mira paced in front of the desk, holding her arms. "Grace, out of anyone in Circe, who would be most likely to be allowed to see the prisoners?"

Grace swallowed, and moved to the door, checking the hallway before locking the door behind her. "The Trio, and anyone in their inner circle."

"And who are they?"

"Circe is incredibly organized and hierarchical. There are different guilds, so to speak, that all work together towards whatever end-goal Circe has at any given time. There could be hundreds of end-goals or one, but the Trio orchestrates it all. Each of the three is over a different guild. Only their inner circle knows who they are. And the inner circle then coordinates with their subordinates."

"Seems complicated." Mira leaned against the desk.

"It has to be. If you were to discover the identity of one of the Trio, and link them to a crime, that entire guild would crumble."

"But people do work with the people in the inner circle?"

"It depends on the job. I've worked with Nathan Poole on occasion at Emoria-Sutherland. He's in charge of general shipping under Number Three."

Mira frowned. Nathan Poole. Why did that name sound familiar? Grace paused and cocked her head in suspicion. "Why are you so interested?"

"Well, if we were to say that we were under orders from someone in the inner circle, they would have to let us see Byron and the ambassador, yes?"

Grace took a deep breath. "That might work. Might being

the critical word here. I suppose it would depend on how well we could convince the guards. If it went wrong, then—"

"I know. Do you have a better idea?"

"No, I don't." Grace frowned. "But how would seeing them help us get them out?"

"Don't worry. I have a plan." Her eyes stilled on the flirtation book. "Meet me at Palace Court at two."

"We're waiting until tomorrow afternoon?"

"No." She looked up at Grace again. "Tomorrow morning. Do you think anyone would recognize you from Emoria-Sutherland?"

"It's possible."

"Good. Come in your nicest dress. We need to make a good impression. And bring whatever you need for those signals."

With that, she turned, unlocked the door, and left Grace's office. If her plan was to work, she needed to move quickly.

HER FIRST STOP WAS SCOTLAND YARD. IT was late, and most policemen had already left the station for the evening. Mira mentally crossed her fingers as she moved to the constable on duty at the front desk.

"Excuse me, but is Officer Wensley still around?"

"He just left. May I take a note for you?"

Mira bit her lip and glanced down for a moment. Taking a deep breath, she looked up at the constable again.

"I'm afraid it can't wait. You see—" Mira faltered, trying to think of a reasonable lie to tell. "I-I have something urgent to tell him. It must be in person."

"What kind of urgent news?"

Mira's face blazed red. "I . . . er . . . well . . ."

The constable paused a moment before breaking out into a smile. "Young love can be hard."

Mira's eyes widened, and she tried to refute the statement, but the constable only laughed and continued.

"I'm afraid you'll have to wait until tomorrow to confess to him. I can't exactly give you his address. But if you leave your name, I'll be sure to let him know that you'll be around. I think he goes on break around one."

"No. It's quite alright."

Mira excused herself and rushed to the door. Byron's files had to have something on Fred, right? As she hurried down the steps, she ran straight into someone, and they both nearly toppled over.

"Oh, I'm terribly sorry." Mira looked up and found herself face to face with Frederick Wensley.

"No need to apologize, Miss Blayse. Were you here talking to Thatcher?"

"Actually, I came to talk to you, but you had already left and—"

"Just your luck that I had forgotten my hat. Come on. We can walk and talk."

He offered her his arm and escorted her back into the building. The constable on duty broke out into a wide grin.

"Wensley! What perfect timing! This young woman needed to speak with you."

"So, I've heard. Have you seen my hat?"

"Oh, I think you left it in the records room. I'll go grab it so you two can have your chat."

Mira's face burned, and she turned to look at a particularly beautiful column.

"What is he on about?" Fred said, standing next to her.

"No idea whatsoever." Mira composed herself and turned towards him. "However, I have an important request for you."

"If you're after records again, I'm afraid I can't help you without Byron around," he teased.

"Byron is missing. He was kidnapped by Circe, and I need your help."

Fred sobered immediately. "What can I do? "

"We've discovered where he's likely been taken. And I think we have a way in. However, if we're going to be convincing, I need to have at least three 'guards' or something of the sort. I was wondering if you could help."

"Anything for an old friend."

"Thank you, Fred. We're meeting at Palace Court at two tomorrow morning. Please don't be late."

"I'll be sure to be there."

A loud cough alerted them to the constable returning with Fred's hat. Mira took the opportunity to leave before anything else was said.

HER NEXT STOP WAS EASY, AS IT was just going home. Landon greeted her and took her coat as she came in.

"Please say that Walker isn't still with Miss Renaldi."

"He's in the sitting room, actually. With—"

"Thank you, Landon!" She practically ran to the sitting room and burst inside. "Walker, I—"

She stopped as she took in her brother and Mr. Durant standing as she entered.

"Mira, are you okay?" Walker moved to her side.

"I'm fine. It's just . . ."

She glanced at Mr. Durant. Did she trust him enough with this?

"I heard about what happened at Victoria Station. Was Mr. Constantine injured at all?" Alexander asked.

Mira hesitated, then took a deep breath and sat in one of the armchairs.

"They took him, along with the ambassador."

Walker pulled a chair from the side and sat in front of her, taking her hands in his. "We'll figure this out. You've been out all day. Have you had anything to eat?"

She shook her head, and Walker looked at Mr. Durant. "Could you ask Landon to bring something in?"

Alexander nodded and left, leaving the twins alone.

Mira leaned forward. "Walker, we've found where he's most likely at. And we have a plan for how we can get him and the ambassador out safely. But I need help."

"Anything I can do?" he asked.

"If you can come with us tonight, we need to have people to pose as guards. I already have one. I can disguise myself as another. But it would be better if there were three."

"What if someone sees through your disguise? Wouldn't it be better if there were three men, and you went as you are?"

"I don't have time to find anyon—" she cut herself off as Mr. Durant came back in.

"He'll be bringing in sandwiches shortly." He tilted his head to the side. "What was this that I was hearing about disguises?"

"Just a plan for how to find Byron." Walker chewed on his lip. "You wouldn't happen to be free this evening, would you?"

"Walker!" Mira hissed.

"What time?" Alexander stood next to Walker.

"See, now we have three!" Her brother looked altogether too pleased with himself.

Mira rubbed at her temples. "I'm not sure this is a good idea."

"It's certainly better than you dressing in my clothes again!"

"I beg your pardon?" Alexander's brow furrowed. "A lady of Mira's standing dressed in gentlemans' clothing?"

"Now both of you are just mocking me. Okay! Okay. We're meeting at Palace Court at two. Can you be there?"

"I'll make it a point to." Alexander smiled.

Walker stood. "Don't worry, Mouse. We'll get him back."

October 23, 1888: Early Morning

THE GAS LAMPS FLICKERED ABOVE THEM WITH hardly a hansom cab or coach in sight. The peaceful darkness shrouded them as they hurried to Palace Court. Despite having Walker by her side, Mira felt strange being out and about so early in the morning. Or was it late? In any case, they reached Byron's around half-past one and Mira unlocked the door, ushering Walker inside.

"Now that we're here, will you tell me the plan?" Walker took off his coat and hung it on the hook in the hall.

Mira repositioned her hat and moved into the sitting room. "Not until everyone else arrives."

"I don't see why you couldn't have explained more of it when we were with Mr. Durant. Then we'd have known better what we are getting ourselves into."

"I have my reasons."

It had taken a fair amount of convincing to get Alexander to leave without knowing the whole plan. Part of her felt bad for keeping him in the dark, as they were doing something incredibly dangerous. Despite that, she couldn't shake the feeling that he had a connection with Circe. Aside from that, she was still formulating a plan, even as she sat in her usual spot in Palace Court. Walker started a fire in the grate, which lit the room in a hazy glow.

The minutes passed, and soon, a knock came at the door. Mira rushed to open it, smiling as Fred walked in.

"So, what's this about you being—what was it?—madly in love with me?"

Mira grimaced, ears burning. "I said nothing of the sort!"

"I thought as much, seeing how bad you have it for Byron. But I'm sure the boys will have something to talk about for weeks, nonetheless!"

Fred laughed and made his way over to Walker. "Good to see you again! Are you part of this rescue party as well?"

"So it would seem." Walker shook Fred's hand and clapped him on the back. "It also seems you have a talent for teasing my sister."

"I've had plenty of experience with my own siblings. And you should know by now that she's easy to tease."

Mira blew a strand of hair out of her face. "Why did I ever think it was a good idea to bring the two of you together?"

A knock at the door interrupted Walker's response as Mira moved to answer it. Alexander Durant stepped in, looking rough around the edges, stubble visible on his face.

"Good morning, Miss Blayse!" He hid a yawn behind his hand as he gave her a slight bow.

"Mr. Durant! The others are in the sitting room, and we're waiting for one more."

He nodded to her but stayed in the entry hall.

"You have a plan, then?" He ran his hand along his hat.

"Of course, I do."

"You aren't worried at all? I mean, we are going after kidnappers."

"If you wish to leave, I'm not going to stop you." She stepped towards the door.

His gaze softened, and he leaned forward, stopping her from reaching it. "I'm more worried for you than I am for me. I'll be coming."

"You don't have to worry about me." She glanced up at him through her lashes.

"I'm afraid it's too late for that."

A final knock came at the door. She jumped, heart pounding as she realized how close they were to one another. Clearing her throat, she stepped away from him, feeling his golden eyes following her. She opened the door, and Grace stepped in, looking every bit as impressive as Mira had hoped she would be. Her white dress floated across the ground, embroidered with red and gold flowers on the sleeves, bustle, and part of the bodice. The rest of the bodice matched the thread of the flowers in a dark red hue. Her hat contained several fluffy white feathers and staggered silk triangles. She carried a parasol, even though the sun would not be in attendance. Her blond hair shone from underneath the hat.

"Grace, you look positively stunning!" Mira stepped back to allow her to come in.

"You did say that I needed to make a good impression. I thought this would do."

"It's splendid. Everyone is here now. Let's get started."

Mira led the way to the sitting room, Alexander and Grace behind her. Fred and Walker were in a fit of laughter befit the late (or early) hour. They looked up as the others joined them.

"Do we finally get to know what we're doing?" Walker leaned forward.

"Yes. Listen carefully because we don't have much time." She turned to Grace. "You mentioned that there are specific signals and codewords that Circe uses to communicate with one another."

Grace shifted uncomfortably, looking between the men. "Er . . . yes."

"Do you think you could convince the guards at the warehouse that we were with Circe?"

"Wait, Circe, as in the group that I inadvertently worked with?" Alexander's gaze hardened.

"Yes, Mr. Durant, please keep up. Grace?"

"It's been a while since I've used the signals but it is possible."

"Good. You are going to be our in. Once you have convinced them, you can talk openly with them. Say we've been sent by Nathan Poole—"

"Who's Nathan Poole?" Walker interrupted.

"A member of Circe's inner circle. From my understanding, and correct me if I'm wrong," Mira looked at Grace, "he is part of the guild of Circe that orchestrated this whole abduction. By using his name, we can convince them to let us move the hostages from the warehouse to another location. We can say that the police have discovered the current location, or something to that effect. We'll bring our own guards to help with the move, of course." She gestured to the three men in the room.

"At that point, they should bring us straight to Byron and the ambassador. Hopefully, they can move on their own, and we'll bring them both back here."

Mira stopped pacing and turned towards the small group. Varying expressions stared up at her. Grace worried at her lip. Walker had a mischievous smile. Fred seemed to be going over the plan again in his head, looking for loose ends. Alexander's brow knit together.

After a few moments of silence, Mira sighed. "Any questions?"

Alexander raised his hand. "What if they don't believe we're with Circe?"

Fred nodded. "That was a concern that I had. Also, do we know how many guards we'll be dealing with?"

Mira's stomach sank. "I know there is a lot that can go wrong, but the longer we wait, the less likely we'll get the ambassador out before it's too late. We have to rescue them before tomorrow evening. Otherwise, the ambassador will not make it to Constantinople in time to sign the treaty. And I can't see how they won't believe we're with Circe. We know the signals, we'll mention Nathan Poole, and we know exactly where they are being held. If the police don't know where they are yet, barring you of course, Fred, then how would we know unless we were part of them?"

"You really think this will work?" Grace said, voice small as a reed.

"It has to. Are all of you in?"

Her gaze spread out across the group as each nodded their affirmation in turn. Alexander was the last, and he stood next to her.

"No time like the present," he said. "Shall we get going?"

THEY FOUND A LONE COACH DRIVER WITH enough seats for them. Mira convinced him to take them down to the docks at Butler's wharf, and once they reached their destination, she paid him to stay put. From there, they made their way down the street towards the large building that housed the warehouse complex. The gas lights were few and far between, but Mira could still make out the few men that were leaning against the walls. They muttered amongst themselves, a small red glow at each of their fingertips. The rank smell of cheap cigarettes affronted Mira's senses, and she bit back a cough as Grace took the lead. She approached one of them, carrying her parasol closed over her right shoulder.

"Good evening, Miss," one of the men said with a rough accent. He stepped forward and tipped his hat into his hand.

"It is a good evening, isn't it?" She hooked the parasol handle on one of her arms and adjusted her right glove.

The man dusted off the crown of the hat. "You're out and about quite late."

Grace nodded, wringing the fabric of the parasol with her left hand. "Darkness is better for discretion."

"Right you are." The man placed the hat back on his head and ran a finger along the brim. "Who sent you?"

"Mr. Poole."

The man took a step back. "So, he's decided then?"

Grace swallowed. "That is none of your concern."

A second man came forward. "Isn't it though, Charlie? We was only supposed to get the one, but we has two now. It's a lot harder to keep two, you know."

"Hush now, Jerry. Let me talk," the first man, Charlie, said, eying the rest of the group. "If you aren't here to give us an answer, what are you here for?"

"I never said I didn't have your answer. We're here to move them to another location. Our police informant sent word that they've narrowed it down to the wharf. We need to move them tonight, or else the whole thing will be ruined."

The men shared a look before turning back to Grace.

"Where are you moving them?" Jerry asked.

Grace's lips drew up into a thin smile. "You don't need to worry about that. Just bring us to them, and we'll handle it from here."

Jerry shrugged at Charlie, who motioned for them to follow him. He took them to a wide door and led them into the main warehouse. Moonlight streamed in from the large windows, casting eerie shadows around the crates. It illuminated the dust that clung to the air and the chains and hooks that hung down from the ceiling. Charlie led them to a room off to the side, which he unlocked before light-ing some of the gas lights within. It seemed like an office space of some sort, with a desk covered in papers and some sort of filing system. Another door stood at the back of the room behind the desk.

Charlie moved to this door next, and pulled out a different key, unlocking and opening it. He took a step in, then hesi-tated, turning back towards them.

"They're in here. Maybe just the gents should come in to move them. Ain't really a pretty sight for you ladies."

"You can't possibly know what I've seen," Mira said, moving past him and into the room, Grace right behind her.

She schooled her expression upon seeing them. The ambas-sador lay on a cot against the far wall, presumably asleep. Byron drooped in a chair at the center, limbs tied tight behind him. His complexion matched the moonlight they had just left, pale and lifeless. She may have thought he was dead until she caught sight of the subtle movement of his chest. Up and down. They had taken his jacket and vest, leaving him in his marred and dirty shirt. It took every inch of willpower not to move to his side immediately.

Charlie moved over to the ambassador, taking a pair of manacles out of his pocket, and shaking the poor man awake.

"Up you get, it's time to move."

The ambassador groaned before sitting up, blinking at the light coming from the office. Charlie snapped the manacles on him and handed Walker the key. Mira turned away in case he recognized her and gave the whole thing away.

"Hey, Charlie?" Jerry said from the office doorway. "There's someone else here to see you."

"They part of the club?"

"Haven't done the signals yet. I always get it wrong. Thought I'd grab you instead."

"Alright. You folks good to get them ready to leave?"

"Of course." Mr. Durant stepped into the room.

Charlie nodded and moved to leave, before stopping next to Byron.

"Don't bother trying to wake this one. He was giving us trouble, so we had to drug him. Gave him a bit of laudanum a while ago and hasn't been a problem since."

With that, he left the room. Mira moved over to Byron immediately, almost crashing into Grace as they tried to untie him. The ambassador blustered behind them as Walker tried to calm him down.

"Here, this will be faster," Fred said, taking out a knife and cutting through the restraints.

Once free, Byron lolled over in a dead weight and Mira tried to catch him. Alexander stepped in, pulling him back against the chair again. With his head repositioned, Mira could see the start of a bruise on his face, as well as some blood coming from a split lip that had dripped onto his shirt.

"Oh, Byron . . . "

Fred moved over to the office door, peeking his head out, while Mira turned her attention to the ambassador.

"Sir, we've come to get you out of here. But we need you to play along. We've told those men that we're transferring you somewhere else."

"Miss Blayse? But how?"

"I'll explain everything, but not now, Ambassador. Can you walk?"

"Certainly. But can you tell me what they've done with Katherine and our children?"

"They are perfectly safe."

The ambassador's shoulders relaxed, and Mira glanced at her brother.

"Walker, if you'll stay by his side?"

Her twin nodded, and she moved back to Byron. Grace dabbed at the blood with a handkerchief.

Mira glanced up at Alexander. "Do you think you can carry him on your own?"

"Are you questioning my strength?" A challenging glint came to his eye.

"Not at all."

"I think we may have a bit of a complication," Fred hissed back to them from the door.

"What kind of complication?" Grace looked up, eyes widening with fear.

"Just that we need to go now. Come on."

He came into the room again and helped Alexander lift Byron up. As they approached the door, Jerry blocked it.

"Who did you say sent you lot, again?"

Grace stood straight as a ramrod. "Nathan Poole."

"Strange. Because he's outside now. So, who's the faker, eh?" Jerry narrowed his eyes.

Mira glanced down, trying to think of a lie. "Well, you see, we—"

A loud crack interrupted her futile ramblings as Fred stepped forward, thrust his elbow into Jerry's chin, and punched him in the face. Jerry crumpled in an instant.

She looked up at Grace, mirroring her shocked expression as Fred and Walker moved Jerry into the back room and locked it.

"Alright then. Time to go." Fred led the way out of the room, running to the nearest stack of crates, and gesturing for them to follow.

As the last of them hid behind the crate, Fred continued to the next, looking for the closest exit. Shouting and footsteps echoed through the warehouse as Jerry was presumably discovered and the prisoners were not.

Mira's breath caught in her throat as she tried to stay as silent as possible. After the first dozen crates, Alexander and Fred switched places, with Fred carrying Byron and Alexander scouting. Walker unlocked Sir William's manacles for better movement. They moved closer and closer to the front of the warehouse and freedom. As they stopped behind another crate, Alexander motioned for them to stop and regroup.

Circling around, he whispered, "There's a second door to the outside about twenty yards away. There isn't much cover, so we'll need to run. Fred, you'll need the most time to run, so you get a head start. I'll take up the rear in case anything goes wrong."

They settled into position, with Fred carrying Byron at the front, followed by Sir William, Walker, Grace, Mira, and finally Alexander at the back. Each person disappeared around the corner of the crate in turn. Alexander tapped her on the shoulder.

"I'm going to see how close they are. Perhaps throw these," he lifted the manacles, "as a diversion. You keep running. If I'm not at the coach five minutes after you get there, then leave without me, okay?"

"What?"

Alexander gave her a grin, squeezed her hand, and disappeared. Taking a breath, Mira peeked around the corner just as the edge of Grace's skirt slipped through the open doorway. Her turn now.

As she picked up her skirt to run, it caught on a chain. She collapsed in a heap of fabric, ankle twisting. A small shout escaped her lips, and she bit down on her finger to quell the pain.

"Did you hear that? They're over here!" Charlie's voice rang out, too close for comfort.

She pulled herself behind the crate again, trying to stay in the shadow. Thinking fast, she pulled a hatpin out, and listened. When she didn't hear anything else, she stood, testing her ankle. A twinge of pain shot up her leg. Twenty yards wasn't that much, was it? She steeled herself and moved around the side of the crate.

Her vision whipped around as someone twisted her arm behind her back and held her in place.

"There now, girlie. Stop squirming."

Charlie pulled her closer to him and she felt his breath on the back of her neck. Mira didn't think twice as she stabbed the hatpin into his leg as hard as she could. He howled in pain and let go of her, stumbling back into the crate. Mira picked up her skirts to run again, but Charlie grabbed her bad ankle and pulled her down.

"That's enough." A new form came around the corner, shrouded in shadows.

He wrenched Mira to her feet, keeping a firm hand on her wrist. As he came into the dusty moonlight, she recognized him as the man from Harding's office.

"Good evening. My name is Mr. Poole. And who might you be?"

"Unhand me this instant," she ground out, seething.

He glanced her up and down. "You seem familiar. Have we met before?"

She tried to pull free, but he twisted her around, pulling a knife to her neck. She stilled.

"That's better. Now, perhaps I don't need a name. But I need to know where the others went, and who sent you."

Mira kept her silence, desperate to think of a way out.

"I'm afraid if you won't tell me, I'll leave you to Charles here, and he's much less accommodating."

Charlie was recovering from the fashion statement in his leg, but leered at her from his position on the ground, nonetheless.

"So, let's try it again." His lips brushed against her ear. "Where did they go, and who sent you?"

Mira's shoulders tightened, and she swallowed, feeling the knife press closer.

The clamorous boom of crates crashing to the ground and

breaking apart caused both of them to jolt. Mr. Poole loosened his hold as he turned towards the sound. It was enough for Mira to elbow him, which caused him to drop her entirely. A moment later, Alexander came careening into Mr. Poole, using a chain and the manacles to swing down and kick him squarely in the jaw. Mr. Poole tumbled to the floor with a crash. Alexander jumped off, pulled her to standing and ran, keeping her hand in his. Halfway to the door, she stumbled, and he slowed to loop her arm around his neck and pick her up over his shoulder. She held on for dear life as he rushed outside and down another alleyway. Once they were relatively safe, he set her down.

"What happened to you running without me?" he said, anger and worry tinging his features.

She winced, and his expression softened.

"Are you hurt?" His hands ghosted over her shoulders as he looked her over for injuries before his gaze settled on her eyes.

"Just my ankle. My dress caught on a chain and—"

She cut off her words as he captured her in a kiss. Time stopped as Mira tried to comprehend his lips on hers. She gasped as his hands found the small of her back, pulling her closer. His stubble scratched her cheek as his soft lips drew her in. Her nose filled with the scent of lavender and citrus, and she relaxed in his arms. Her knees wobbled as he pulled away just as suddenly, eyes wide as he dropped her like a burning match.

"I'm sorry, I-I . . ." he stuttered, flustered and red.

Mira's head spun, and she struggled to regain her balance, stomach fluttering. Her hand strayed to her lips.

"You kissed me." Her voice slurred, entirely confused and enamored and upset and besotted.

"It's just you were . . . and the knife . . ." He looked around for any of the guards. "I can't apologize enough, Miss Blayse. But we must get out of here."

He picked her up again, moving towards the coach. His

strong arms wrapped around her, and she kept her head down, eyes most certainly not straying to his lips several times. The wind pulled at her hair as he picked up speed. He slowed as they came near the coach.

"There you are!" Walker said, moving over.

Alexander let her down to the ground, careful of her foot. She couldn't help but stare at him, feeling lost at the lack of contact, only coming out of her daze as Walker took her arm.

"What happened?"

She shook her head. "I'll tell you later. Where are the others?"

"Byron's in the cab with the ambassador and Miss Trimbell," Fred said, coming over. "I think we should change our plans. Circe knows where Byron lives, and they might try to follow us there."

"Good point," Alexander said, frowning.

"We can bring him to his brother in Bolton Street. They likely don't know about him, and they won't know to follow us there," Fred said.

"There's not enough room for all of us." Alexander avoided Mira's gaze. "I can stay behind and try to throw them off our path even more."

"You're injured," Fred said, and Mira noticed a spot of red seeping through Alexander's sleeve.

"It's really not that bad."

Fred shook his head. "I'll stay behind to divert them and then head back to my place. That way all of you can get looked after. I'll come to Bolton at first light."

"Thank you, Fred. Please be careful," Mira said.

"Careful? Never knew him." Fred smirked and ran off, presumably to create a diversion.

Mira purposely ignored Alexander and opened the carriage door. Grace sat on the far side of the back-facing seat, Byron slumped onto her. The ambassador sat across from Grace in the front-facing seat. Considering her options, Mira stepped in and settled next to Byron.

"How is he doing? Has he stirred at all?" she whispered to Grace.

"Not at all. I'm a bit worried."

Walker and Alexander climbed in next, and the cab jostled on the journey to Bolton Street. They let out a combined sigh of relief, yet Mira's stomach roiled with confusion and butterflies. Her whole body tingled from head to toe. She pushed the memory of the kiss away and focused on their next steps. They were all out and safe. If they could just get to Castel's, everything would be fine. She glanced over at Byron, still ghastly and pale. His hair stuck to his forehead, sticky with sweat. She noted Grace held his hand in hers. Somehow, she wasn't quite so jealous.

As the cab traveled over a hole in the road, Alexander's legs bumped into hers. She turned towards him, and he looked down. After a moment, he cleared his throat.

"How's your ankle?"

"I'm not feeling it now." She averted her gaze.

"What happened with your ankle?" Walker asked.

"I fell and twisted it."

"Are you hurt anywhere else?" Walker leaned forward.

"I'm perfectly fine. Just tired, that's all. I'm certainly not bleeding." She gave a pointed look to Alexander.

"It was only a nick."

"Still."

They settled back in silence, the adrenaline from the evening wearing off bit by bit, but the emotions still swirling within her.

THE DRIVER PULLED UP AT NUMBER 12 Bolton Street. Alexander helped Mira out and she limped to the door. The butler answered after a few minutes, wearing his nightclothes.

"May I help you?"

"Please wake Mr. Sherard. His brother has been injured. We'll be bringing him in, along with the ambassador."

He looked past her to where Walker and the ambassador carried Byron out of the cab while Grace hovered around them. The butler stepped to the side.

"The first guest room is up the stairs to the left. I'll fetch Mr. Sherard."

They carried Byron up the stairs and set him on the bed in the guest room. The men helped to settle him in the bed, and Grace removed his shoes. Castel rushed in soon after, rubbing the sleep from his eyes.

"What the devil is going on?"

"We found them, and with a day to spare. We thought it would be safer for them here than at Palace Court," Mira said.

Castel furrowed his brow.

The ambassador stepped forward. "Mr. Sherard, thank you for orchestrating a search party so quickly. I'm afraid it's quite late though, and I know if I'm exhausted having had some sleep this evening, these young people must be dead on their feet. Is it possible we could rely on your hospitality for the rest of the evening?"

Castel straightened with a nod and turned to his butler. "Davies, if you could make the arrangements?" He paused and glanced at Alexander's arm. "But first, if you'll find some medical supplies?"

The butler nodded and left. Castel turned to them again. "If you'll all wait in the sitting room, we'll get everything ready for you. Miss Blayse, if you'll stay a moment?"

Walker and Alexander left first. Grace hovered for a moment, then followed. Castel stood next to Mira, following her gaze to Byron's face.

"Where were they?"

"Butler's Wharf." She rubbed at her arms. "They had them in a warehouse."

"What happened to him?"

"They drugged him with laudanum. I'm not sure when it will wear off."

Castel nodded. "I had hoped he wouldn't end up here like this again." He walked back towards the door and paused. "I seem to have underestimated you, Miss Blayse. I'll be sure to remedy that in the future."

Mira nodded as he left the room, then turned her attention back to her detective. Her stomach twisted in knots of betrayal, roiling in confusion from the kiss while her heart still leapt at seeing Byron safe and sound. She gently brushed the hair off of his forehead and adjusted the pillow underneath his head. Grace had wiped up most of the blood from his split lip, but Mira went to the dressing table and wetted a cloth, nonetheless. She cleaned up the remaining blood and dabbed at his forehead, trying to clear away the sweat and grime. When he didn't stir, she sighed, and set the rag on the side table.

"Please wake up soon, Byron." She kissed his forehead and felt a spark run through her before she went down to find the others.

HER ANKLE TWINGED AS SHE CAME DOWN the steps, and she was glad to find an armchair again once she made it to the sitting room. She passed Davies as he left the room, having delivered the medical supplies. Walker was helping Alexander with his arm. Grace sat, straight as a ramrod. Did she always have to be so graceful? Mira bit back a groan and sat up to be more ladylike to match.

"That's fine! It'll heal just the way it is," Alexander said, wincing as Walker dabbed at his cut with iodine.

"Just a bit more and we'll wrap it up. Mira, can you grab that bandage?"

Mira went to stand, but Grace beat her to it. "Wouldn't want you to injure your ankle more."

"I can walk on it," Mira said, but stayed seated just the same.

"Why are you trying to kill me?" Alexander gritted his teeth.

"It's quite the opposite, in fact. If this got infected, it could kill you. How did you manage this kind of a cut, anyway?"

"I had a run in with a knife. Or rather, the knife had a run in with me."

"A knife?" Grace paled.

"Don't ask." Mira gave up on being ladylike and slumped back in the chair as best as she could.

Walker gave a final tug on Alexander's bandage and moved to Mira, kneeling in front of her.

"Which ankle?"

"The right one."

He nodded, and carefully unbuttoned her shoe, slipping it off. He held her foot in both of his hands for a moment, then frowned, turning to the others.

"Do either of you know how to tell if an ankle is broken?"

Alexander hesitated, gaze flitting to Mira's expression before he nodded.

"I can look at it. If that's alright with you, Miss Blayse."

She bit her lip and gave a sharp nod. Alexander took Walker's place. She could feel the warmth of his hands through her stockings. A familiar flush came to her cheeks, and she looked away.

"I'm not feeling any bones out of place." He moved one of his hands up to her ankle. "Let me know if this hurts at all."

She flinched back as he rotated her foot and a spike of pain rushed up her leg. "Just a bit."

"I don't think it's broken. But you certainly bruised it."

He looked up at her, and her traitorous heart skipped a beat.

"You'll want to stay off of it as much as possible for a day, at least."

"Since when were you a doctor, Durant?" Walker cleaned up the medical supplies.

"I'm only doing what I've seen doctors do for ankles in the past. It still may be a good idea to have an actual physician look you over." Alexander stayed kneeling at her feet. "Do you want the shoe on, or off?"

"Off, I would think," Mira said.

He nodded and stood as Davies returned.

"Your rooms are prepared, if you'll follow me."

Alexander insisted on carrying her up to her room. Once they reached it and the others moved on, she understood why. He set her down in a chair and stepped back.

"I must apologize once again. I wish I could say that I didn't know what got into me, but that would be a lie. Honestly, Miss Blayse, I try to keep up this facade of ambivalence, but today . . ." He looked down. "I don't know if I've ever been more terrified in my entire life. To see that knife at your throat . . ."

Mira's hand moved up to her neck of its own accord.

"I should never have kissed you, especially considering your feelings for Byron, and the situation. Please forgive me."

Before she could respond, he fled out the door, leaving Mira with a throbbing ankle, and a confused heart.

October 23, 1888:
Late Morning

To say that Mira was sore when she woke would be an understatement. She let out a soft moan and pushed herself up to sit against the headboard. Her overgarments, corset, and bustle lay in an untidy heap on a chair, abandoned in an attempt to sleep more comfortably. She grimaced at the thought of having to get dressed again, especially since some of the skirts were torn and dirty. Despite the overall ache throughout her body, her ankle felt quite a bit better. Until she tried to get it into her boot, that is.

By the time she was dressed and somewhat presentable, it was almost eleven. Would Cyrus even notice that she and Walker were missing? Wincing, she made her way down to Byron's room to check on him. She knocked, and upon hearing nothing, she gave the door a gentle nudge, easing it open.

A bit of color graced Byron's cheeks as he lay sleeping. His messy hair still clung to his forehead. His stubble had darkened, and his shirt seemed dirtier in the morning light. But his chest moved routinely up and down. She smiled and sat on the edge of the bed, taking his hand in hers. The door opened behind her, but she didn't turn. Grace came around the bed and sat on the opposite side.

"They're serving a late breakfast downstairs. I can stay with him."

Mira looked between her and Byron, then nodded. She gave his hand a light squeeze, a promise that she'd be back soon.

Walker and Alexander sat at the table with half-eaten plates in front of them. Fred paced by the window and Mira felt a wave of relief wash over her that he made it home safe. As she limped in, Alexander jumped up and moved to her side. The dreaded butterflies returned.

"Should you be on that foot?" He supported her to the table.

"It's fine! Just a bit sore."

She settled herself into the seat and served herself. Alexander sat next to her, and Fred moved closer to the table.

"I was right about not going back to Palace Court. I passed by there last night on my way home. There were plenty of people loitering about." Fred leaned over the back of a chair. "I stopped by the Yard this morning and let everyone know we found the ambassador and Constantine."

"Oh, where is the ambassador?"

"Castel left with him early this morning. They needed to adjust the plans for his departure, and he wished to meet with his wife and children as soon as possible," Walker said.

Mira nodded and took another bite of breakfast. Her stomach grumbled, hungrier than she expected.

"How's Byron?" Fred asked, finally sitting down.

"Still asleep. I'm afraid he was injured somehow. Along with the laudanum, he's having trouble waking up."

"I hope it wasn't another blow to the head." Fred frowned. "Wouldn't want his memory to get any worse."

Mira nodded and remembered that she needed to pick up his journal from Palace Court. He'd need it once he was awake. Fred cleared his throat and stood.

"I ought to get back to the police station. Keep me updated on him, will you?" His eyes pleaded, and Mira nodded.

With Fred gone, an uncomfortable silence fell over the remaining three, a particular tension between Mira and Alexander. Walker pushed his plate out and looked at the two of them.

"I ought to go as well. Uncle is probably worried sick about us, and I'm guessing you'll be wanting to stay here for the time being, eh Mouse?"

"For now, yes." She fidgeted with her napkin. "Do you have to leave?"

"How long do you want your lecture to be?" He raised an eyebrow.

She sighed. "You'd better leave, then."

Walker nodded. "Take care of her for me, will you Durant?"

"I'll be sure to keep her out of trouble."

With that, Mira was alone with Alexander once more. She focused on her breakfast, feeling entirely out of place. After a moment, he cleared his throat.

"Did you sleep well?" His heavy gaze fell on her features, and she resisted the urge to squirm.

"Enough. And you?"

"About the same."

"Good."

The silence hung between them, thick and intricate like the tapestry on the dining room wall. Mira tucked a stray piece of hair behind her ear, her pulse in her throat.

"I ought to check on Byron." She stood and limped out of the room, leaving her unfinished plate behind.

Her heart leapt as she approached Byron's room, the soft rumblings of his voice reverberating down the hall. The door stood ajar, and she moved to open it further, but paused as she heard the conversation inside.

"You're my guardian angel once more, Grace." Byron's voice sounded hoarse and low.

"Hush now, save your breath," Grace said, soft and loving.

Mira stood frozen outside the door.

"But I have to thank you. I don't know how you found us or—" A coughing fit cut off his words.

"You have more than just me to thank for that. The plan was entirely Mira's."

"Who?"

"Your secretary?"

"I don't have a secre—"

Mira turned on her heel, unable to hear anymore. She stumbled back to the stairs, moving too fast for her ankle, holding her tears at bay. Her insecurities came rushing back, and she didn't care to give him the benefit of the doubt. Here she was, feeling guilty about Alexander kissing her, while Byron still didn't remember her. And more importantly, he didn't need her anymore. She had half a mind to go straight to Palace Court and tear herself out of his written memory, burning every page with any mention of her. But what would that do, other than hurt him more?

She made it to the bottom of the stairs before a few tears slipped out. Would it be hurting him? If he never remembered her? Would it matter? She went to the sitting room, hoping to compose herself and rest her foot again, but found Alexander there reading instead. As she turned to go back to her own room, he looked up.

"Mira?"

And with that simple utterance of her name, not forgotten, and entirely informal, she burst into tears on the spot. He came to her side in an instant, offering her a handkerchief, which she dabbed at her eyes.

"What happened? Are you unwell?"

She tried to form a sentence several times, but burst into a new round of tears each time she opened her mouth. Eventually she settled on shaking her head. He led her to a chair and eased her into it, then rubbed his hands anxiously.

"Do you need some water? Shall I fetch Walker?"

She shook her head again, face wet and hot, while Alexander panicked.

"Is there nothing I can do whatsoever?"

"I'm sorry," she squeaked out between gulping breaths.

"What are you doing, apologizing? I'm the one who is utterly and completely useless!"

A laugh bubbled up amongst the tears and she looked up at him. "You aren't useless."

"Well, that's a lie if I've heard one." He continued to pace, throwing his hands up. "I have no idea what to do in this situation!"

Another laugh followed the first, and soon she was laughing more than crying. After a few calming breaths, she tried to compose herself again.

"I'm sorry about that. I-I normally don't cry like that in public."

"Perfectly alright. It's just me. Nothing to be ashamed about. But whatever is the matter?" He sat beside her.

Mira clutched at the fabric of the handkerchief, grounding herself.

"It's silly."

"To cause you to cry? Mira, I didn't even see you cry when they arrested your uncle. Or when we found Mr. Sutherland dead."

"I've been holding it all in." She shook her head. "It's just, I overheard Grace and Byron a moment ago and . . ." She felt the pressure behind her eyes building again, and she closed them, leaning her head back. "He's not going to remember me, is he?"

"We don't know that for certain."

She took a deep breath. "But I can't count on it. I can't trust that from one day to the next, he won't decide that he's in love with someone else. What if he only believes that because it's what his journal tells him? Hearing them just barely, there's something there. And she loves him. What if I'm in the way?"

Alexander sat silent for a moment, pensive. He cocked his head.

"What do you want, Mira?"

"What?" she stuttered, startled at the frankness of his tone.

"You can't change whether he remembers you. But you can change whether you want to continue this dance of memory with him, dance on your own, or" —he drew out the word and smirked— "switch partners."

She rolled her eyes at him, and he sobered again. "There is the possibility that he loves you, and that in the future he will remember you." He took her hand in his. "But are you willing to get from here to there when that isn't a certainty? Do you love him that much?"

"I don't know." Her voice sounded hollow to her ears.

They sat in silence for a few minutes. The ticking of the clock grinding on Mira's ears. A servant of time, not memory. She hadn't considered the possibility of leaving. Could she do it? Knowing how much she loved him, even now as her heart tore itself to shreds? How many times could she sew it back together before it wouldn't beat? She glanced up at Alexander, his hazel eyes caring, deep, and warm. She relaxed.

"Can you take me home?" she whispered.

"I'll go call for a cab now." He squeezed her hand as he stood to leave.

Once he acquired a cab, Alexander informed the butler that they were leaving, and escorted her outside. He helped her into the seat, careful of her injury, and settled in beside her. Mira tried to smooth out her skirts. In this state, she was sure to get a lecture from her uncle. Somehow, that comforted her, and she focused on that rather than the turmoil brewing within her.

At Swan Walk, Cyrus came out to meet them, a frenzy of worry.

"Goodness, child! Look at the state of you!"

"I know, Uncle." Mira limped up the steps, Alexander at her side. "I'll wash up as soon as I'm able."

Alexander continued to follow as Cyrus ushered her into the house, but stayed in the entryway.

"Come in, Mr. Durant, and make yourself comfortable in the sitting room!" Cyrus blustered. "I'll be in after I see Mira up to her room."

"If I may, sir, she's injured her ankle. Perhaps you can retrieve some items and she can change and freshen up in another room without navigating the stairs?"

Cyrus whirled on her. "Why didn't you say something, Mira?"

"I . . . well . . ."

"Don't worry, I'll take care of it!" Walker called from up the stairs. His footsteps echoed down the stairwell.

"You can wash up in my study. Come now." Cyrus guided her in that direction and called over his shoulder, "Be with you in a moment, Mr. Durant!"

The lecture she expected didn't occur when they reached the study. Instead, he sat her in a chair and left for a moment, returning with a basin, mirror, and a pitcher of water. Walker came in soon after, carrying her slippers and a decorative wrapper. Mira stared at it a moment, not recognizing it at first. She hadn't worn a wrapper in months, as she hadn't spent much time at home at all since meeting Byron. Of course, it was entirely against society norms to wear one so late in the day, and with Mr. Durant, a gentleman, visiting, it was unheard of. Then again, it would be more comfortable than just about any other gown she owned. She glanced at her uncle, who nodded his approval.

"Good thinking, Walker," Cyrus said.

Mira blinked at his reaction, and he turned to her.

"Will you need any help? I can call for the parlormaid."

"No, I should be fine. Now, shoo."

Uncle and brother thus banished, and door locked, she set to work cleaning herself up. A glance at the mirror showed the damage done by her tears. It was a wonder she hadn't frightened Mr. Durant off. Her curls hung in knots. She rinsed her face in the basin, did what she could with her hair, and removed her damaged gown, bustle, and second petticoat. From there, she freed her aching feet from her boots and sat for a moment to give her ankle a break.

She blessed Walker when she realized that the particular wrapper he'd grabbed closed all the way in the front. She didn't want to send someone to get her cleaner, more decorative petticoats at this point. The cool silk felt amazing on her skin and reminded her of how tired she was. Perhaps after a nap, she'd feel better. After all, they were up for half the night trying to save Byron and the ambassador. But Alexander was waiting for her, and after all of his help, she couldn't just leave him there, could she? So, she slid into her slippers, set her abandoned clothing items on a chair, and went to find the men in the sitting room.

They had moved a chaise in from the parlor, which she gravitated to, bringing her injured foot up to rest.

"I can't thank you all enough," she said, not feeling the least bit of remorse for reclining a smidge.

"I'm just glad you're safe. I was out of my mind this morning when I realized the two of you were missing." Cyrus leaned against the mantel, puffing his pipe. "Thank you for bringing her home again, Mr. Durant."

"It was my pleasure; I can assure you." He suppressed a yawn. "Pardon me, but it would seem the late evening is catching up to me. Perhaps it is time to bring myself home."

Mira went to stand, but Alexander held a hand out. "I'll come back to check on you again tomorrow, Miss Blayse." He gave a slight bow, and Cyrus followed him out.

Walker sat on the bit of chaise that Mira didn't occupy.

"He really likes you, you know."

"Please, not now," she whispered, heart fit to burst again.

"Did something happen?" Walker frowned.

"No," she lied. "I just—not now."

"Right. Byron's still recovering. You must be worried."

She averted her gaze. "He was awake when I left. I'm sure he'll be fine."

Walker evidently missed the tone of her voice as he responded with, "That's good to hear," and stood to move over to another chair.

Landon came in with a small bag.

"I heard you hurt your ankle, Miss."

"It's just sore."

"Nonetheless, it would be best if we did something with it. Can you take off your slipper and stocking while I prepare something for it?"

Mira nodded while Landon mixed some sort of reddish-brown paste in a bowl with some water.

"What is that?" Walker leaned in.

"A mixture of clay and water."

"Mud? Really?" Mira sat back as Landon smeared the substance on her ankle.

"It should take down the swelling."

He wrapped it up tight in clean strips of fabric and replaced her slipper.

"You can wash it off tonight and see how it does tomorrow morning."

"Thank you, Landon."

His eyes twinkled as he packed up his things and left the room. "Of course."

Walker shifted in his seat. A few moments later, he stood again, messing with his hands.

"You don't have to stay here, you know," Mira said, raising an eyebrow.

"I don't? I mean, of course, I don't. I just . . . I feel like I ought to talk to Liza—er—Miss Renaldi. But here you are with a twisted ankle and—"

"Go. I'm perfectly fine here."

He grinned. "I'll send my regards!" Leaning over, he gave her a kiss on the forehead and left the room.

Mira sighed. Now that no one fussed over her, she couldn't distract herself. The fears of him only loving her because she reminded him of Grace danced in her mind's eye. How could she have seen the conversation between Byron and Grace as anything but loving? She over-examined memories of every interaction that could be considered the least bit romantic.

Right after their fight with Molly and her thugs, she wasn't sure what her feelings for Byron were. They had just discovered the full extent of her parents' murder, and it overwhelmed her. She had been so certain that he was in love with her, though. That surety was a lifeline that brought her closer and closer to him until she couldn't imagine not being in love with him. And yet the moment Grace came into the picture, the line had snapped, and it left her floundering. She finally knew her own feelings but couldn't determine if his were real or only illusions.

Yet did she really know her own feelings? When Alexander kissed her, it was like a fire, passionate and burning. If she didn't care for him at all, would she still be reeling from it? Her feelings for both men were confusing and muddled. Emotions and logic unable to come to any conclusion whatsoever.

"Mira, are you crying?"

She brought a hand to her face, surprised at the wetness, and turned to see her uncle in the doorway. He pulled a chair over and sat by her, passing her a handkerchief.

"What's happened?" he asked, gentle and soft.

"Have you ever been in love?" Her voice barely above a whisper.

Cyrus sat back for a moment, then nodded.

"I have. There was a woman I met while in India. The daughter of someone working for the East India Company. Unfortunately, she was in love with another man."

Ice filled Mira's chest, and she sat up further. "Did it ever feel like she loved you?"

"No, she was forthwith from the start."

Mira looked away, and Cyrus leaned forward again.

"You're in love, aren't you Mira?"

She swallowed, thinking that perhaps she was in love twice-over. "I'm surprised you didn't know."

"I had an inkling. Perhaps I let myself entertain the idea once I knew he was a Sherard."

She gave a halfhearted laugh and leaned back. "He doesn't love me, though."

"Are you quite certain of that fact?"

She turned towards him again. "Uncle, how can he love someone he doesn't remember?"

"I'm not sure. The human brain is a complex and mysterious thing, and so are memories. But the heart is even more unpredictable. Does the heart need the head to feel?"

"I don't know."

"Perhaps you need some time away from him. Even if I don't mind the two of you courting," he gave her a pointed look, "I'd rather you do it properly. At the moment, you're spending too much time together. How are you to understand your feelings when you never have time to think on them alone? Without his influence?"

"You may be right. After all, he doesn't need me anymore." A bitter tone crept into her voice.

"What do you mean? I thought you helped with his memory?"

"He's gaining bits and pieces of it back. Never me, mind you, but the day-to-day events and things. He doesn't need me to keep track of things."

"Then this is the perfect opportunity to take some time away. Resign as his secretary, and if he actually loves you, he will make it a point to court you. And in the meantime, you can determine if you actually love him."

"But I do!"

"Yes. But I also see the way you look at Mr. Durant, and the way he regards you. In either case, I approve of your decision."

Mira's cheeks flushed, head swimming in uncertainty. He gave her a soft smile and kissed her forehead.

"Do you want me to get your sketchbook and watercolors? Or a book? After all, I'm not letting you off that couch until bed."

Mira groaned. "It's not that bad!"

"And it won't get worse. Do you want something to do, or not?"

"Watercolors, please."

He nodded and left the room, leaving Mira's gut churning in knots. What was she to do?

October 24, 1888

*A*FTER HER CONFINEMENT TO THE SITTING ROOM the day before, Mira's energy burst at the seams, determined to get out. Especially after coming to a decision about the whole Byron situation. Her uncle was right for a change. She needed some distance to figure things out. And perhaps Byron did too. But for that to happen, she needed to resign. Seeing him every day and having him forget every day taxed her emotions. And since he clearly remembered things without her—she took a deep breath and re-centered herself, pinning the last of her hair up—then he didn't need her to be his secretary.

Testing her foot for the umpteenth time that morning, she found she could walk with only a slight ache. Landon's mud did wonders, and she could even fit into her boot with little discomfort. And despite growing bored with reading, painting, and playing cards the day before, resting it had done her some good. She chewed on her lip. Before meeting Byron, she could happily spend an entire day in leisure. Had he ruined those activities for her? They weren't quite as exciting as scouting out crime scenes and chasing leads. Would she be able to give it all up? Perhaps she shouldn't resign so quickly.

No! She shook her doubt away. She made a decision, and she was sticking to it! Just as soon as she sneaked past her uncle.

She crept down the steps, careful to avoid the ones that were sure to squeak, and slowed near his room. But just as she reached the bottom step, a knock came at the door. Dash it all! She slipped into the parlor, hoping Landon didn't see her.

Muffled voices came through the wall, and Mira moved to the window to try to make out who was at the door. She only caught a glimpse of the side of his coat, but that coat seemed awfully familiar. Landon opened the parlor door and gave her an accusatory glance at seeing her walking dress.

"Going out, were we?"

"Just for a short walk, and my ankle doesn't hurt in the slightest!" She took a step forward to demonstrate. "And how did you know I was in here?"

"You forget that I know your tricks when you are ill or injured, young lady." He raised a brow at her. "Luckily for you, you have a visitor. Shall I show Mr. Constantine in?"

Her eyes widened. "He's here?"

"I wouldn't suggest it if he weren't, Miss." A small smile formed on his face.

"But he was—he's alright?"

"He seemed to be in good enough spirits. Shall I leave him on the doorstep?"

"No, please." She composed herself, hand flitting up to check her hair. "Let him come in."

Landon nodded and moved back to the entryway. Soon enough, Byron burst in. Relief swept over her, seeing him up and about, but her insides still tied themselves in knots.

"Mira!" His eyes lit up, and he gave her a grin, but somehow his sunshine didn't touch her.

"Good morning, Byron." She moved to the window.

"Are you well? I heard you hurt your ankle and—"

"I'm perfectly fine."

"Oh. Good. I couldn't help but worry, because once I read my journal, I realized you weren't there, and Grace tried to explain, but" —he sucked in a breath— "I had to see you."

A warmth spread over her, and she attempted to squash it down. "I needed to come home, and you know how my uncle worries."

"Well, the prime minister has asked us to come and explain what happened, and the meeting is at ten." He looked her over. "Were you on your way to Palace Court?"

"Bolton actually. I assumed you'd still be on bedrest."

"Oh, I've slept far too much in my life. But brilliant! That means we can be off, then!"

"To the prime minister?"

"Exactly."

He whirled around and left the room. Mira stood stunned. This was not how the morning was supposed to go. She attempted to speed after him, ankle protesting, but Byron was already out the door.

"Byron! Wait a moment!"

He froze and turned back towards her. "Oh, I'm sorry. I forgot about your ankle! Are you able to travel?"

"Well enough, especially if we get a cab. But why are you in such a hurry? We have plenty of time before ten."

He shook his head. "I'm not sure. Ever since I woke up, I've had this energy. Had a devil of a time sleeping last night. Kept having these strange dreams."

"What kind of dreams?"

Frowning, he turned back towards her. "You know, I don't even remember them."

With that, he moved to the street and signaled for a cab.

Once one stopped, he helped her in. As he climbed in after her, he grinned again. "Oh wait! I do remember one of them!"

MIRA WASN'T ABLE TO GET A WORD in edgeways as they travelled to parliament, the meeting place for this particular encounter with the prime minister. His leg bounced up and down as he regaled her with the intricacies of his dream, getting lost in the minute details. Every so often he would punctuate his sentence with a yawn.

At first, she marveled at how certain parts of the dream seemed to match up with things that had happened to them during their investigation. Almost like little flashes of memory trying to help him remember. But as his descriptions veered away from reality, she found herself caught in her own thoughts. How could she explain her resignation? How would he respond? She glanced over at him as he rambled. Tangents weren't normal for him, and he still seemed pale. Had something else happened?

Five minutes from their destination, she put a hand up. This silenced him in the middle of a discourse on whether you could actually attach a bicycle to a hot-air balloon.

"While that is all well and good, Byron, are you alright? Are you sure you shouldn't be in bed?"

"What makes you say that?" He bristled at her comment.

"You are just" —she paused trying to find a tactful way of describing the change— "much more exuberant this morning."

He paused then nodded. "My mouth does seem to have a mind of its own today, doesn't it? I think it was the laudanum. My thoughts are racing, and I can't seem to keep anything straight. That's why I avoid alcohol as well. Just makes things fuzzy. Although in this case—"

"We're here," she interrupted.

That quieted him down as they hopped out of the cab and moved towards the parliament building. Byron showed a letter to an attendant who escorted them into a hallway more lavish than Mira had ever dreamed. The wood paneling, exquisite and dark, made way to ceilings filled with murals and chandeliers. Prince Albert (may he rest in peace) had outdone himself with the architecture and art. The attendant continued on until he led them to an inner office. Prime Minister Salisbury, Sir William Arthur White, and Castel stood to greet them.

"Good morning, Detective, Miss Blayse." Salisbury nodded to both of them.

"Good morning, Prime Minister," Mira responded.

The First Lord gestured for them to take a seat, which they did.

"I've called this meeting to determine exactly what led up to the attack at Victoria station. We need to know who was involved so that we may avoid this on our second attempt. It is imperative that Sir William leave today for Constantinople. Detective Constantine, if you'll start?"

"Of course, sir. I met Sir William at his residence around five-thirty on the twenty-first. We intended to put him on the train at Victoria at six-fifteen, which would take him to Dover, where he would board an airship to Paris. Then boarding the Orient Express, travel from Paris to Constantinople."

"Yes, Mr. Constantine, we are aware of the itinerary." Castel glowered.

"Oh. Right. Sorry. Erm." Byron ran a hand through his hair. "Things got sticky at Victoria station. Two old women approached the ambassador and asked him for help moving luggage."

"They were going to miss their train, you see," Ambassador White supplied.

"While I felt suspicious about it, we followed them to the edge of the station, away from the other passengers, where some men ambushed us and knocked us out. When we woke, we were in a dark room with a single cot and a chair. When our captors came to bring us food and water, I tried to incapacitate one of them, but they called for another guard, at which point they forced something down my throat. I have no memory of anything else until I woke up at Mr. Sherard's residence yesterday morning." He turned to the ambassador.

"It is exactly as he told it. They came twice in the time we were there, and both times they drugged him, with what the guards said was laudanum. Then early yesterday morning, Miss Blayse, among others, got us out."

The prime minister turned to Mira next. "How on earth did you find them and get them out safely?"

She sat up straighter. "When I read of the attack in the paper, I immediately went to Palace Court, where I met with Grace Trimbell. She was also worried about Byron as they are old friends, and we discussed what could have happened." At this point she faltered. Should she be honest about Grace's involvement in Circe, or not?

"It just so happens that she's a secretary at Emoria-Sutherland. She had overheard Mr. Harding, the acting director, speaking about the warehouse to some workers. He asked them to go to Butler's wharf and see if a backroom in a warehouse could be fitted with a cot and other necessities. He said it was for a surprise inspection. However, he had never done such a thing before, which made her suspicious. Along with that, the order still went through despite the fact that he was arrested."

"Arrested?" The prime minister looked down his spectacles at her.

"Well, yes. For the murder of Mr. Sutherland."

"Why, he wasn't at the party at all!" The ambassador sat straighter in his chair.

"It's more complicated than that. May I continue, though?"

After varying nods and assents, she continued to explain the details of her plan, excluding anything that could incriminate Grace. At the end, the prime minister removed his spectacles and rubbed at his eyes.

"Miss Blayse, I find it quite incredible that you were able to pull that off. However, next time I must ask you to leave the heroic exploits to the authorities."

"I'd say she did just fine on her own," Byron said, then he leaned closer and whispered, "I'm glad you are alright," to her alone.

Salisbury turned to the ambassador. "This time around, we'll send more guards with you. Those guards will accompany you all the way to Dover for extra security. And you are not to stop for any reason. Understood?"

"Yes, Prime Minister." Ambassador White nodded.

"Good. You have an hour to get everything together. Constantine, I expect you to pick up some constables from Scotland Yard and report to the ambassador's residence within the hour. Any questions?"

"Am I to go with them, then?" Byron asked.

"You are more likely to pick up on any threats based on your deductions," Castel sighed. "Just don't get yourself caught this time."

THEY RECRUITED THE CONSTABLES AND PICKED SOME essentials for Byron to travel with in less than thirty minutes. With the remaining time, Byron insisted on a stroll across Westminster bridge.

"I think I know what went wrong last time." He leaned against the railing.

"Oh?" She glanced up at him.

"You weren't there." He looked over his shoulder at her, eyes soft.

Mira averted her gaze. "You don't need me, Byron."

"The circumstances would suggest otherwise." He took his hat off and gestured with it.

"No, I would have been the first to help those old women. Then we'd all have been kidnapped, and then where would we be?"

"Ah, yes. Didn't account for that." He rolled the brim of his top hat between his fingers.

"If you aren't careful, you'll drop it into the river." She peered over the railing. "Quite a wet way to go for a hat."

"Don't you worry. I've got a firm grip on it."

She gave him half a smile and turned around, back against the railing. It was easy being with him. When no crimes were forcing them to run about, and they could just be together.

Her thoughts drifted to Alexander. How he always seemed to be there for her, despite their rough start. She let out a sigh at the memory of the warehouse. That kiss was nothing like she thought it would be. Did she love him, too? She glanced at Byron and found herself wondering what it would be like to kiss him.

But she couldn't ignore the way he forgot her. How he lived his life without knowing she existed. How could he love her when he couldn't recognize her on the street? Claim to know her when he wasn't even aware of her until he read about her in a book or saw her in a shoddy self-portrait? Both were made of paper that could burn as bright and fast as his feelings seemed to. The thing was, the brighter something burned, the faster it smoldered into nothing. This couldn't continue, could it?

"And what are you thinking about?" He turned to look at her.

She looked down, feeling the weight of her tears on her eyelashes. She shook her head, tired of crying.

"I resign."

"What was that?" He stared at her.

"I can't do this anymore, Byron."

"What?!"

His brow furrowed, and she turned away so he couldn't see the first tears fall. She wiped them away with her glove.

"All of this." She shook her head and took a step away. "It's like we're playing pretend. That you love me, and I love you, and somehow, despite you not remembering me, that everything will work out." She looked up at him, eyes wet and glassy as emeralds. "In the beginning, it worked because you needed me, and I didn't know what I needed. But now, you don't need me, and I—"

"Mira, I don't understand." He stepped closer. "Of course, I need you."

"But you don't. I've seen it more and more over the past couple of weeks." She let out a soft laugh. "You're remembering more every day, and I am so happy I can't even describe it. You're remembering things after years of being in the dark. You can wake up and know what you need to do, remember what day it is, and live your life hoping that one day you won't forget anything."

She took a shuddering breath and turned away again. "But that joy is overshadowed because you don't remember me. You never do. Every day, you remember more and more, but it is somehow impossible for you to remember me. When I am with you every day, by your side."

She leaned back over the railing as the colors of the sky rippled in the water. The sounds of the city swept over them. Byron stood next to her, and she felt his scrutinizing stare trying to deduce where this tirade of emotions came from.

He swallowed and spoke, placing a hand on hers. "I want, more than anything, to remember you, Mira. To wake up and have the first thing I think of be you. Little by little, my memory is coming back, you're right. We just have to be patient. It will come."

"But what if it doesn't?" She threw her hand out over the railing. "And what if these feelings you are having are just words on a page? Are they real? Or are we still pretending?" Her voice caught in her throat.

"My feelings are as real to me as you are standing here in front of me." His voice lowered to a whisper. "How can you say that they aren't?"

"Because all you know about me is ink on paper." She blinked the tears back. "You can't possibly love me from that."

He caught her by the shoulders and locked his gaze with hers. "And how do you know that, Mira? Why is it so impossible for you to believe that I—"

The chimes of Big Ben chirped, announcing that it was quarter to the hour. Their time was up. Byron's mouth snapped shut as he looked up at the time. She took a deep breath.

"You'll be late."

"I don't care." He took her hands in his.

"You have to go, Byron." She pushed his hands away.

He glanced up at the clock again and she took the opportunity to leave.

She hastened down the street away from him, ankle stinging. At the end of the bridge, she glanced back and caught him staring before he turned away and rushed off in the other direction.

MIRA HUNG HER COAT ON THE HOOK with a sigh, numb all over. That wasn't how she wanted it to go at all, and yet once she started speaking, it was like she couldn't stop. It all came tumbling out. She squeezed her eyes shut, trying to push Byron's lingering gaze from her mind. A murmur of voices came from the sitting room, and she turned towards it, curious.

She approached the half-open door and peeked inside. Alexander grinned at something Walker had said. She almost pushed open the door to make herself known when Walker continued.

"But what if I'm misunderstanding things?"

Her twin paced in front of the fireplace. Alexander sat in an armchair, focused on their conversation. Mira leaned closer to the door. Misunderstanding what?

"It's obvious that Liza likes you."

"Yes, but what if this is too fast? I don't want her to feel uncomfortable."

A small smile grazed Mira's lips. Walker was never flustered by girls.

"Why don't you ask her?"

"I can't just ask her!"

Alexander laughed, and Walker scowled at him. "This isn't a laughing matter, Durant."

"I can't help but laugh when you are being so dense. Why are you making it so complicated?"

"Because it is!" Walker threw his hands up.

Alexander shook his head and stood, moving over to Walker.

"You're overthinking things. You already talked to her father about it. Bring up courting and see how she responds. Then you can stop running circles around each other."

Walker leaned against the mantle. "I'll think about it."

"Good. Because it's a rather good idea, and I'd hate for it to go to waste." Alexander folded his arms.

"If you're so keen on it, maybe you should try it," Walker scoffed.

Alexander sighed and turned away towards the window. "Ah, but I have the complication of her not liking me."

Mira froze. Were they talking about her now?

"She's warming up to you, I think."

"And what makes you say that?" Alexander glanced over his shoulder.

Mira turned to leave, as none of this was her business whatsoever. In turning, she stepped on a squeaky floorboard. The men stopped their conversation, and Walker whipped the door open.

"Mira!" He said her name louder than usual, his gaze flickering back to Alexander. "How long have you been back?"

"Not long," she lied. "Just came in, actually."

"Well, look who's here!" He grabbed her by the arm and brought her into the room.

"Mr. Durant! How good of you to visit." She smiled at him, and he had the good sense to look ruffled.

"Good afternoon, Miss Blayse. I was surprised to hear you were out and about."

"Just needed some fresh air."

Walker looked between the two of them, then made a subtle move for the door. "I'll see about getting some tea put together."

Mira fiddled with her gloves. Alexander moved over to her.

"Have you been crying again?"

"Is it that obvious?" She glanced up at him.

"Only to someone who's seen you cry before." His arm twitched by his side as if he wanted to wipe her tears away.

"Walker must be oblivious then." She turned her face away from him.

Alexander chuckled and moved back towards the window. She came over next to him.

"Miss Blayse, about the other day—"

"Mira."

"What?"

"Please." She looked up into his eyes. "Call me Mira."

"Mira."

He opened his mouth to continue, but she beat him to it.

"It was unexpected." She pulled her hands into her chest. "And perhaps a bit too fast."

"I understand." He rubbed the back of his neck.

"I forgive you for it, though. It's made me pause for thought."

"Oh?"

She leaned against the side table. Her gaze landed on the globe, and she set a hand on it, giving it a soft spin.

"Do you ever want to run away?"

"Not often," he sighed, wistful. "But sometimes, when things get too hectic, I think about it."

"Where would you go?" She turned towards him.

"Everywhere. Sometimes I think I was born too late." He placed a hand on the globe to stop it. "I'd love to have been an explorer."

"Somehow I don't see that," she laughed.

"What about you? Where would you go?"

"Paris," she whispered, trailing a finger over France. "I've always wanted to go to Paris."

"It's a lovely place. I'm set to travel there in a few days."

"Really?" She glanced up. "What for?"

"My employer has some things he wants me to look into."

He paused a moment, then cocked his head, looking at her. "Do you want to come with me?"

She blushed and averted her gaze.

He continued. "You did say you wanted to go."

She laughed again. "Just run away?"

"Is it such a ludicrous thought?"

"Perhaps not." She held a breath. "But I'd have to say no."

He nodded. "And what a wise 'no' that would be."

The sky darkened outside, threatening to rain. Mira reached up and closed the curtains.

"For the record, I don't dislike you."

His head shot up, shocked. "You heard that?"

"I didn't mean to eavesdrop. Not at first. But I've never heard Walker talk so seriously about a woman before, and I was curious."

He nodded and licked his bottom lip. "I, well—" He laughed a little and looked up at her again. "If you don't dislike me, then . . ."

Her mind fled back to Byron's figure, standing on the bridge. She shook her head, moving for the door.

"You challenged me to solve you not too long ago, and I think I've done that. But I still need time to solve me. Good afternoon, Alexander."

October 25, 1888

*M*IRA WANDERED THE NEXT MORNING, AIMLESS. HER uncle left in the early morning for Emoria-Sutherland. He needed to settle the issue of Spenston Park, as it hadn't been touched since the murder, and it technically belonged to him. Walker disappeared soon after, shouting something about losing his nerve. She found herself drawn towards the butler's pantry to find Landon.

"Good morning, Miss Mira." He smiled up at her from where he stacked dishes. "How is your ankle holding?"

"Your remedy worked wonders. I hardly feel anything now."

"Good." He paused and took in her expression. "Is something else the matter?"

"No. Not at all."

He gestured to the silverware. "You rarely seek me out. Make yourself useful while you decide what's bothering you."

Mira gave a begrudging groan, picked up a polishing cloth and grabbed a fork.

"Does something have to be wrong?"

"You didn't touch your breakfast, aside from moving it around your plate."

He raised an eyebrow at her as he put the dishes away. She rubbed harder at the fork in her hands, hoping he would drop the subject. He picked up another polishing cloth and turned his attention to the knives, giving her a look.

"I think I made a mistake," she said, relenting.

"Can it be fixed?"

She shook her head. "I don't know. But maybe it shouldn't."

"Why don't you start from the beginning?"

And so she did. About her feelings turning from a trickle of love for Byron to a vast ocean that spread through her entire being. Her insecurities about Byron's memory, particularly after Grace stumbled into the picture with her strewn packages. From the elation she felt every time they discussed a proper courtship to every pang she felt as he continued to forget her. How Alexander Durant swept her off her feet and made her feel things she'd never felt before—although she stopped herself from telling Landon about the kiss.

She continued to speak about how conflicted she felt in having feelings for Alexander, while at the same time she knew she loved Byron more than anything or anyone else. And she couldn't set that aside. She explained her plan to resign from working with the detective so they could both figure out their feelings. And how that plan fell to ruin when everything spilled out the moment she opened her mouth.

"What I said was terrible, but I can't say that I didn't mean it because I still feel like it's true. He doesn't love me. He couldn't. If anything, he loves me because I remind him of her. But she's here now. He doesn't need me."

She set down the last polished fork and picked up a spoon.

Her voice softened to a whisper. "The worst thing is, at this point, he could put down his journal forever and forget me altogether. But I could never forget him."

Landon polished the candlesticks, and she fell into silence next to him, focusing on the bevel of each spoon. After a few minutes, Landon set his cloth down and turned to her.

"I don't think this has anything to do with Byron's memory."

"What, but I—"

Landon gave her a sharp look, and she closed her mouth.

"This stems from you, Mira. For over a month, you happily worked with Byron, and you fell in love with him despite him forgetting you every day. Now you're having feelings for Mr. Durant."

Mira set the spoon down, looking at him. Landon continued.

"I want you to ask yourself this question: Has he changed? Or have you?"

A HAZY LIGHT STREAMED THROUGH THE PARLOR windows. Mira sat on the floor in one of the mid-afternoon sunbeams staring at a blank page. Never mind the fact that she had been staring at the white abyss for the better part of an hour, she still didn't have a single idea of what to paint. A fog planted itself in her mind. It held her captive, unable to move or escape. She leaned back against the base of the couch with a sigh. Nero mewed and rolled into another patch of sunlight.

"Knock, knock!" The professor rapped his knuckles against the half-open door.

She glanced up at him and moved to stand. He put a hand up.

"Don't get up for me. The floor is as good a place as any."

He sat next to her and set the black box he was carrying

between them. Nero rubbed against his leg, and the professor gave him a scratch behind the ears.

"Can't find inspiration?" He touched the blank page.

She screwed her lips together and shook her head. He opened up the black box and pulled out his stereoscope, handing it over to her.

"I thought you could use some entertainment. After all, your ankle is still healing, isn't it?"

"I can barely feel it today."

"Well, you need some cheering up, either way, if you aren't finding it in you to paint." He reached into the box and pulled out some new slides.

Mira smiled and slipped one into place. "Oh, I love it when they are in color!"

She pulled the stereograph forward and back, making the tropical scene appear real. The hand-painted sections sprung to life. Mira laughed and passed it over to the professor to look through.

"This is just like when you came to visit after I broke my wrist. Except, I don't need you to move the photographs for me."

He handed it over to her again. "I've also grown too old for sitting on the floor, it would seem." He stretched out his back and moved over to an armchair.

"Did my uncle tell you about what happened?"

"He gave me the general gist. He also said that you've been moping, and invited me over for a dinner party of sorts."

"He didn't mention anything to me."

"That's because it was meant to be a surprise," Walker said, coming in. "But now I suppose we have to let you in on the secret." His eyes twinkled as he sat next to her and reached for the stereograph. She reluctantly handed it over.

"And for the record, it was my idea." Walker shifted the stereograph back and forth. "We never did properly celebrate our uncle's release, and I've got several pieces of good news, so why not?"

"Will it just be us, and Uncle?" Mira pulled out a new set of pictures to look at.

"And a few other guests. You'll see." He winked.

Mira shook her head with a smile and looked through the stereoscope again. "What time?"

"Oh, in about forty-five minutes."

She whipped her head up. "Walker, that's barely enough time for me to get ready!"

"Then you'd better get on it." He took the slides from her, and she rushed upstairs.

SHE FELT FOOLISH COMING FASHIONABLY LATE TO a party held in her own house, but with the time she had, it couldn't be helped. She readjusted the bow on the collar of her royal blue dinner dress and gave herself a once over before heading downstairs.

Landon greeted her on the landing. "They have already adjourned to the dining room, if you'd like to join the party."

She nodded her thanks and headed in that direction.

The table had been opened to its fullest measure; the place settings as extravagant as they had ever been. Mira noticed china she hadn't seen since she was ten. She sent a quick glance around the table, recognizing, of course, her uncle at the head of the table, with the professor to his left. There was an empty chair to the right of Cyrus, which Mira guessed was her spot. Mr. Durant was next, followed by Walker, who sat next to Miss Renaldi. Two individuals that Mira recognized as Liza's parents occupied the chairs to the left of the professor. She made her way to her seat, only stopping as Alexander stood to pull out her chair.

"You look stunning as always, Miss Blayse."

"Thank you."

A heat burned her cheeks, and he returned to his seat. The murmur of conversation spread across the table.

After the first course, Landon moved about the table, retrieving dirty dishes. Walker stood, and the conversations died down.

"May I make an announcement?"

"Of course, dear boy, we've been waiting all night!" Mrs. Renaldi said, with a wide smile.

He grinned and turned to Liza. "Just this morning, Miss Renaldi and her parents agreed to a formal courtship."

Mira found herself clapping with everybody. She stood to hug her brother, and he squeezed back.

"I'm so happy for you."

She moved to Liza next, hugging her tight as well. Cyrus stood with his glass.

"May I propose a toast?"

"Hear, hear!" said Mr. Renaldi as the rest of the party raised their glasses.

"To new beginnings!"

After everyone took a sip and sat back down, Mira turned to her uncle.

"That toast applies to you as well, with your new involvement in Emoria-Sutherland."

"And after that dreadful business with the murder, too!" Mrs. Renaldi added.

"It was ghastly, wasn't it? Thank goodness it's over." Cyrus leaned back.

"I'm just glad Liza wasn't involved. To think, the first party we allow her to attend by herself, and someone ends up dead!" Mrs. Renaldi continued, patting her lips with a napkin.

"The one thing I don't understand is where that second shot came from." Liza set her glass down in front of her.

Mira frowned. She had forgotten about that.

"You heard it too?" Cyrus asked.

"What second shot?" Mr. Renaldi asked.

Cyrus gave a thoughtful look. "When I was on my walk in the woods, I heard a shot, and as I walked back to the estate, I saw Dr. Kelley come down the ivy. As he ran around the house, I heard a second. But if he was already down the ivy, why would there be another?"

"I hadn't thought about it that way." Liza frowned. "But I know for a fact I heard two! I hadn't gone to bed yet."

"I only heard one. Didn't you, Miss Blayse?" Alexander asked.

"That's what I thought." She glanced at her brother. "Walker, you were asleep, weren't you?"

"Neither shot woke me up if there were two. Maybe the second shot went off when he threw the gun coming down?"

"He didn't throw anything. Wouldn't I have seen it?" Cyrus asked.

"But the pistol was in the grass. Although, it could only hold one bullet," Walker trailed off.

"Are you sure you heard two, Cyrus?" The professor asked, swirling his glass and taking a sip.

"I'm positive because—"

A loud clattering banged through the room. Mira started, sitting back to find Landon picking up a dropped ramekin behind herself and Alexander.

"My sincerest apologies!" Alexander said, hopping to his feet to help pick up any broken pieces.

"It's my fault entirely, sir. I had miscalculated."

AFTER THAT, THE CONVERSATION RETURNED TO THE meal, and whether Walker would be accepted as an apprentice where Mr. Durant worked and then Mrs. Renaldi asked whether anyone had been to the theatre recently. However, Mira didn't hear most of it, mind far away from the conversation. She reviewed the particulars of the night of the murder over and over again in her head. If there had been a second shot, then something was terribly wrong.

She continued to stew over the matter for the remainder of the evening. Shortly after dinner, the party moved to the parlor to play cards. Mira sat near the window, declining to play, but writing everything she could remember from the night of Sutherland's death. Alexander came over to her after a particularly bad hand.

"And what are you working on so studiously?" He placed a hand on the wall behind her, leaning over to see what she wrote.

Mira closed the notebook she was writing in and looked up at him. "Just a personal project. That's all."

He smiled and sat next to her. "I almost wish this night would never end."

"It has been rather nice." She nodded.

Walker gave a small yell of victory as he won the round at the table, with Liza giggling beside him.

Mr. Renaldi set his cards down. "I'd say it's about time for us to go home."

His wife nodded. "It's been a wonderful evening."

"Is it alright if I stay on a bit longer?" Liza asked.

Her parents shared a glance. Walker spoke up.

"Perhaps you two can ride on in a hansom cab, and I'll walk Liza back. Mr. Durant and my sister can act as chaperones."

Mr. Renaldi heaved a sigh. "If it's alright with you Cyrus, I don't see the harm in it."

Uncle Cyrus nodded. "Go on then."

M IRA AND A LEXANDER GAVE QUITE A BIT of distance between themselves and the newly courting couple. That way, they could keep an eye on things, but still give them some privacy. At the same time, Mira felt like a hypocrite. After all, she was walking unchaperoned with a man she had already kissed. Her cheeks heated just thinking about it. He shifted closer, and she looked up at him.

"I'm leaving for Paris tomorrow," he said.

"So soon?"

"We've had to move things up." He hesitated. "You could still come with me, you know."

"You know I couldn't." She turned away.

"I could convince Walker to come. All of us on a grand adventure!"

She gave him a soft smile. "That kind of thing requires days of planning. Besides, I doubt he'd want to be so far away from Miss Renaldi now that they're courting." She gestured to the couple ahead of them, who were deep in conversation.

He sighed, following her gaze. "You're right. Of course, you are. I just hate to think of the company I'm losing."

"How long will you be gone?"

"A week, maybe more."

"That is hardly any time at all. You'll be back in London in no time."

He nodded. "Yet, every minute I'm not with you feels like an eternity."

She couldn't help but laugh. "You are so dramatic."

"Yet, I'm entirely serious."

She stopped walking and turned towards him, searching his face. His warm eyes poured into hers and flicked down to her lips. Her breath caught in her chest, fit to burst. She glanced down the street at Walker and Liza. Alexander placed a hand on her cheek, pulling her gaze back to him. His thumb rubbed down the side of her face and a tingle ran down her spine.

"I love you, Mira Blayse. I want you to always remember that."

She swallowed. "I'm sure that it's a difficult thing to forget."

His hand gently pulled her forward, and a bubble of confusion and fluttering butterflies burst in her stomach. She closed her eyes, lips parting. A soft warmth burst on her cheek, and she opened her eyes as he pulled away.

"We ought to catch up to the other two. Who knows what kind of trouble they might get themselves into?" He chuckled and offered his arm.

She took it in a daze, touching a hand to her cheek.

AFTER DROPPING LIZA OFF AT HER HOUSE, Alexander tipped his hat to the twins and disappeared into the mist. Mira stared after him, confused. Walker stood next to her.

"Shall we go home, then?"

She nodded mutely, and they turned towards home. After a block or two of silence, Walker cleared his throat.

"You've been awfully quiet this evening. And you've never turned down a game of cards before. Is something the matter?"

Mira's mind jumped back to the night of the murder, and she picked up the pace, her brother following behind.

"There were two shots."

October 26, 1888:
Morning

MIRA PACED IN FRONT OF PALACE COURT, trying to muster up the courage to approach the door. She yawned, blinking back the exhaustion that came from staying up half the night, worrying about the second shot. It wasn't likely that two individuals imagined the same thing, was it? And she hadn't heard it herself, so what did that mean? In any case, the answers had to be back at Spenston Park, and if she was to get to the truth, she couldn't do it alone. She fingered her key and stared up at the building, anxiety rising within her.

She let out a laugh and turned away again. What was she nervous about? He likely had forgotten their argument entirely. She glanced back at the door. Or perhaps he had hidden his journal away and wouldn't know her whatsoever. In any case, standing out on the street wasn't doing her any good. But how was she to breach the topic of conversation?

Oh yes, I was your secretary, but you never remembered me, so I resigned. Also, I love you, but that's irrelevant.

She groaned and turned to pace again.

The door to Palace Court swung open, and Byron peeked out. "Are you lost?"

She froze. If she came back tomorrow, she'd have another try. But the longer they waited, the less likely it was that they would discover anything. As considered her options, he came down the stairs and stood in front of her.

"Because, I had thought I wouldn't be seeing you again." He rubbed the back of his neck. "Or . . . I suppose meeting you for the first time, again."

She took a deep breath and looked down. "You read your journal?"

"Of course, I did. You may be intent on my forgetting you, but I refuse."

Mira swallowed, the corners of her eyes burning. "I didn't come here to argue."

"Then why did you come?" He crossed his arms.

"There were two shots." She brought her gaze up to meet his eyes, and his brow furrowed.

"What?"

"At the party. There were two. Dr. Kelley came down the ivy and ran around the house, and then there was a second shot."

Byron's eyes flickered from her to the pavement, then to the building opposite. He stepped aside and gestured to the door.

"I suppose we have one last mystery to solve."

Mira's heart sunk at the statement, even if it was likely to be true. She moved into the sitting room and took her usual place. Byron followed, but instead of moving to his chair by the fire, he sat beside her on the sofa.

"So, how do we know there were two shots?"

"We have two witnesses. My uncle, who heard them while he was on his walk, and Miss Liza Renaldi, who was still awake at the time. That being said, Alexander and I both only heard one shot, and we were the ones to discover the body."

"So, if there was a second shot, why didn't you hear it?" He leaned back and ran a hand through his hair.

"I haven't the faintest idea. It's been bothering me all night."

"Well, we could try to track down each of the guests to interrogate them, however most of them would have been asleep at the time." He sat up, eyes brightening. "What were you thinking?"

"We need to go back to Spenston Park. I know that it hasn't been touched since Sutherland died, because my uncle received the property and hasn't quite figured out what to do with it. He's given most of the servants the month off. I know it's been two weeks, but maybe we can find something?"

"It's as good a place to start as any. Is that why you're dressed for traveling?" His gaze flicked down to her dress.

"I thought it might come in handy, although I don't plan on staying all day."

He nodded. "Give me a moment to put myself together, and we'll be off."

IT FELT STRANGE BEING WITH BYRON AGAIN after spending so much time apart. Save the day she resigned (which really shouldn't count), she hadn't spoken with him in two days. Which wasn't long in the grand scheme of things, but it felt like an eternity. After a near silent ride to the station, they bought their tickets and found a compartment to themselves. Mira sat nearest to the window, and Byron sat in the center of the seat across from her. He took off his top hat and passed it from hand to hand. It occurred to Mira that they had a two-hour ride ahead of them, and it could prove incredibly awkward if they didn't at least attempt a normal conversation. Once the train was moving, she cleared her throat.

"Did the ambassador make it to Dover alright?"

Byron nodded. "He'll make it with time to spare to Constantinople."

After a moment, he added, "In many ways, thanks to you."

"I didn't do it alone. It wouldn't have been possible without Grace being able to convince those men that she was part of Circe."

His eyes widened. "She told you about her involvement with them, then?"

Mira nodded. "You must be relieved to know what caused your memory loss."

Byron leaned back. "They aren't the most pleasant memories to have back." He glanced up at her, a pained expression filling his eyes. "But I suppose it's better than not knowing."

Silence fell over them. Mira tried to distract herself with the scenery moving outside the window, but the atmosphere suffocated her. So much needed to be said, but she couldn't bring herself to open her mouth.

"Is that part of why you resigned?" He ran a finger along the crown of his top hat, averting his gaze.

"What?" She turned back towards him.

"I worked with Circe and they killed your parents. Is that part of it?" He glanced up at her.

She shook her head. "That was entirely necessary for your investigation."

He nodded. "I just want to understand. My shorthand of the conversation wasn't helpful in that regard."

Mira closed her eyes, a thousand answers coming to mind, but none of them tactful in the least.

"I'm not sure what could be misunderstood."

Byron hummed and retrieved his journal from where he stowed it, thumbing through the pages. He pulled out a loose sheet of paper and glanced over it.

"Ah, here we are. On October seventeenth, I wrote about a

young woman who came to see me at Palace Court." His gaze
flickered up to hers before he continued. "She was extremely
upset about me forgetting about her, as I hadn't read my journal
that day. Yet she asked me not to read it that day. Of course, she
said nothing about writing anything down. This was you, yes?"

Mira nodded and turned away, eyes tracking the countryside through the window. A page turned behind her.

"The next day, I tried to apologize, because really I should
have read my journal. And what did you do?" He paused for a
moment, giving her a chance to answer.

She remained silent, and he continued. "You apologized
instead, because, as my former self wrote, you believed it was
your fault for being upset. And yet these are the only two
instances that I have recorded where we've talked at all about
my forgetting you, and how it affects you. That is, until the
twenty-fourth, when you decided to resign, saying that I don't
need you anymore. Is everything correct and in line with your
impeccable memory so far?"

Mira furrowed her brow, looking over at him. He leaned
over his journal, fingers steepled.

"So far, yes," she said.

"Well, then." He snapped the journal closed and stood,
shoulders tense. "What I don't understand is why you haven't
brought this up to me before. Why is it you don't want me
to remember you when you are upset, and downplay how
you actually feel?" He paused a moment, voice rough with
emotion. "Why is it you think for a second that I don't need
you anymore?"

Mira's heart quivered, and she faltered for an answer. He
threw the journal on the seat.

"Yes, I've never remembered you before without my
journal, but that doesn't mean I can't love you now, with you
here in front of me." He choked on a laugh. "Even now as I'm
arguing with you, I can't help but love you." He moved closer

to her, extending a shaky hand, before faltering and pulling it back. "Every morning in the past week I've woken with new memories, yet I know they're not complete. I know that the most important thing is gone, and it drives me mad. I'm not certain how I know, other than the overwhelming sensation that something is just out of reach." He looked away for a moment, taking a steadying breath. "It's like when the city is drenched in fog and you know something is in front of you, but you can't quite make it out. Not until you come face to face with it. Each morning, I'm left wondering what it is that I'm missing until I discover that it's you." His eyes shone as his gaze flickered across her face. "I don't need ink and paper to tell me how I feel. Mira, I've never loved you for what you could do for me. I love *you*."

Mira swallowed. Could she honestly say it back? After everything?

"Byron, I can't." Her voice cracked. "I just can't."

Byron ran a hand through his hair, turning away from her. He took a long deep breath. Then, with a glance over his shoulder, he picked up his journal and left the compartment.

HE DIDN'T RETURN UNTIL THE CONDUCTOR ANNOUNCED their station, and he didn't attempt to rekindle their conversation. For her part, Mira felt numb again, wishing that she had come to Spenston Park on her own. Instead, they traveled from the station to the estate in silence.

Once there, Byron took a deep breath and turned to her, voice hesitant. "Did you bring a key or something?"

Mira nodded, having retrieved the key that morning from her uncle. She moved up the steps and unlocked the front door.

The door creaked open. Spenston's once lively and bright entry hall teemed with shadows, desolate and lonely.

Byron stepped in. "Let's first retrace your steps. Where were you before the first shot?"

Mira led him to the conservatory. The poor plants wilted with neglect, with a few strong survivors trying their hardest. The fish in the pond seemed alright, if a bit sluggish. Perhaps it had been hasty of her uncle to excuse the staff for the month.

"Alexander and I were in here." She turned around to face him.

"Discussing his feelings for you?" He studied the withered leaves of a nearby plant.

"Among other things, yes." Her face flushed. "Is that relevant?"

"Just trying to get the full picture here." He stalked over to the koi pond. "Then you heard a shot?"

"Yes, and we ran from here up to the office."

He paused, nodded, then moved to the doorway.

"Wait here until I call for you, then run as you did the night of the murder."

Byron disappeared up the stairs. A minute later he hollered for her to run, but as she reached the steps, her ankle twisted again, more painful than the last time. She crashed to the ground with a bang. Byron came rushing down to help her up.

"Are you alright?" His eyes screamed concern, and she forced herself to look away.

"It's just my ankle. It hasn't quite recovered from when we rescued you."

"Can you stand?"

She nodded. He hesitated a moment before wrapping his arm around her waist to pull her up, supporting her against the bannister. Pain shot up her leg, and she winced.

"I'm sorry, Mira. I should have realized." He faltered. "May I?"

She gave a short nod. "Please."

Mindful of her skirts, he picked her up and carried her up the stairs, settling her into a chair in the study. He knelt in front of her and checked over her ankle, grimacing as she winced in pain.

"Tell you what, I'll do the running from here on out, alright?"

"I can't argue with that."

She leaned into the chair as he stood and paced over to the door. After a moment, he fished in his pocket and pulled something out, handing it to her. The metal of his pocket watch felt cool in her fingers. She frowned as he set his satchel on the desk.

"What is this for?"

"I'll go back down to the conservatory and holler when I'm about to run. You'll count to see how long I take to get from the conservatory to here."

She nodded, and he disappeared out the door again. Mira stretched her feet out.

"Are you ready?" He hollered up the stairs.

"Ready! Shall I count down?"

"Go ahead!"

She counted down from three, and a moment later, his footsteps barreled up the stairs. She counted the seconds on the watch, stopping as Byron came into the room.

"Less than forty-five seconds." She glanced over at the splintered door. "But we still had to break down the door. That took about a minute."

"So, a minute and forty-five seconds for you to come into the room. Then what did you see?"

"Mr. Sutherland." Mira swallowed. "Dead and bleeding over his papers."

The constables had cleared the room of papers on the night of the murder; however, the pools of blood still stained the desk.

"Hmm." Byron moved around the desk.

"What?"

"Well, it doesn't seem like Dr. Kelley's style, does it? The other murders involved poison or drugs. Making it appear like natural causes. He had access to the victim as their physician. And as far as we know, he'd never shot anyone before."

"But we know he was the one who climbed down the ivy. It had to have been him."

"Where was your uncle when he heard the first shot?" He turned back towards her.

"He said he was a bit out into the woods." She gestured towards the window.

"And he saw Dr. Kelley through all the trees?"

"No, as he was walking back."

Byron hummed again, moving to the window. He opened it and leaned out, looking down at the ivy, then out towards the woods.

"It's a fair bit of a walk back. Definitely more than a minute and a half. Yet he saw Dr. Kelley climbing down the ivy."

"Yes?"

"That doesn't add up, does it?" Byron pulled his head back in, the breeze from the window tousling his hair.

"Maybe my uncle remembered it wrong?"

"Just a moment."

Byron opened his satchel, retrieving his journal and leaving a white notebook. He flicked the journal open and skimmed over the pages.

"Katherine White saw Dr. Kelley that night too. Thought he was a ghost." He held his place with his finger and looked up at her. "Did she hear two shots?"

Mira paused, trying to remember. "I think she said that she heard the gunshot after she saw the ghost."

"Well, then that definitely doesn't add up." He snapped the journal closed. "Because how would Dr. Kelley shoot Sutherland if he were outside haunting Lady White? There were definitely two shots."

"But then why didn't I hear both?"

"What happened after you found the body?" He moved over to the edge of the desk, leaning against it, and folding his arms.

"I went downstairs to telephone the police."

"I need details, Mira. Which route did you take and what did you see?"

Mira took a deep breath, closing her eyes to focus on the memory. "I took a shortcut through the ballroom. The servants were still cleaning up after the party. I ran through and figured out how to dial the telephone."

"Anything else?"

Mira frowned. "Wait. I ran into one of the servants and knocked over some trays." Her eyes shot open. "They clattered so loudly, if the second shot happened . . ."

"You wouldn't have heard it. But Durant would have."

"Maybe not if he were banging on doors at the opposite end of the house."

"Right." Byron turned back to examine the room. "The pistol used was taken from this display." He traced a finger over where the missing pistol hung. "The murderer would have had to have brought their own bullets. But why take the time to load another shot if Sutherland was already dying?"

"What if the murderer missed on the first shot?"

"And Sutherland just let his killer stand there and load another bullet? I'd think he would have had a few more survival instincts than that."

Byron crouched down to examine the floor. "And we still have the issue of the residue on the floor."

As Mira leaned over, trying to see what he was up to, something caught her eye in the fireplace grate, glinting in the sunlight from the window.

"Byron, what's that in the fireplace?"

He shifted his weight so he could turn towards the grate. He sifted through the ashes, pulling out several pieces of metal.

"What is that?" She craned her neck to see.

"Looks like fragments of a bullet casing and a bit of charred rope. We wouldn't have seen it the night of, as the fire was still lit."

Byron set the fragments on the desk and turned to the closet. He opened it and crouched to the floor again.

"Scuff marks. As if someone dragged a pair of boots across the ground." His eyes trailed towards the desk. "They disappear about here." He traced the spot with a finger. "I'd guess because someone else helped to carry them."

He gave her a grin of triumph. "I know how it happened."

Byron stood and positioned himself at the center of the floor facing Mira and gestured to the door.

"Mr. Sutherland was mingling with guests in the ballroom when Dr. Kelley, or some other agent of Circe, approached him in conversation. They talked for a bit, and during that time the agent slipped something into his drink, and he became tired. Unfortunately, he still had some edits to make to the merger before everything was finalized. So, he excused himself and headed to his study to finish up his work and get to bed."

Byron turned towards the desk, leaning both hands against the edge.

"Alone in his study, he fell into a drug-induced sleep. Perhaps it was laudanum, as that stuff is fairly powerful in larger doses. Whatever it was, it made it incredibly easy to come upon him without him being aware of anything."

He paced over to the closet and opened it, pointing to the scuff marks on the floor and their relation to the closet door.

"Dr. Kelley and his accomplice tied and gagged Sutherland, in case he woke up too soon, and stuffed him in the closet. Then they returned to the party to continue to make their alibis."

He snapped the door shut with a bang and moved back to the desk, circling around to the side closest to Mira.

"Once the party was over, and all the guests had nearly gone to bed, the two of them set to work. Kelley was the right build and coloring to play Mr. Sutherland. He changed clothes, and they used pig's blood, or something of the sort to make him look as if he had been shot." Byron bent over and gestured to the blood stain on the desk.

"That's why the blood clotted so fast. Who knows how fresh it was? At some point, they placed a bullet in the grate, Kelley locked the door, and took his place at the desk."

Mira glanced between the fireplace and the detective. "So, the shot that I heard with Alexander wasn't an actual shot. Just a bullet exploding from the heat?"

"Exactly." Byron turned on his heel and paced over to the door, rubbing his hands together. "You run up and see someone who looks like Sutherland slumped at the desk. But did you even enter the room?"

"No. I went immediately down to the telephone."

He walked over to the desk, eyes set on where the corpse had been. "If you had come closer, you would have seen him breathing. Once you had seen what you thought was the corpse, Kelley could move Sutherland into position, still asleep, mind you, and climb down the ivy. Lady Katherine White sees a man drenched in blood and assumes he's a ghost."

Byron moved over to the pistol display and took one of the pistols from its slot, moving into position directly in front of the desk. He raised his arm as if to shoot, and Mira could picture the night of the murder clearly in her head, almost hearing a phantom sound.

"While Kelley escaped, his accomplice shot Sutherland, hence the second shot."

"But why go to all the trouble? If they wanted Sutherland dead, then why not poison him?"

"Because it had to look like murder. Mira, when I was captured, but before the laudanum, I heard them talking about a failed attempt to delay the ambassador. If the police hadn't settled on your uncle so quickly due to him being in the wrong place at the wrong time, they would have had to detain the entire party, or at least not allow them out of the country until the case had been solved."

"But why didn't Kelley just shoot Sutherland himself? Why pretend to be him at all?"

Byron paced, gun in hand, and manic with the prospect of finishing the case. He tapped the pistol against his hand a few times as he thought, and briskly turned as the answer came to him. "We know Kelley's expertise is poison, and while it is a nasty thing, it is less hands-on than a gun. Let's call it an irrational fear, or maybe warped professional pride. Something to that effect." He turned towards her. "No. Kelley was only there to help to drug Sutherland and be his doppelgänger." He slid the pistol back into the display. "And if the real murderer shot Sutherland outright, the likelihood of him being caught would increase. He needed to establish his alibi, and Kelley could be the scapegoat, should the need arise."

Mira frowned. "Then who was the real murderer?"

He rubbed at his hands. "Well, if I am right about how it was done, there's only one person who could have helped Dr. Kelley."

Mira trailed over the guest list in her head, mulling over the people she saw that night. Her breath hitched. "No."

He rubbed the back of his neck. "It would explain why they needed it to be so complicated. He needed an alibi."

"No, Byron. I know you don't like him, but—" She brought her fingers to her lips and turned away. "There has to be another explanation!"

Out of all the people he could accuse—and yet it made perfect sense. Had she kissed a murderer? Her throat constricted, lungs gasping for air. She had to get out, but as she went to stand, her ankle gave out again. Byron caught her before she collapsed completely, and set her back in the chair.

"Are you alright?"

She shook her head, still struggling to breathe.

"Look at me, Mira. Take deep breaths."

He took both of her hands in his, kneeling in front of her.

Her breathing evened out, but the room loomed over her, bloody and cold. She looked up at Byron, voice wavering.

"Can we talk somewhere else?"

He nodded and picked her up, cradling her to his chest. His heartbeat thrummed in her ear, and she relaxed as he brought her down to a parlor. He settled her on the couch, helping her to elevate her ankle, then pulled a chair over to sit next to her.

"I didn't mean to upset you."

"All the evidence does point to him." Her voice shook. "It's just difficult to grasp."

He nodded. "I know that the two of you have," he cleared his throat, "become close in the past few weeks."

She bit her lip and looked away, thinking of the night before. They had almost kissed again. She had *wanted* him to kiss her. Especially with him going away. She gasped and turned back to Byron.

"He's leaving for Paris today. He said it was only for a week, but if he truly murdered Mr. Sutherland . . ."

"We have to stop him before he leaves the country." Byron stood. "I'll see if I can phone Scotland Yard. They're closer."

He left the room, and Mira sighed, slumping further into the couch. A few minutes later, he returned.

"I can't get the telephone to work." His gaze darted around the room.

"I know they've got one in town. It's not that far, and you could take one of the horses." She sat up. "My uncle kept the groomsmen employed to look after them."

"And leave you here?"

Mira went to stand, and winced, laying back down. She paused, thinking of a solution. "You can have a groomsman set up a carriage and take me to the train station. He can take your horse there, and we can go back to London to deliver the evidence."

Byron hesitated. "I still don't like it."

"We can't let Mr. Durant leave the country. That's more important than fussing over my ankle."

He frowned, turning the idea over in his head. In the end, he sighed and nodded.

"I suppose I'll see you at the station, then."

Byron moved to the door and paused, looking back at her. He opened his mouth as if to say something, then simply left the room.

October 26, 1888:
Afternoon

*A*FTER BYRON LEFT, MIRA BROKE DOWN. NOT in sobs as she had when she overheard him speaking with Grace, but slowly, mechanically. She cried without tears. A pain wracked her chest as she came to grips with the fact that she did in fact love Alexander. Yet she didn't know him at all. She fell in love with him despite her reservations. Despite the voice in the back of her head telling her he was dangerous. The voice proved to be right. She fell in love with a murderer. With his charismatic grin and the way he seemed to know when she was hurting, and came to the rescue. All of it, a lie.

With Byron, it was the same, only almost opposite. She loved him and he said he loved her, too. But he didn't know her. She was his ghost, his figment, a fairytale. Flickers of the truth caught between blurred lines. But his version of her was still only real in his imagination. She wanted him to love her for who she was outside of his journal, who she truly was.

Footsteps echoed in the entry hall. She let out a sigh of relief and composed herself. That would be the groomsman. It took him less time than she realized to get a carriage ready.

"I'm in here!" she called out.

The door opened. Mira's heart froze.

"Why, Mira, how nice to see you again."

Alexander Durant strolled into the room, shutting the door behind him. He set something down that she didn't quite see and moved over to her.

Mira flinched and pushed back into the couch. Her gaze darted about for a way out. His expression morphed into something more complex. Something between annoyance, pity, and idle curiosity.

"Ah, don't bother getting up for me." He put a hand up and came closer. "I wouldn't want you to hurt that ankle of yours."

She swallowed. "I thought you were going to France."

"Just had to make a quick stop." He cocked his head. "Although, you seem to have beaten me here."

"We know you did it. Don't deny it."

He raised an eyebrow, almost surprised. "I'm aware of that. Byron's voice does carry quite well when he's enthused."

Mira frowned. "How long have you been here?"

"Long enough to hear your theories and cut the telephone wire. I had hoped to get here first to clean up the evidence I had neglected to retrieve. After Miss Renaldi's comment last night, I knew you weren't likely to leave well enough alone."

He paused to glance around the room, eyes settling back on her. "Although, I am surprised you made up with Byron so fast. If I had known, I would have come on an earlier train."

"You were counting on me fighting with Byron?"

Her mind trailed back to Grace. Had she helped to set this up?

"That was part of the plan, yes." He settled into an armchair with a smile.

"You mean to say that you and Grace drove us apart on purpose?" She glared at him.

"Oh, no." He stifled a laugh. "Miss Trimbell was a happy accident. I didn't even know she worked with Circe until the night we went after Byron and the ambassador."

He leaned forward, eyes dangerous and dark. "Of course, I've since done my research on her. According to rumor, this isn't the first time she's stepped out of line to help Byron. I can't imagine the Order will let that go so easily this time."

Mira's stomach dropped, thinking of Grace's stiff corpse found on the street somewhere. Anger and nausea boiled within her, but she kept her expression calm.

"You've been working with Circe all along, then?"

"I'm afraid so." He glanced around the room. "Are you cold?"

She refused to answer, meeting his gaze with a hard glare.

He shrugged, moving over to the fireplace. He placed a log in the grate and set to work lighting it.

"My cover story worked rather well, don't you think? You see, my job was to dissuade you from working with Byron. It's too dangerous for us to have him working at full capacity. Solving a crime here and there isn't an issue. But you nearly destroyed the entire smuggling guild after a single case." He glanced in her direction. "Circe doesn't take threats lightly, you know."

A spark latched onto the log, and soon the fireplace blazed to life.

"So why stop the threats then? Why pretend like you weren't with Circe?" She sat forward.

"Well, you didn't really respond to the threats to begin with." He stood and shook the soot off of his hands. "You kept calling my bluff. And seeing as Number Three didn't want you to be killed or hurt, he came up with a different idea that I rather liked."

He came over and sat on the couch, sitting on her skirts, and pinning her in. As she tried to shift away, her ankle twinged with pain. She was stuck. He leaned closer, eyes more gray than golden in the light.

"You see, the goal was to separate you from Byron. It didn't matter how I accomplished that as long as you weren't hurt." His eyes flicked down to her lips. "And I didn't lie when I said I was jealous of Mr. Constantine. I was quite taken with you from the moment we met. Still am."

He leaned back but kept her pinned in place. "And wouldn't the problem be solved if you were in love with me instead of him? No muss, no fuss, no threats. Just a simple change in priorities."

Bile rose in Mira's throat. "The only problem is that you're a murderer."

"It was a necessary move." He adjusted his cuffs.

"You shot him in cold blood."

"That shot should have killed two birds with one stone." He turned to her again. "Do you know how much planning went into those two shots? You might ask why we even bothered with such complication, but aside from my flair for the dramatic and the good doctor's reservations about guns, it was all quite necessary. We needed Sutherland dead, but we needed the ambassador out of the picture as well. This meant avoiding any suspicion at all costs and carefully crafting a motive for the ambassador. We ensured that the two of them were seen together multiple times, even managed to get them to leave the room together at one point. Unfortunately, we couldn't account for your uncle being on a stroll at the time of the murder. Not only did he see Kelley, but he heard both shots as well."

He paused a moment, soft but dangerous gaze trailing back to her. "I am sorry he was caught up in everything. That wasn't the plan. And even though they caught Kelley, I'm glad your uncle was released."

Adjusting his cufflinks, he continued. "I thought I got off entirely with the alibi we created, but I suppose you and Byron are too clever a pair, even for me. Pity too. This whole scheme required three members of Circe to be in attendance that night."

Mira furrowed her brow. "Three?"

"Myself, of course, Dr. Kelley, and one of the servants. She slipped the drug to Mr. Sutherland, and later crashed into you at exactly fifteen after so that you wouldn't hear the second shot." He laughed.

"It all worked quite wonderfully until we realized your uncle was outside. All in all, it was complicated chaos, but still organized. And it would have been worth it, too. Circe would have had another method for smuggling after you and Byron dismantled the first, and with our efforts, the ambassador would have been framed. With him unable to go to Constantinople, the likelihood of war would increase tenfold."

"You'd send thousands of men to their deaths?" Mira recoiled.

"You and those blasted morals." His lips pressed into a thin line, and he tilted his head to the side, studying her. "If I had more time, I'm sure I could have persuaded you to come to our side."

She scoffed, and Alexander leaned in.

"We're trying to change the world, Mira. Right now, England has stakes in almost every continent on the planet."

His face came closer, inches from hers, and she shrunk further into the couch.

"The sun never sets, and all that. But that won't be forever. The power dynamic will shift again, and when it does, we'll be the ones who step in."

His breath was hot on her lips, her heartbeat erratic. He smiled and pulled back.

"In any case, if that plan had worked, I'd be happily married to a gorgeous and fascinating woman, Byron would be floundering again, and you'd be kept far away from the inner workings of Circe. Safe, protected, unknowing."

"I'd have never married you."

He smirked. "No, Miss Blayse. I know for a fact that if you hadn't found out about my involvement, and I had a little more time, that you would have been mine."

He stood and moved over to the door, crouching to pick something up. As he returned, Mira recognized it as Byron's satchel. Her eyes widened, and she sat up.

"Give that to me. Now." Her voice hardened.

"And why do you care?" He pulled Byron's journal out and flicked through it idly. "After all, he doesn't remember you. If I recall, you were worried he didn't love you, that none of this," he gestured with the book, "was real."

He threw the satchel to the ground, keeping a firm hold on the journal.

"That isn't any of your business."

"It could be, though. You still have the choice."

He stopped on a particular page and pulled out the loose-leaf watercolor paintings Mira made for Byron to help him remember. He sifted through them.

"You have such a distinctive style, Mira. And such a talent for capturing likenesses. This is meant to be me, isn't it?"

He turned the sketch towards her, and she glared at her rendition of him. He laughed and shifted onto the next one.

"Yet I'd still say your self-portrait doesn't do you justice." He compared it to her. "With formal training I could see you becoming a great artist."

He removed the two paintings and folded them carefully, slipping them into his pocket. Afterwards, he tucked the remaining paintings back into the journal and set it on the side table. In two steps, he pinned her into the couch again, resting one arm on the back of it as he leaned over her, lowering his voice.

"I do love you. And I remember you. We could go to Paris, and you could study art with the French masters. All you have to do is forget all of this."

He tucked a wisp of hair behind her ear, leaving his hand on her cheek, and a shiver ran up her spine. He leaned closer until there was only an inch between them.

His dark eyes roved over her face. "Forget the man who never remembers you."

"You honestly think I could love you, knowing that you're a murderer?" Mira whispered, voice brittle. "That I could set that aside and go with you? Even if I don't know if Byron actually loves me, at least I can trust him. At least I know that he's a good man, instead of a coward who hides behind lies and false promi—"

He pushed her into the couch and kissed her, rough, passionate, and greedy. She pushed against him, trying to turn her face away, but he kept her in place with one hand on her neck. After an eternity, he pulled back and nausea swept over her. She slapped him hard across the face. His expression darkened, and his eyes became dangerous and threatening.

"While I hoped you would reconsider, I suppose I'll take that as your answer."

"You're despicable." Mira sat up again, fuming. She rubbed at her mouth.

He moved over to where he had placed the journal. He stared at it, then picked it up, looking at her.

"I suppose there's no more use for this then."

He tossed Byron's journal into the fire.

"No!" She jumped to her feet, ignoring the pain, but he threw her back onto the couch.

"That contained his memories of you, didn't it? All of them?" He laughed. "He'll never remember you now. And if he doesn't remember you, he won't know to come back for you."

"He'll come back when I'm not at the station waiting for him." Her shoulders shook. He lowered his voice and leaned in again.

"Unless he thinks you've already left. It's amazing what people will do for a simple bribe."

It occurred to Mira that the groomsman had never come, and she looked at him in horror.

"We would have been great, Mira." He ran a hand down her cheek to her jaw, breath hot on her face.

Then he pulled back and straightened his jacket. "But I suppose it wasn't meant to be. I'm off to Paris, and since you won't come with me, there's no one to stop me. Circe needed me over there as it is. I suppose it will just be an extended stay."

"We will track you down." Mira kept her head high and leveled her gaze with his.

"Will you?" He gave a sharp laugh. "Your detective isn't going to remember you, Mira. You forget, I heard your little plans. I've been here this whole time. He'll get to that train station and meet with the groomsman who will tell him that you left on the previous train, anxious to return. He'll get on the next train, intent on following after you. By the time he gets to Swan Walk and discovers that you aren't there, the last train will have already left. He'll have to sleep. He'll have to forget. The only person who will know where you are is me, and I'll be locking the door on my way out."

He held up the key to Spenston Park. Mira reached in her pocket and glared at him, realizing he had stolen it along with the kiss.

"You wouldn't dare."

"Oh, don't worry. I'll send an anonymous note to Walker once I'm safely across the channel. I don't think you'll starve in that time."

He picked up her hand and kissed the back of it. "Au revoir, Miss Blayse."

With that, he left the room, the click of the lock behind him. She picked up a blanket from the back of the couch and stumbled over to the fireplace, using the pokers to save the journal as it went up in flames. She set it on the floor and tried to squelch the fire with the blanket. Tears rose to the surface, which gave way to sobs. She pulled the blanket off and tried to open the book. The cover cracked as she touched it, burning her fingers as she tried to salvage Byron's precious memories.

Alexander was right. Byron would have to sleep. He'd forget her all over again, and this time it would be for good. Without the journal, it would be impossible to convince him of anything. Almost every page was singed down to the middle, with most of the words illegible. The remaining paintings were ashy and grey. As she tried to turn through the pages, they disintegrated under her touch. She set it down, not wanting to damage it further, tears streaming down her face.

The only thing left was to try to escape on her own. The windows were shuttered, and he locked the door behind him. Was there any way out? Byron's satchel caught her gaze, and she pulled herself over to it. Opening it, she found the white notebook he had taken to carrying around with him. She opened it to the first page and sobbed at seeing Byron's perfect script.

> *October 12*
> *I remember.*
> *Yesterday I met with Chief Inspector Thatcher about the new case that I'm on. I also remember bumping into Grace Trimbell the day before that. Seeing as I'm remembering bits and pieces again without reading the main journal, this notebook is to keep track of what I'm remembering day to day, and to compare what memories stay for multiple days at a time. Perhaps, if this keeps up, I can find the reason why I'm remembering things all of a sudden. At any rate, I've remembered my journal two days in a row!*

Mira gasped. These were his memories, his actual memories. The things he remembered from day to day, ever since he had bumped into Grace. She bit back another round of tears, realizing that this was no help at all, since she wouldn't be mentioned on any of the pages. He didn't remember her. He never had. He never would. Despite this, she continued to read over every day, savoring his handwriting and style. That is, until she noticed a pattern.

> *It seems that big portions of my memories are blocked and fuzzy. As if there was another person I was with, and yet when I try to picture them, I come up with nothing. And then there are these feelings that I can't quite seem to understand.*

She pushed forward a few pages.

> *I know for certain that I'm in love. These feelings can't be anything else. Yet, I don't know who I am in love with. I know it can't be Grace.*

Each snippet she caught made a hope build up in her chest. Byron really loved her, didn't he?

> *I caught a whiff of perfume in the sitting room this morning, and a sense of euphoria came over me. I love her, whoever she is. Why can't I remember her?*

She turned another page and held a hand over her mouth, crying in silence.

> *Does she even exist? Or am I in love with the dream of someone? No, I must assume she is real. There are too many dark spots in my memory that point to there being someone. It must be her! How is it that she seems so far away when she's within arm's reach every day?*

The more she read, the more the journal turned away from his memories and turned towards the "dark spots" that he

310 ◆ NATALIE BRIANNE

focused on remembering. It was perfectly clear that those were
the memories with her in them.

> *My master journal must know who she is. At this*
> *point, she seems to be the only thing I'm forgetting,*
> *barring minor details. Perhaps meditation would*
> *bring her to my remembrance?*

The journal continued with entries about his multiple
experiments and attempts to remember her. Each morning he
woke with no recollection of her and a growing frustration at
the failure. As she reached the end of the entries, it seemed that
nothing he did worked. But did that really matter?

He loved her. And she ruined everything because of her jealousy. Because she felt confused and hurt and, in the end, she
couldn't blame anyone but herself.

At some point before nightfall, Mira limped back to the
couch to sleep. Her entire body was sore and aching, and her
soul seemed to be weak as well. She took off her bodice, skirts,
bustle, and corset so she was only in her chemise and drawers.
She covered herself up with the blanket and curled in on herself.
Her stomach growled. She hadn't had anything to eat since
their ride down. Shivering, she held the notebook close to her
chest and wept.

October 27, 1888

MORNING CAME FAR TOO EARLY, AND WITH it, the reminder that Alexander trapped her in the room, alone with her guilt. She dressed, but forewent the shoes, as her ankle still throbbed with pain. Despite this, she resolved to get out, one way or another.

She started with some hair pins at the door. Pulling out two, she felt around the inside of the lock, trying to find the best way of getting the pins to all align, using the second pin to create tension. Her first pin broke during her first attempt, and she pulled out another to use. In the end, she had a pile of broken hair pins, stinging fingers, and a still-locked door.

Her next attempt involved searching the room for any additional exits. She couldn't exit through the main door or windows. But she held out hope for a hidden door or a cupboard or something that she could use to escape. She scouted it out from the couch, and then, when she found something of interest, she would make her way over to check it out. Each one came to a dead end.

Her last attempt was to pound on the door and yell for help, hoping that one of the groomsmen could hear her. This was short lived as she quickly recognized how thirsty she was. Aside from this, with all of the staff dismissed and the stables so far away from the main house, no one would hear her. So why try?

She settled onto the floor next to the remains of Byron's journal. Would Alexander actually send word to Walker? Would it be in time?

Her ears picked up the sound of hurried footsteps in the front entryway. She stood and limped over towards the couch, picking up a vase to throw in case had Alexander decided to return. Then the person shouted, and her name echoed throughout the house.

"Mira?!"

She dropped the vase, and it shattered to the floor as she stumbled to the door. Tears pricked at her eyes.

"Byron, I'm in here!"

The footsteps became louder until they stopped on the other side of the door. The handle jiggled.

"Mira! Thank heavens! Are you hurt?"

"Just my ankle."

"I'm going to get you out. Step away from the door."

She did as he said and moved against the far wall. After a couple of kicks, the door splintered, and Byron stepped in. He locked eyes with her and rushed to her, lifting her up in a tight embrace.

"Don't ever do that again."

He kissed her cheek and continued to hug her as if letting go would make her disappear. She relaxed in his arms, tears streaming down her face.

"I didn't think you would come. Without your journal . . . "

She pulled back to look at him. While the mussed-up hair and faint circles under his eyes worried her, nothing suggested that he had stayed up all night.

"Did you sleep?"

He swallowed. "Actually, I did. I didn't realize you were missing until this morning."

"What?" Her voice cracked.

"It's not that I wasn't worried! Heaven forbid. But when the groomsman told me that you had gone on ahead, I had time to think on the trip home. I wondered why you had left without me and realized it must have had something to do with why you had resigned. I decided to give you some distance. Aside from that, I was helping Thatcher and Fred try to track down Mr. Durant, who has vanished from London. I didn't even realize my journal was gone until this morning."

"But if you didn't realize I was missing last night, then how . . . "

His smile softened as he held her in his arms, gazing over her features with his deep blue eyes.

"Why, I remembered you."

She broke out into a wet laugh and smiled up at him. "Say it again."

"I remember you, Mira."

She pulled him down by his collar into a kiss. And while her first kiss with Alexander burned like fire, kissing Byron filled her senses with the sensation of a perfect spring afternoon, green and vibrant and beautiful, with sunlight bursting all around. It washed over her, cool and refreshing like the air after a rainstorm when the world feels clean and new. His lips, soft as velvet, felt rich and warm as drinking hot chocolate. It reminded her of every good thing in life, wrapped up in an embrace that she never wanted to leave.

But then he kissed her back, and her heart sang. His fingers found the small of her back, and pulled her closer, deeper. The smell of sandalwood encompassed her, like ripples of sunset on the Thames. It tasted of laughter and hope and love. She pulled back from the kiss, needing to breathe, and she placed her head on his chest. His heart beat fast and steady at her ear, and a rumble spread through him as he laughed.

"You didn't let me finish," he said.

She kept her head on his chest, and he kept his arms loose around her.

"I remember the very first time we met, when you followed me, and each day after that as I grew more and more fascinated. I remember the first time I wrote your name in my journal." He ran a hand over her hair. "When you showed up at my doorstep and helped me find my journal for the first time. I remember the way your eyes lit up when the airship lifted off, and the way you scrunch up your nose when you are shading a sketch."

His voice softened.

"I remember you yelling at me for not reading my journal. I remember the moment when you found out how your parents died. I remember that you took Mr. Graham's mums so that you could take care of them after he died. I remember almost everything, I think."

He pulled away so he could look at her face.

"And most importantly, with all of those memories together, I love you more than I ever thought was possible."

She let out a breathy laugh and choked on another sob. "And I love you too."

He leaned down and gave her a quick peck on the cheek. "I'll remember that."

She laughed and held a hand to his face.

"You really remember," she whispered, scarcely daring to hope this wasn't a dream.

He turned his head and kissed her palm. "Yes, dear one. I do."

She laughed again, and he shifted his weight. His hand moved to her waist to support her better.

"How's your ankle?"

"It's difficult to walk on."

He picked her up and brought her over to the couch, settling her down. He caught sight of the white notebook and flushed.

"Oh. Did you . . . did you read that?"

Mira swallowed. "Yes."

"Ah, well. I did write some rather . . . erm . . ." He picked it up and flipped through it, clearing his throat. "Everything in it is true, you know. I started it as a sort of exercise, to keep track of what memories stayed from day to day."

He set it down again and locked eyes with her. "But soon enough, it showed the evidence of what I lost. I've tried dozens of ways of keeping you in my memory from dusk to dawn. None of them seemed to work."

"And what did you do last night?"

He faltered. "I was so certain my memory had ruined everything between us. That I'd lost you. And I was so worried about you and how you were feeling. When I woke up, I had just finished the most amazing dream." He glanced over at her. "And you were the only thing I could remember."

Tears threatened to cloud her vision again, and Byron pulled a handkerchief from his pocket and knelt next to her.

"I would have thought you'd be happy about all of this," he teased, wiping the tears away.

"Oh, I'm fit to burst with happiness, Byron."

She caught one of his hands and held it close. He squeezed her hand and pulled himself up onto the couch, careful not to pin her dress as he took in the room. His eyes widened at the mess of charred leather and paper on the floor next to the couch. He picked up the remains of his journal.

"What happened here?"

"Alexander. He was here when we were investigating the office. He heard our plan, and when you left, he bribed the groomsman to pretend as if I had made it on the train. Then,

I guess he went up to take care of the evidence we found and discovered you had left your journal."

"He was here?" His expression darkened, voice lowering to a growl. "Did he hurt you?"

She hesitated. "Not really. He wanted me to go with him to Paris. When I told him no, he burned your journal and locked me in. I was afraid that no one would find me in time."

"I'm glad that I did." His shoulders relaxed.

Mira frowned. "But if Alexander left yesterday, he could very well be halfway to France by now. I'm not sure if we can catch up with him."

Byron dropped his journal and stood to pace, tapping a finger on his chin. "You're right. But at least we've stopped Circe in their tracks, for the moment. If we could only trace them back to their source, then we could resolve all of this once and for all."

He glanced back at her and softened. "Although there's not much we can do about that right now. We ought to get you back to Swan Walk. Your uncle and brother are worried sick."

"You saw them?"

"I went over first thing this morning to speak with you, and your uncle let me know you hadn't come home last night. Walker was already out searching for you."

"I didn't mean to worry them. Or you."

"Well, you couldn't exactly help that. Come on, I told the coach driver to wait."

After helping her painfully into her boots again, he picked her up and carried her out of the house. They settled into the coach, and Mira smiled, leaning her head against Byron's shoulder. The coach driver drove them back towards the station.

THEY REACHED LONDON BY MID-AFTERNOON, AND MIRA relaxed, more than happy to be back. Byron offered her his arm for support as they went to find a hansom cab to take them home.

"Is it alright if we make a stop at Castel's before heading to Swan Walk?" he asked as he helped her into the back of a cab.

"I don't mind." She smiled at him as he gave directions to the driver.

"You really need to stop getting into so much trouble, Mira," Byron teased once they were bustling up the street.

"Well, I'm sure I won't get into nearly as much trouble now that I'm not your secretary." She smirked.

Byron tensed. "What?"

"Don't you remember? I resigned."

She pulled back and looked up at him. He schooled his shocked expression upon seeing the mischievous glint in her eye.

"Well, what if I refuse your resignation?" He crossed his arms.

"You wouldn't dare!"

"Oh, but I do. Miss Blayse, I refuse your resignation." He leaned in closer and lowered his voice to a whisper. "I love you too much to let you go again."

"Well then, Mr. Constantine. What trouble should we get into next?" She laughed.

Byron hummed. "Oh, I don't know. Shall we go to Paris?"

Mira grinned up at him. "Really?"

"Of course. We've got a villain to catch, don't we?"

She fidgeted with the cuff of her sleeve. Even if her uncle could be convinced, it wouldn't be simple to track down Alexander. "You really think we could find him?"

"We can certainly try."

Mira nodded and pressed into him. She sighed. Her forgetful detective remembered her. Had actually remembered her.

And they finally had a new lead on Circe. But could they find Alexander? He needed to be stopped, that much was certain. To think that she had fallen for him so easily and allowed him to separate her from Byron. She shivered, remembering the way his cold eyes met hers.

The cab stopped in front of Bolton Street, and Byron asked the driver to wait a few minutes as he helped her out. Davies answered the door.

"Mr. Sherard is expecting you, if you'll wait in the sitting room."

Byron nodded, and Mira followed him in. As they opened the door, Miss Grace Trimbell stood from where she sat at the window.

"Mr. Constantine. I didn't expect to see you again." She brought a hand up to touch her cameo brooch, and she glanced at Mira. "Nor you, Miss Blayse."

"I thought it would be good for all of us to say our good-byes." Byron stepped into the room.

"Goodbyes?" Mira echoed, looking between them.

"If I am to be free of Circe, I have to go where they can't find me. And as soon as possible," Grace said.

Byron turned to Mira. "Castel has arranged for her to go to America. Circe doesn't have as much of an influence there, and it will be easier for Grace to start a new life."

Grace nodded. "It will certainly be a new adventure." She gave a small smile.

"When are you leaving?" Mira asked.

"First thing tomorrow morning."

Davies appeared in the doorway. "Mr. Sherard is in his office, Mr. Constantine."

"Won't be a minute!" Byron squeezed Mira's hand and left the room.

Mira glanced down. "I'm sorry you were pulled into all of this. If it weren't for me, you wouldn't have to leave London."

"It's alright. Really it is. I've been wanting to be free of

Circe ever since I met Byron the first time around. If this is my chance . . ." Grace shook her head and moved across the room. "It really isn't your fault. If we must blame anyone, then let's blame Byron," she teased.

"I suppose I can agree to that." Mira smiled.

Grace sighed and stepped away again. "I hope someday I'll learn not to envy you. But I always knew he wouldn't love me." She bit her lip. "Especially once I saw how he was with you."

Mira flushed. "Well, I have heard that American men are quite handsome."

Grace laughed, high and light-hearted. "I can only hope." She cocked her head. "Perhaps that should be my new name? After all, Grace Trimbell must die when I leave Europe."

"Hope?"

"Yes." Grace turned towards the window, wistful. "I think it could suit me."

"I think you're right." Mira moved to stand next to her, keeping her weight on her good foot. "What do you think you'll do?"

"Oh, I'm not exactly sure. I suppose I have some skills in secretarial work I could put to use." She glanced up at Mira. "Who knows? Maybe I'll be my own kind of private detective."

Mira laughed. "You've had a bit of practice there, too."

They stood in silence a few moments more as the leaves blew around on the pavement below. Mira swallowed.

"I'm not sure I ever thanked you for saving him. Without you, he would have died years before I ever even met him."

Grace shook her head. "You don't need to thank me. Even with everything that has happened, I will never regret that decision."

The door opened behind them, with Byron and Castel coming into the room.

"We've finished up the itinerary for your trip, Miss Trimbell," Castel said. "I hope you don't mind staying here another night."

"Not at all." She smiled.

"Until we meet again, Miss Trimbell."

Byron kissed Grace's hand. She pulled him into a hug.

"Thank you for everything you've done for me." She pulled back and turned to Mira, hugging her as well.

Grace whispered into her ear, "Take care of him for me."

Soon enough, Byron and Mira settled in the carriage on the way to Swan Walk. Mira relaxed into his side, and he kissed the top of her head. He sighed.

"Sometimes I wonder if Circe would be taken care of if it weren't for my memory."

"We've still done quite a bit to hurt them in the last few months."

"I suppose you're right. But their roots run deep. Hopefully now that we've maimed the smuggling ring again, we can focus on the other branches."

Mira nodded and closed her eyes, thinking back on their experiences with the smugglers.

"Byron." She sat up to look at him. "I just realized something."

"What's that?"

"Circe is ruthless. If someone is in their way, they just kill them. I mean, perhaps it could be tricky depending on the person's connections, but . . ."

Byron furrowed his brow. "But?"

"Why didn't they just kill me? They've had ample opportunity." She sat forward. "Alexander mentioned that Number Three has a specific interest in me."

Byron narrowed his gaze, deep in thought.

She stared at him, wide-eyed. "Byron, why would they need me alive?"

Author's Invitation

Welcome to the end of the book! Since you've made it this far, I have a favor to ask. Whether you enjoyed the book or not, please leave an honest review on Amazon or Goodreads. It only takes a few minutes and makes a significant difference for the future of this book. Reviews are essential for its success and longevity, and you'll be helping other readers decide if it's worth their time. If you loved the book, don't hesitate to recommend it to your friends!

To make it even easier, scan the QR code below to go directly this book's page on Goodreads:

AND IF YOU WANT TO KEEP UP with my news and inklings, you can join my newsletter by scanning the QR code below.

Acknowledgements

A fond thank you from the bottom of my spleen to those who have reviewed any of my books, including this one. Why spleen? While heart is the cliché/overused organ to thank someone from, spleens are often overlooked but vital parts of the body-- much like how reviews are to a book. Yes, books can survive without reviews, but it certainly makes life difficult.

If you haven't left a review yet, consider taking a moment out of your day. It will certainly make mine.

Thanks to the MMMN girls--Alayna, Eliza, Erica, and Heather. I'm a great fan of murder mysteries. This love was ingrained in my soul from the myriad of movies my family watched growing up. I foolishly thought it was just my family, but lo and behold a group for murder mystery movie night appeared almost overnight. This was highly unexpected, unanticipated, and unbelievably fantastic! My thanks to you comes in part because you helped me realize just how many friends I have and could have during this whole crazy pandemic. And that those friends could be sophisticated, hilarious, and incredibly cultured.

Michelle, you are one of the coolest people I know. You bring out the joy in me every time we're together! I admire your adventurous heart and brave soul and I am so grateful to be your friend. Also, thank you for helping me figure out that the best way to power through writer's block is to reread my own work. Past Natalie knew what present Natalie needed to do. I just forgot. Or maybe Byron is rubbing off on me again.

To the publishing staff at Immortal Works:

Holli, I feel like you've taken me under your wing and allowed me to grow in so many ways I didn't expect. From taking a chance on Constantine 1, to bringing me in as a freelance editor and audiobook artist, you really have helped me to succeed and progress in my author journey.

John, once again your edits made my book significantly better. Although I must say I am proud that I'm down some since the last book! Also, I love that you aren't sure who the lurking bad guy is. Maybe you'll find out in book three.

Ruth, your kind warmth has helped me through bouts of imposter syndrome, even if you didn't realize it. From the moment we met, I have felt nothing but acceptance from you. And that's made all the difference in the world as I've stumbled my way through marketing and publicity. Thank you!

Rebecca, Lenore, and the whole design team, thank you for your work on the covers and interior! People do judge a book by its cover, and it's a terribly difficult job to have. I salute you!

Staci thank you for everything that you do from acquisitions to copyfitting. And especially thank you for letting me join your writing group. It's helped me to realize that even when it feels impossible to get a "flow" state in 15 minutes if you just sit down and do it you can create so much.

A nod to my mother and brother for being rubber ducks at all times of day. Particularly when it came to plotting the murder of Mr. Sutherland. I still laugh thinking of mum talking about blood spatters, bullets, and the best way to murder a fictional character whilst walking around a hospital.

Welcome to the final acknowledgement! If you're still here, thank you!

It's truly a pleasure to have you here, dear reader. This is the only place in the book where I can talk to you directly. After all, the dedication was likely not for you, the author bio is in third person, and the hundred some-odd pages before this point were about Byron and Mira. And while that was written for you to enjoy, this part is written for you.

Thank you for reading my book. My darling predecessor, Dorothy L. Sayers, had a theory that creativity comes in three sections. First, when the idea is in its purest, perfect form in the author's head. Second, when it is brought into the real world via pen, ink, and paper. Third, when it is brought back to the ideal through the reader's imagination.

This book couldn't have come to its final creative state without you. Your unique voice, the way your brain formed the descriptions in your mind, and the moments that may have made you want to jump for joy, gasp in anticipation, or throw the book across the room. And so, I acknowledge you, the finisher of my work. My partner in crime.

About the Author

NATALIE BRIANNE'S love of writing might be traced back to an old Rainbow Macintosh Laptop she received for her 8th birthday. Perhaps it came from years of improv storytelling and the discipline of wonder. Or maybe, she was born to write and didn't realize it until her first book sprung out of her fingertips somewhere between a house in Pleasant Grove, Utah and a bus on its way to Edinburgh, Scotland.

She received her degree in Interdisciplinary Humanities from BYU. While she could have studied English or Creative Writing, she opted to learn more about culture, distant lands, and people in hopes of writing better stories. Much of her first book, *The Pennington Perplexity* was written when she lived at 27 Palace Court, London, walking the streets as if she were her characters.

When Natalie isn't writing, voice acting, playing the guitar very badly, traveling, and forgetting that she has vegetables in her fridge.

Looking For More?

CONSTANTINE CAPERS SERIES:

The Pennington Perplexity
Flashes of Memory
There Comes a Midnight Hour

THE 13TH ZODIAC SAGA:

Keepers of the Zodiac
Heart of the Meridian

SHORT STORIES AND NOVELLAS:

FROM CONSTANTINE'S CASEBOOK

Byron's Oblivion
The Great Sheep Panic
In the Silence of the Catacombs

FROM SAMIRA'S SKETCHBOOK

A Constantine Christmas

GENERAL FICTION

The Glade of Sionn O' Shea

www.ingramcontent.com/pod-product-compliance
Lightning Source LLC
Chambersburg PA
CBHW021534250626
47154CB00006BA/2118